Emerald Tide

a story in the
RomantiSea Serenades
series

J.D. Harbor

Ebook ISBN: 979-8-9921213-2-2

Paperback ISBN: 979-8-9921213-0-8

Cover Design: J.D. Harbor

Editing and Proofreading: Mehkala Spencer, All The Proof Editing

Formatting: Nicole Kincaid, Naughty Nook PR

To my parents – Thank you for always encouraging my creativity, for believing in my dreams even when I doubted them, and for fostering a love of storytelling that has shaped who I am. Your support means everything.

One

The kitchen of Murphy's Irish Pub was a chaotic symphony. The thud of feet on grease-slicked tiles mixed with the metallic scrape of spatulas and the sharp sizzle of meat searing on the grills. Steam hissed from pots, dimming the vibrant colors of vegetables under a smoky haze. The kitchen was a whirlwind of shouted orders and precise movements.

Heat and motion thickened the air, carrying the pungent scents of sweat, caramelized onions, and rosemary. Once pristine, Aidan's chef's coat was streaked with dark gravy and melted butter, a faint scorch mark branding one cuff. With his sleeves rolled up, you could see his sweaty forearms, all scarred from years of cooking.

"Chef, two shepherd's pies up!" Declan's voice boomed, the plates scraping across the counter.

"Yup!" Aidan barked back, his hands working swiftly, plating the food with mechanical precision. Every movement was ingrained, second nature. His body carried on, even as his mind wandered. Somewhere in the chaos, he'd stopped thinking.

He should have found comfort in that.

The heat was relentless, radiating from burners that hadn't cooled since lunch. Sweat pooled at the base of Aidan's neck, dampening his collar. The old ventilation system wheezed uselessly, the air heavy and unmoving. The smell of oil and caramelized onions clung to him like a second skin.

Tickets kept fluttering onto the rack, thin paper strips slapped into place. Declan and the kitchen staff moved like soldiers under siege, their shouts blending with the clatter of pans, the hiss of sauces, and the rhythmic chop of knives. Above it all, Aidan's voice rang out, pushing them forward.

He had lived for this rush. Or at least, he used to.

Then, Seamus filled the doorway.

His broad shoulders blocked the faint light from the dining room, his figure a shadow carved out of stone. Arms crossed, he stood silently, surveying the chaos. The faint scent of pipe tobacco lingered, cutting through the kitchen's sharper aromas. It was a scent that had followed Aidan since childhood, tied to early mornings and late nights before he'd understood the weight of the restaurant on his father's shoulders.

Seamus's presence sent an uneasy ripple through Aidan's chest, breaking his tenuous focus. He didn't need to say a word. Just standing there, he was a weight pressing down on the room.

"How's it going, lad?" Seamus asked, his low voice carrying a quiet authority. It wasn't a question; it was an order.

"Busy," Aidan replied curtly, slicing into a piece of Guinness-braised beef. The knife slid cleanly through the tender meat, but the tightness in Aidan's chest refused to ease.

Seamus's eyes flicked to the clipboard hanging crookedly on the wall. "Bring the lamb stew up for the specials. It's what they come for."

Aidan's jaw clenched. The same lamb stew. The same shepherd's pie. The same menu, unchanged for thirty years was as rigid as the man who stood before him.

"I was thinking of running something new tonight," Aidan said, keeping his tone clipped. "Maybe the blackened salmon I've been working on. Something lighter."

Seamus's expression hardened, his sharp eyes narrowing as he stepped further into the kitchen. His boots clicked faintly against the tile floor. "Lighter? Salmon?" His voice dropped lower, each word measured, but the authority in it was unyielding. "We don't need fancy twists, lad. The customers don't come here for 'light.' They come here for what they know. The food I built this place on."

Aidan's frustration flared, rising like a pot ready to boil over. He bit back the retort burning at the back of his throat and turned to the cutting board instead, his hands moving faster, his knife chopping more sharply. Each strike against the wood reverberated in his ears.

"This place needs some new dishes, Da," he mumbled, just loud enough for Seamus.

Seamus cocked his head slightly, his eyes steady and sharp, pinning Aidan in place. "Tradition keeps us in business," he said, his tone firm but quieter now, almost as if testing the words against himself. "Maybe you'll understand that when you're running the place."

When you're running the place.

The words landed on Aidan's shoulders like a lead weight. His dad laid out his future, but it sounded more like a prison sentence than a promise. Day after day of serving the same dishes, running the same kitchen, walking the same path Seamus had carved out.

Seamus lingered a moment longer, searching Aidan's face. For what, Aidan couldn't tell—disapproval, frustration, or maybe something else his father would never admit aloud. Then Seamus clapped him on the shoulder, the gesture meant to be encouraging but only making the weight on Aidan feel heavier.

"Get back to the line, lad," Seamus said, turning and disappearing into the restaurant beyond.

Aidan forced a tight smile that faded the moment Seamus was out of sight. He returned to the line, the roar of the kitchen swallowing him again. A quiet inner voice grew stronger with each difficult night and tense exchange.

He wanted something else. Something more.

The oven timer beeped, jolting Aidan back to the present. He reached for the pan, pulling out a tray of golden-brown soda bread. For a moment, his hand hovered over the warm loaves, his mind elsewhere. Then, with a sigh, he set the tray down and moved on to the next dish, his heart a little heavier than before.

The restaurant bustled on, indifferent to the cracks forming beneath his surface.

The kitchen door swung open with a clang, and in walked Jazz, hips swaying to an interior beat only she could hear. A mischievous grin stretched across her face, highlighting the dark curls piled high on her head; the curls smelled faintly of woodsmoke and sunshine. Clutter and chaos didn't faze her; she thrived in it, moving through the whirlwind of Murphy's like a dance she knew by heart.

"Oi, Chef!" she called melodiously, her voice cutting through the din like a burst of music. She propped one elbow on the counter, her weight shifting to one side as she let out an exaggerated sigh. "What's the holdup on that side of colcannon? You've got one very impatient customer at the bar asking about it. Furthermore, he wants your autograph on them mashed potatoes ... says they'd better be extra special coming out tonight."

Aidan glanced up from the dish he was plating, a smirk tugging at the corner of his lips. "He wants my autograph?" He wiped his hands on the dish towel slung over his shoulder, tossing a quick look her way. "Tell him it's extra. Five bucks per signature. Nah, make it ten. I'm feeling generous."

Jazz laughed, warm and infectious, her eyes sparkling as she crossed the kitchen to lean beside him on the counter. "I'll let him know, but I'm keeping half of that. Bartender's tax."

"You're merciless," Aidan said, shaking his head as he slid the side of colcannon toward her. "There you go. Fresh off the line. Tell him it's so good, it'll change his life."

Jazz winked, lifting the plate with ease. "I'll tell him it's magic, but we both know the truth." She leaned in slightly, her voice dipping into a teasing tone. "Speaking of which, what time do you plan to dazzle me with your presence at the bar tonight?"

Aidan's smirk grew as he played along. "Depends. What's the special? And don't say Guinness—I can get that for free back here."

"Oh, you're so picky," Jazz said, rolling her eyes dramatically. "Lucky for you, we just got a new whiskey shipment in. Something smooth, just the way you like it. I'll even pour it myself so you know it's made with love."

Aidan let out a gentle laugh as he shook his head. No matter how insane the night got, Jazz always managed to lighten the mood. Where Seamus's presence weighed him down with tradition and obligation, Jazz brought lightness—a certain ease he had come to rely on over the years.

"Ah, all right," Aidan said, mock defeat in his voice. "You win. I'll come by when things settle down here. You know I can't resist when you bribe me with whiskey."

Jazz grinned triumphantly, but before she turned to leave, she leaned a hip against the counter and studied him, her expression softening. "You know, you really should give yourself a break sometime, Chef. It's not all on your shoulders, you know."

Aidan exhaled, his smile faltering just a little. "Feels like it is," he muttered, wiping his hands on his towel. "I just want this place to work—really work. Not just scrape by on the same old menu and tradition. I've got ideas, but ..." He trailed off, shrugging as if to brush the weight of it aside. "Let's just say my dad and I don't exactly see eye to eye on it."

Jazz hesitated for a moment but didn't push. Instead, she offered him a small, knowing smile. "For what it's worth, I think Murphy's could be more than it is. And I think you're the one who could make it happen—if you don't let him wear you down first."

Aidan huffed a quiet laugh, though there wasn't much humor in it. "Easier said than done, Jazz."

"Most good things are," she said with a shrug, then lifted the plate again. "Now stop sulking and get back to work. I'll see you at the bar later. Don't make me come back here and drag you out myself."

"Wouldn't dream of it," he replied, a trace of a real smile breaking through as she spun on her heel and headed out the door.

He watched her go, shaking his head as he returned to the line. The banter was familiar, a brief reprieve from the relentless pressure surrounding him. But as the kitchen roared back to life, the weight of Seamus's words lingered, coiling around him like the heat of the ovens.

Tradition keeps us in business. Maybe you'll grasp that when you're running the place.

The thought gnawed at him as he plated another dish. *When you're running the place.* It wasn't just a promise—it was a life sentence. And no amount of whiskey or laughter could drown out the quiet voice in his head, the one asking: *What if I don't want to?*

The rhythm of the kitchen pulled him forward, one order at a time, but the question lingered. Always there. Always louder.

"Smart man." Jazz's voice floated back into the kitchen as she nudged him playfully with her elbow before heading back to the bar. Before disappearing through the swinging door, she glanced over her shoulder, her smile softening. "Take a break when you can, Aidan. You're looking too serious back there."

Aidan exhaled, the weight of the evening pressing on him again, though her words lifted it, if only a fraction. "Yeah," he said, giving her a quick nod. "I'll try."

"You better," she tossed back, her laughter lingering in the air as the door swung shut behind her.

For a moment, the kitchen felt lighter, the pressure dialed down just a notch. Aidan watched the door sway in her wake, a half-smile lingering on his lips. That was what Jazz did for him—she put cold water on a sweltering day. She made nights like this bearable, even when the weight of everything else threatened to crush him.

But the din of the kitchen roared back as the door settled, the unrelenting cadence pulling him back into the rhythm: the next ticket, the next order, the next obligation. Despite everything, the brief moment of banter with Jazz clung to him, a subtle reminder that not everything in his life was defined by duty and tradition. Some things—some people—still brought a spark of light.

He reached for the next plate, his movements a little slower, his mind drifting back to their exchange. Later, after the last order went out and the kitchen cooled, he'd slip into the bar and let Jazz pour him that promised drink. Let the world fall away for a moment. Maybe tonight, for once, he wouldn't overthink everything.

But for now, there were orders to fill and plates to perfect.

The rest of the crew—a mix of line cooks and dishwashers—shifted into cleanup mode, their chatter a low hum as they restocked shelves, scrubbed counters, and stacked dishes in the walk-in. The clatter of pots and pans softened into a steady rhythm as the night wound down.

Aidan wiped the sweat from his brow, grabbed a cloth, and began cleaning the counters. The repetitive motion was almost meditative, but his mind churned restlessly. His earlier confrontation with Seamus gnawed at him like a pebble in his shoe, small but sharp. Lately, every conversation with his father felt the same—less like a discussion, more like a reminder of a future that felt less like an opportunity and more like a cage.

The creak of the kitchen door pulled him from his thoughts. He didn't need to look up to know who it was. The faint scent of lavender and rosemary drifted in, as familiar to him as the kitchen's ever-present heat.

"Still at it, are ye? Goin' at it like you're twenty-five?" came Maureen's voice, soft and warm, with just the slightest edge of concern. "You should be sittin' down by now, mo ghrá."

Aidan's lips twitched at the sound of the old nickname—mo ghrá, my love. She'd been calling him that since he was a boy, back when he'd run around the kitchen chasing stray potatoes and stealing nibbles of raw dough when Seamus wasn't looking.

"Not done yet, Ma," he said without turning, still focused on scrubbing the grill. "If I stop now, the place'll be a disaster in the morning."

Maureen stepped further into the kitchen, wrapping her arms around herself the way she always did when she was worried. Her sharp blue eyes scanned him, missing nothing—from the exhaustion carved into his face to the tightness in his movements that betrayed just how much he was holding back.

"You look tired," she said softly, though her tone carried a quiet firmness. "And don't tell me you're fine. You're always fine."

"I am fine," Aidan replied, scrubbing a little harder than necessary. "It's just another busy night."

Maureen didn't respond right away, but he could feel her eyes lingering, her silence heavier than words. He knew what was coming before she even opened her mouth.

"Your father," she began, her voice cautious but steady, purposeful. "I know you two haven't—"

"Ma!" Aidan interrupted, his tone sharp but pleading as he set the rag down. "Not now. Not here. Please."

He glanced over his shoulder, catching sight of the crew still moving about, cleaning and tidying, close enough to overhear if Maureen pushed the issue. He didn't want anyone else knowing how fractured things felt between him and Seamus.

Maureen sighed, the sound heavier than she meant it to be. She stepped closer, lowering her voice. "I'm just worried about you, Aidan. You've been taking on too much. And I don't mean just here in the kitchen."

Her words sat heavy in his chest because, of course, she was right. The pressure from the restaurant, the weight of his father's expectations—it was all bearing down on him, more than he knew how to handle. He wanted to make Murphy's better, to help it grow into something stronger, but the constant battles with Seamus were draining. They were both too stubborn, too set in their ways, and it felt like nothing would ever change.

"I'll handle it, Ma," he said finally, his voice low but steady. "I just need some time."

Her lips pressed into a thin line, unconvinced, but she nodded anyway. "You need to take better care of yourself, mo ghrá," she said softly. "You've always pushed yourself past your limits and told everyone you were fine. Just ... don't forget to slow down every once in a while."

Aidan gave her a faint smile, though it didn't quite reach his eyes. "I won't."

She lingered for a moment, the weight of unspoken concern settling between them. Then, with a tenderness that caught him off guard, she reached up and brushed a stray lock of hair off his forehead, the gesture as familiar as it was comforting.

"I'm going home," she said quietly. "I'll see you Sunday for family dinner, yeah?"

"Sunday," he echoed, nodding.

"You better be," she teased, a small smile breaking through. "Or I'll send your father after you with a wooden spoon."

That got a real smile out of Aidan, brief but genuine. "I wouldn't put it past him."

With a light laugh, she gave his shoulder a gentle squeeze before departing the kitchen, leaving behind a trail of lavender and rosemary.

When the door swung shut behind her, Aidan let out a long breath, leaning his hands on the counter. The weight of the night, the tension with his father, and his mother's quiet concern all pressed down on him like the heat of the ovens.

Sunday dinner loomed ahead, another ritual steeped in obligation. Another round of lectures about the future, the restaurant, and the Murphy name. Aidan wasn't sure he wanted to carry it anymore. But what choice did he have?

He sighed, picked up the rag again, and resumed scrubbing.

The kitchen wasn't clean yet. Neither was his head.

Two

Aside from the hum of the road, the car was quiet except for the faint murmur of some classic rock tune on the radio. Aidan glanced at his older sister in the passenger seat, her arm dangling lazily out the window, fingers tapping the door in time with the beat. Aisling sat relaxed, the breeze tousling her dark hair. In contrast, Aidan's knuckles gripped the wheel tightly, his shoulders stiff, the tension radiating off him palpable.

Aisling broke the silence first, her voice calm but probing. "So, are you happy?"

Aidan blinked, startled by the question. He glanced at her, confused. "What kind of question is that?"

"It's not a trick question, little brother." Aisling smirked, but there was a sharpness behind her smile. "You've been working in the restaurant for how many years now? Don't you ever wonder if it's where you're meant to be?"

Aidan sighed, his grip on the steering wheel tightening. "It's the family business, Ais. It's what we do."

Aisling let out a soft, dry laugh. "Right. What we do. You sound just like Dad."

"That's not fair," Aidan shot back, his tone defensive. "It's different for me. You got out. You left for law school. You didn't have to deal with—"

"With what?" Aisling interrupted, her voice sharper. "With Dad? With his expectations? Believe me, Aidan, I dealt with plenty. You think it was easy walking away from all that?"

Aidan hesitated, his eyes fixed on the road. He could still remember the years of cold tension between Aisling and their father after she left. The way Seamus had barely spoken her name, as if acknowledging her absence would give it power. He'd never forget the way their mother's voice would tighten when she mentioned Aisling, caught between pride and worry.

"You saw what it did to him," Aidan said quietly. "To the family. When you left, it nearly broke him."

"And staying broke me," Aisling said softly, her voice losing its edge. "Aidan, you don't have to keep carrying all of this just because Dad expects it. If you're not happy, you can walk away."

"It's not that simple," Aidan muttered, his jaw tightening. "I can't just abandon the pub. Not like you—"

"Don't," Aisling said sharply, cutting him off. "Don't make this about me. This is about you. And it's not about the pub, either. It's about whether or not you can see yourself doing this for the rest of your life. Can you?"

Aidan didn't answer right away. He couldn't. The truth was, he didn't know. All he knew was the weight of responsibility pressing down on him, the endless grind of running the kitchen, and the constant, nagging fear of disappointing his father.

"I don't have a choice," he said finally, his voice low and heavy. "You don't get it, Ais. You got to leave. You got to chase your dreams. I don't have that option."

Aisling sighed, leaning back in her seat. "You always have a choice, Aidan. The question is whether or not you're brave enough to make it."

They fell into silence after that, the only sound the hum of the car and the faint strains of the radio. Aidan kept his eyes on the road, his jaw clenched, trying to shake off the weight of her words. But they lingered, sinking into the back of his mind like stones.

Pulling into the driveway, Aidan looked at the familiar brick house, its chimney puffing faint wisps of smoke into the crisp air. A combination of wistful remembrance and apprehensive expectation always surrounded that house. Once a haven, it had become a stage for routine tension, week after week, without fail.

The faint hum of football commentary seeped through the windows, and the sight of Declan's truck parked neatly to the side confirmed what Aidan already knew: his brother was inside. The living room curtain fluttered slightly, and he imagined Declan stretched out on the couch, already making himself at home.

As Aisling climbed out of the car, she gave Aidan a wry smile, shaking her head. "You look like you're bracing for battle."

Aidan smirked, though it didn't reach his eyes. "Sunday dinner, Ais. It's always a battle."

She patted his shoulder lightly as they walked toward the door. "Let's hope Dad's in a good mood. Or at least distracted enough by the game to let us eat in peace."

Inside, the familiar warmth of the house wrapped around Aidan like a heavy, well-worn coat. The scent of garlic and rosemary mingled with the savory aroma of roasting lamb, and the rhythmic scrape of a wooden spoon on the bottom of a pot came from the kitchen.

"I'll grab us beers," Aisling said as she hung her coat on the rack near the door. She glanced toward the kitchen, where Maureen was likely bustling about. "Might as well get ahead of it before Dad starts with the restaurant talk."

"Good luck in there," Aidan muttered, nodding toward the kitchen.

"Please, I have Ma wrapped around my finger." Aisling smirked over her shoulder as she disappeared through the doorway, leaving Aidan to navigate the living room alone.

The low murmur of a muted football game drifted down the hall, mingled with the occasional clink of glass. Aidan stepped into the living room to find Declan and Seamus sitting side by side on the worn leather sofa. Both held pints of beer, their eyes fixed on the screen. Neither spoke, but the room hummed with an unspoken understanding between them, a quiet camaraderie built on routine.

"Lad," Seamus greeted without looking away from the game, tipping his beer slightly in acknowledgment.

"Da," Aidan replied, mirroring the subtle nod as he slid onto the opposite end of the sofa. The cushions gave way beneath him, familiar and just slightly too soft, like sinking into a memory he wasn't sure he wanted to revisit.

For a few moments, the only sounds were the faint commentary from the game and the occasional creak of the couch as one of them shifted. Aidan's eyes flicked between his father and brother, the silence heavier than it needed to be. He tapped his fingers on his knee, debating whether to speak.

Finally, he turned to Declan, his voice low but casual. "So, how'd the bookcase delivery go this morning?"

Declan's lips curved into a grin as he sipped his beer. "Went pretty well, actually. Guy in Dilworth was thrilled with it—said it was even better than he'd imagined. Rustic charm, hand-carved details, all that jazz."

Aidan nodded, feeling a small flicker of pride for his brother. "Good to hear. Sounds like you're getting pretty good at this whole custom furniture thing."

"Not too shabby, huh?" Declan said, leaning back into the couch with a satisfied grin. "I'm thinking of putting a few more pieces together, maybe seeing if I can get into one of those artisan fairs in the spring."

Before Aidan could respond, Seamus cleared his throat loudly, his eyes still glued to the television. "Can't hear the damn game with all this chatter."

Declan rolled his eyes, muttering under his breath. "Because it's so riveting ... they run around, kick the ball and maybe the ball will go into the net."

Seamus's looked toward him, sharp and pointed. "I didn't ask for commentary, Declan. Just a bit of peace while I watch."

Aidan shifted uncomfortably, leaning forward to rest his elbows on his knees. "We're not exactly shouting over here, Da."

Seamus grunted, his eyes still glued to the muted television. "Could've fooled me," he muttered, taking another long sip of his beer.

Declan rolled his eyes, clearly biting back a retort. He slouched further into the couch, resting his pint on the armrest. The room fell into a tense silence, the football game on the screen providing the only sound as the commentators' lips moved soundlessly.

Aidan scanned the room again, his eyes shifting between the framed photos on the walls and the soft, flickering light of the fireplace. The quiet felt like it was pressing down on him, heavy and unrelenting. He glanced sideways at Declan, who was tapping his fingers idly against his glass, his jaw tight.

The tension was only broken when Aisling breezed back into the room, balancing two frosty beers in one hand while holding a third to her chest. "Alright, gentlemen," she announced, her voice cutting through the quiet like a gust of fresh air. "Beer delivery's here. Try not to fight over them."

She handed one glass to Aidan, who took it with a quiet, "Thanks" and passed the other to Declan. With the third glass in her hand, she perched herself on the oversized arm of the sofa beside Aidan, crossing her legs gracefully as she took a sip of her drink.

"So," Declan said after a moment, his tone deliberately casual as he glanced at Aidan, "come up with any new recipes lately, Chef Extraordinaire?"

Aidan blinked, caught off guard by the question. He hesitated, glancing toward Seamus instinctively before replying. "Not really. Haven't had much time for experimenting lately."

Declan raised an eyebrow, tilting his head. "Come on, you've gotta have something up your sleeve. You're always playing around with new ideas. What about that seafood special you mentioned last month?"

Before Aidan could respond, Seamus cut in, his voice sharp. "Not in my kitchen, he isn't."

The room froze for a beat, Aidan's stomach twisting at the comment. He turned his head toward Seamus, whose eyes were still fixed on the television but whose grip on his beer had tightened noticeably.

Declan, always the one to poke the bear, let out a low whistle. "Jeez, Da, relax. It's just a question."

Seamus's gaze snapped to Declan, his expression hard. "The kitchen runs just fine the way it is. We don't need any fancy 'specials' mucking things up."

Aidan's jaw tightened, his grip on his beer glass growing firmer. "It's not mucking things up to try something different every now and then," he said evenly, though there was an edge to his tone.

Seamus snorted, shaking his head as he leaned back in his chair. "We've been running Murphy's the same way for years, and it works. You don't fix what's not broken."

Aidan opened his mouth to argue, the words already forming on his tongue, but before he could speak, Maureen's voice rang out from the kitchen.

"That's enough shop talk before dinner!" she shouted, her tone firm and cutting through the room like a bell. "I don't want to hear another word about the pub until after we've eaten—and that includes you, Seamus Murphy!"

Seamus grumbled under his breath, turning his attention back to the screen with a tight-lipped scowl. Declan smirked, clearly amused by their mother's ability to shut down even the most heated discussions with a single shout.

Aisling raised her glass in mock salute toward the kitchen. "Cheers to Ma for keeping us all in line," she said lightly, though she spared a fleeting look at Aidan, lingering just long enough to catch the tension in his expression.

Aidan exhaled slowly, the crisp bitterness of his beer doing little to ease the knot tightening in his chest. The brief relief he'd felt when Aisling joined them had already dissolved, replaced by the same simmering frustration that always seemed to linger in this house.

The tension was familiar, like a clock ticking down to an inevitable confrontation. No matter how much they avoided it, he knew the topic of the restaurant—and what Aidan owed to the Murphy name—would rear its head again before the night was over. It always did.

But not yet. For now, Aidan tried to push it aside, sinking into the moment and letting the quiet clink of glasses and the grunts toward the football game fill the silence.

"Alright, the food's ready!" Maureen's voice rang out cheerfully from the kitchen, cutting through the heavy air. "Come to the table before it gets cold!"

Seamus stood with a grunt, the sound almost as gruff as the man himself. He clapped Aidan on the shoulder as he passed, the weight of the gesture heavier than it needed to be—more expectation than affection. Aidan sighed, setting his beer down and rising reluctantly.

Declan, already heading for the dining room, caught Aidan's eye and shot him a quick thumbs-up, his grin lopsided and knowing, as if to say, *Hang in there.*

Here we go, Aidan thought, his shoulders tightening as he followed his brother. Whatever storm brewed beneath the surface tonight, they'd face it.

Just not yet.

Maureen had artfully arranged the roast lamb, mashed potatoes, roasted carrots, and her famous gravy on the elegantly set dining table. The silverware clinked as the family settled into their seats, the warm hum of conversation wrapping the room in a sense of normalcy. But the tension was unmistakable to Aidan, humming just beneath the surface like an engine ready to stall.

He speared a piece of lamb with his fork, trying to let the meal's warmth anchor him. Yet his thoughts wandered to the chaotic kitchen: the towering stack of invoices Seamus needed to review, the stressed whispers of the waitstaff as they rushed to fix a wrong order, and the ceaseless, overwhelming grind of the restaurant. He could feel the weight of his father's expectations pressing on him, even here.

Maureen broke the quiet. "Aidan, love, you've been looking a bit run-down lately," she said as she passed the roasted carrots across the table. "I'm starting to worry about you."

"I'm fine, Ma," Aidan replied, his tone deliberately steady. He didn't look up as he sliced into his food. "Just busy. You know how it is."

Across the table, Declan snorted. "Busy? You're always busy." He leaned back in his chair, balancing it on two legs like he had as a kid.

"Seriously, man, when did you last take an actual break? You've been running yourself into the ground."

"I'm fine," Aidan repeated sharply, the words cutting through the table like a knife. He glanced at Declan with a glare meant to end the conversation. But Declan leaned forward, setting his chair back on four legs with a soft thud.

"Hear me out," Declan said, his voice more serious, "You really should take some time off. A week. Two, even. I can handle the kitchen while you're gone."

Aidan let out a dry laugh. "You? Handle the kitchen?" The doubt was evident in his voice. "You'd burn the place down in a week."

Declan bristled. "Come on, give me some credit. I've been your sous chef for years. You think I can't manage it without you hovering over me?"

"It's not about that," Aidan shot back, his fork clinking against his plate as he set it down. "It's complicated. The restaurant is ..."

"Complicated?" Declan interrupted, his voice softening, though frustration still simmered. "It's not complicated, Aidan. You just don't trust anyone else to do the job. And I get it—I do. But, come on, man, you're running yourself ragged."

Aidan's chest tightened. "No, the problem is that running a kitchen isn't a hobby you can half-ass while off playing with wood scraps in your workshop. It's a real job. It takes focus."

Declan flinched, his jaw tightening, but instead of snapping back, he took a breath and leaned forward, resting his elbows on the table. "I know it's a real job, Aidan. I've been in that kitchen with you for years. I've seen the hours you put in and the weight you carry. But you don't have to do it all alone. Do you think I'm just standing on the sidelines here? I'm not. I'm trying to help, but you won't let me. You're my brother, and I hate seeing you like this."

Aidan looked away, his grip tightening around his fork. Declan's words pressed against a wall he'd built up over years of grinding through the same routine, day after day. Though he wanted to reject and dismiss Declan, the earnestness and openness in Declan's voice struck him.

Declan leaned closer, his voice quieter now, almost pleading. "You're burning out, Aidan. And it's not just me who sees it. Ma sees it. Even Da probably sees it, even if he won't admit it. You're trying so hard to hold it all together, but you're human, man. You can't keep this up forever."

"I said I'm fine," Aidan snapped, his voice sharper than he'd intended, the edge unmistakable.

The table fell silent, the weight of his words settling heavily in the air. Maureen's hands stilled as she folded her napkin neatly in her lap, casting quick looks from one son to the other. Finally, she reached out and placed a calming hand on Aidan's arm. "Declan's only trying to help, love," she said softly.

Before Aidan could respond, Seamus cleared his throat, leaning forward slightly. His voice, low and steady, cut through the silence. "Your brother's right."

Aidan froze, his stomach twisting. He looked up, startled to see his father's sharp eyes fixed on him. Seamus's hands clasped on the table, his expression unreadable.

"You can't do everything yourself," Seamus said, his tone firm but quieter than usual. "You need a break. Maybe that's why we've had an uptick in orders getting sent back."

Aidan's head jerked up, his jaw tightening. "You're blaming me for that?" he demanded, his voice taut with anger. "You're the one who keeps pushing the same outdated menu and barking at the staff like they're soldiers. Maybe the problem isn't me, Da."

"Watch your tone, lad," Seamus issued his warning, his jaw clenching, a cold edge darkening his expression. "You're not invincible. You've been pushing yourself too hard, and it's starting to show. That's on you."

"That's on me?" Aidan's pulse raced, his voice rising. "You're the one who dumps all your stress on me. Every time something goes wrong, it's my fault. I'm always the one who ends up fixing it, never you."

"Aidan," Maureen interjected, her voice soft but urgent, trying to stem the tide. But it was too late.

Seamus shoved back his chair abruptly, the loud scrape of wood against the floor cutting through the room like a knife. He stood, his fists clenched at his sides, his expression dark. "Enough," he said tightly, his voice low and clipped.

Aidan opened his mouth, but Seamus was already walking away. His boots thudded heavily against the hardwood as he disappeared down the hall, the slam of his bedroom door reverberating like a gunshot.

The table remained still, the argument hanging like a heavy smog. No one spoke. No one moved.

Aidan sat back in his chair, staring at the now-empty seat at the head of the table. His chest ached, his frustration roiling just beneath the surface. He dragged a hand down his face, trying to collect himself, but the weight of the evening clung to him.

He glanced at Declan, who sat stiffly, staring down at his plate. Maureen meticulously straightened the silverware across the table, her careful movements clearly indicating she was avoiding eye contact. Aisling swirled the last of the lager in her glass, her expression neutral, though her silence pointed.

This was how it always ended.

Declan finally broke the quiet, his voice low but steady. "Look, I wasn't trying to push you, Aidan. I just ..." He trailed off, rubbing the back of his neck awkwardly. "I don't want to see you burn out. That's all."

Aidan let out a slow breath, his fingers gripping the edge of the table as he forced himself to calm down. "I'll think about it," he said after a long pause, his voice quieter but firm. He glanced at Declan. "Maybe I could take some time after the St. Paddy's rush is over. But until then, it's just not possible."

Declan nodded, his expression softening slightly. "Fair enough."

Maureen, who had been silent until now, reached out and gently touched Aidan's arm again. "You've always had a knack for butting heads with your father," she said softly, a faint smile tugging at her lips. "But, love, try not to be so quick to meet him with fire. I know he doesn't like to open up, but ..." She hesitated, her eyes flickering toward the empty doorway where Seamus had left. "He's been under a bit more stress lately."

Aidan's jaw tightened as he studied her face, searching for the unspoken meaning in her words. "What kind of stress?" he asked, his tone tinged with suspicion.

Maureen shook her head gently as though she'd already said more than she intended. "Nothing you need to worry about, mo ghrá. Just … give him a little grace. He doesn't show it, but he carries a lot."

Aidan wanted to press her further, to demand what exactly his father was dealing with, but the quiet weariness in her voice gave him pause. She knew more than she was letting on—of course, she did—but Maureen had a way of drawing lines when it came to family matters. If she weren't ready to share, he wouldn't get anything out of her by pushing.

"I'll try," he muttered, his voice reluctant.

Her smile softened, and she patted his arm before rising from her chair. "That's all I ask."

The tension in the room ebbed slightly, though it didn't dissipate entirely. Aidan let out a heavy breath, studying the meal's scattered remains. The roast sat half-carved, its juices pooling on the serving platter. The mashed potatoes were untouched, the bowl was still full. It was funny, in a way. They always prepared too much food for these dinners, as if expecting some miraculous moment of peace to stretch the meal into hours.

Instead, they got this.

Every week. The same fight, unresolved silence, and an ache in his chest.

Three

The night was tranquil, considering it was a Tuesday. Dinner service had been unusually slow, a peaceful change from the weekend's rush. Only a few customers remained, their quiet chatter and the clinking of glasses filling the mostly empty restaurant. Warm light reflected off the rows of whiskey bottles behind the bar, casting everything in a cozy caramel hue.

Aidan sat at the bar, elbows propped against the polished wood, nursing a glass of amber lager. His muscles ached with the familiar soreness at the end of a long stretch in the kitchen. He could still smell the lingering scents of shepherd's pie and roasted lamb clinging to his skin, no matter how many times he'd scrubbed his hands between services. The pub's familiar presence felt suffocating tonight, a heavy weight he couldn't entirely dismiss.

Jazz leaned casually against the bar beside him, wiping glasses. Her dark curls spilled over one shoulder as she shot him a playful glance. "You look beat, Chef," she teased, her voice light but tinged with an undercurrent of concern. "Tough day perfecting casseroles and Guinness stew?"

Aidan snorted, shaking his head. "Yeah, real tough. You know, mastering the ancient art of boiling potatoes. Can't let the craft die."

Jazz laughed, warm and familiar, and tapped her glass against his. "Here's to you, culinary hero. Saving us all, one potato at a time."

With a quiet laugh, he took another sip of his beer. The ease of their banter came naturally, honed by years of working side by side. Jazz had a gift for lightening even the slowest nights, her sharp wit cutting through whatever weight Aidan had been carrying.

The door to the pub swung open with a gust of cool air, pulling Aidan's attention as a familiar face stepped inside. A tall, broad-shouldered man with an affable grin strolled in like he owned the place, wearing a worn leather jacket and a baseball cap emblazoned with his brewery's logo. His saunter exuded swagger, as always.

Jazz's eyes sparkled as she leaned against the bar, propping her chin in her hand with mock interest. "Well, well, well," she drawled, her voice dripping with flirtation as she gave MJ a slow once-over. "Look what the cat dragged in. If it isn't Marcus 'I'm-too-cool-for-this-pub' Johnson, gracing us with his presence."

MJ grinned, swaggering up to the bar and leaning in just a bit closer than necessary, his voice low and teasing. "Jazz Castillo, looking as fine as ever. You miss me or something? I'm feeling all kinds of love right now."

Jazz rolled her eyes, but her smile gave her away. "Oh, please. I'm trying to figure out what poor soul you're here to harass tonight. You can't be here for my stellar bartending."

"Stellar bartending? That's what we're calling it these days?" MJ shot back with a wink. "I'm here for the ambiance, obviously. And maybe a little of that Jazzy charm. You know how it is."

Aidan shook his head, smirking into his glass. MJ and Jazz had always danced around each other like this, the playful back-and-forth just shy of admitting they liked each other. It was sufficient entertainment, anyway.

"I'm going to start charging you for compliments," Jazz said, pretending to be serious as she poured MJ's usual. "First one's free. Next one? That'll cost you."

MJ laughed, accepting the beer with a grin. "Put it on my tab."

Jazz rolled her eyes again, but Aidan noticed the way she lingered for a moment longer than necessary, her smile lingering as she turned to tend to a customer at the other end of the bar.

MJ slid onto the stool beside Aidan, clinking his glass against Aidan's lager. "What's up, man?" he said, leaning in slightly. "You look like you could use something stronger than a beer."

Aidan smirked, shaking his head. "Nah, the gods' elixir is just right for now." He tipped his glass back for another sip. "What brings you by? Thought you'd be busy over at the brewery."

MJ stretched out, kicking back like he owned the place. "Had a little time tonight. Figured I'd drop in and see how the culinary master's doing. Plus, I needed to scope out some competition," he said with a wink, nodding toward the tap lines behind the bar. "Speaking of which, when are we getting some of my beers on tap here? I could give your customers something more exciting than Guinness and Harp."

Aidan let out a low laugh, shaking his head. "You know how my dad is. He's practically married to the same old same. If you want to pitch that to him, you'd better come armed with a lifetime supply of Jameson and a convincing Irish accent."

MJ groaned theatrically, though his eyes danced with amusement. "Man, you've gotta let him off the leash sometime. This new stout is amazing, deep, rich, with a hint of coffee. Would kill it in here. The old-timers wouldn't know what hit 'em."

Aidan rubbed the back of his neck, a flicker of temptation creeping in despite himself. MJ's brewery was the talk of Charlotte, and Aidan had to admit, his beer was amazing. The thought of bringing it up to Seamus, though ... well, was a headache waiting to happen.

"I'll think about it," he said, sipping his beer. "But don't hold your breath."

MJ grinned, raising his glass in a mock toast. "That's all I ask."

They fell into a natural rhythm, years of friendship making the conversation effortless. Aidan asked about the brewery, wanting to hear from MJ how they managed the wild success he'd only read about.

MJ leaned forward, his face lighting up with excitement. "It's been wild, man. We just expanded the taproom and added a private event space; demand is through the roof. I mean, we're still small compared to the big guys, but we've got people coming in from everywhere now. Hell, we even started doing beer tours on weekends." He paused for a sip, then grinned. "It's exhausting, but it's worth it."

"Yeah," Aidan said quietly, swirling the last of his lager in his glass. Something in his chest tightened as he listened. MJ didn't just take pride in his work, he was passionate about it. A kind of passion Aidan hadn't felt in years.

"So ... what's it like?" Aidan asked, his voice almost hesitant. "You know ... actually following your dream."

MJ studied him for a second before answering, his tone softer now. "Honestly? It's everything. Don't get me wrong—it's hard as hell. Some days, I'm pulling sixteen-hour shifts and barely sleeping. But the thing is, it's mine, you know? I built it. Even when I'm dead tired, I don't mind because I love doing it."

"Ah, that sounds ... nice," he said softly.

The words lingered, striking a chord deep within Aidan. His fingers tightened around his glass. *It's mine.* The idea sat heavy in his chest, almost foreign.

Because nothing about Murphy's felt like his.

Though he wouldn't confess it, a part of him deeply envied that. Aidan turned back to his glass, staring at the faint traces of foam clinging to the sides. The weight of the past few months bore down on him: the endless days at the pub, the constant fighting with his dad, and the overwhelming sense that he was stuck in a life that wasn't entirely his.

MJ's smile dimmed just a little as he leaned closer, his fingers tapping idly against his glass. "You ever think about doing your own thing, man? I mean, don't get me wrong, Murphy's is great and all, but ... is this what you want? Long-term?"

Aidan's jaw tightened as he turned toward the liquor bottles lining the bar's back wall. It wasn't the first time someone had asked him that, but the question hit a little harder every time. He didn't know how to answer it. He wasn't even sure what he wanted anymore.

"I don't know," Aidan admitted, barely above a whisper. "I just ... I don't know."

MJ clapped him on the back, his grin softening. "No rush. But if you ever feel like shaking things up, you know where to find me. Murphy's food with MJ's beer? We'd be unstoppable."

Aidan's low laugh didn't warm his eyes, which remained cool and unreadable. "Yeah ... maybe."

Even as he said it, something inside him shifted. Maybe it was time to stop settling for "fine."

Declan popped his head out from the kitchen, a towel slung over his shoulder. "Hey, Aidan! The new guy left half the pans a mess. Can you check if we're good, or do I have to redo everything?"

Aidan sighed, the weight of the day settling back on his shoulders. "I'll take a look," he muttered.

MJ smirked as he slid off his stool. "Duty calls. Guess I'll get out of here before Seamus finds out I'm corrupting his head chef."

Aidan snorted. "You're always trouble."

"That's what you love about me," MJ shot back, pulling Aidan into a quick hug. "Hey man ... look, you've got talent; I hope you're not wasting it to carry on a legacy instead of pursuing your dreams."

"It's always good visiting you too, MJ."

On his way out, MJ called back to Jazz, who was wiping down the far end of the bar. "Hey, Jazz! When will you quit this place and come work for me at the brewery?"

Jazz sauntered over, grinning. "You couldn't afford me."

MJ laughed, throwing up his hands. "Had to try."

Aidan watched their teasing, a small smile tugging at his lips. For a moment, the tension in his chest loosened. But as the door swung shut behind MJ, the familiar weight returned, heavier than before.

He pushed off the bar and headed toward the kitchen. The clang of pots and swish of soapy water reached him before he stepped through the doorway. The nightly scrubbing, rinsing, and stacking plates were in full swing. Tonight, it felt suffocating.

He stopped just inside the door, rubbing a hand over his face. Declan was laughing it up with a dishwasher; he seemed so comfortable. A pang of envy stabbed at Aidan. Declan didn't carry the weight of the pub's legacy. That was Aidan's burden: the gospel of Seamus Murphy. Keep the menu the same. Stick to what works. Leave well enough alone.

What if it wasn't well enough anymore?

Heat rose in his chest. New ideas were consistently rebuffed with the same familiar argument: tradition, stability, and loyalty. These words felt less like values and more like chains.

His attention lingered on the washed plates. He was burning himself out, throwing everything into Seamus's kitchen to keep the grind going. But it didn't feel like his anymore. The routines that once gave him purpose now felt suffocating. Did he want this? Did he want to spend the next thirty years running into someone else's kitchen? Following someone else's vision?

What's my vision?

The question hit him hard. His thoughts drifted to MJ; he was so proud and pumped to build his own thing. MJ had taken a risk and created something he loved.

Aidan scrubbed a hand down his face. I don't even know what I want. That was the problem, wasn't it? Every day at Murphy's felt like another step away from figuring it out.

Maybe a break would help me figure it out.

The thought lingered, raw but freeing. He was not about to abandon his family or the restaurant. But perhaps he needed space to clear his head and figure things out.

He sighed, rolled up his sleeves, grabbed a rag, and began wiping the counters. It was all muscle memory: scrub, rinse, wipe. But his mind was somewhere else entirely.

He was tired. Tired of Seamus's gospel. Tired of the grind. Tired of pretending that "fine" was good enough.

Four

The tall front windows filtered in the soft morning light, casting golden rays that bathed the restaurant and warmed the worn wooden tables. The silence that only existed before the doors opened, before the rush of voices, clattering plates, and shouted orders enveloped Murphy's Irish Pub. Aidan cherished this time of day, these quiet moments when the pub transcended its commercial nature and felt like a time capsule.

The bar gleamed, its dark oak polished to a sheen, and the rich aroma of freshly brewed coffee mingled with faint traces of last night's whiskey and stout. Aidan sat at one of the corner tables, his hands wrapped around a steaming mug, letting the silence soak in. Across from him, Jazz sipped her coffee, and her legs crossed under the table, her posture so relaxed it was as if they were sitting in a cafe instead of an empty pub that would soon swarm with customers.

"You know," Jazz said with a smirk, glancing around the room, "if it weren't for the fact that I've seen this place packed to the brim and crazy as hell, I'd almost say it looks kinda charming right now. Peaceful, even."

Aidan dragged a hand through his hair, letting his eyes track hers across the familiar space. He hadn't really looked at the pub like this in a long time. Most of the time, it was just noise—an endless churn of barking orders, clattering dishes, and the grind of service. But now, with the soft glow of morning settling over the room, he noticed the details again: the hand-carved wood on the chairs, the faded copper mugs hanging behind the bar, the sconces that cast a warm, welcoming light over the booths. It felt ... different. Quieter. But also distant.

He found himself drawn to the far wall's collection of mismatched photos. Many frames held pictures of family and friends at celebrations, holidays, and milestones spanning decades. The frames were dusty but not overly neglected. Yet one photo stood out, not just because of its content, but because it was spotless. The frame gleamed, the glass perfectly clean, as though someone had taken extra care to preserve it.

It was a picture of his parents, Seamus and Maureen, standing on the Cliffs of Moher during their honeymoon in Ireland. His mother's hair whipped wildly around her face from the wind, but she was laughing, her eyes bright with unrestrained joy. Seamus stood beside her, younger and leaner, a rare, genuine smile breaking across his usually serious features. They looked ... free.

Aidan studied the photo, their happiness suspended in a single, perfect moment. It all felt unreal: his mom's laughter, his dad's grin. The pub had always been a part of his life, but seeing his parents like that, so full of light, made him wonder.

Had his father been the one to keep that particular photo spotless? The thought gnawed at Aidan, subtle but insistent. He wasn't sentimental, or so it seemed, but maybe he held onto that picture—that moment—to who they had been before the weight of the pub settled on their shoulders.

When was the last time I felt like that? Aidan wondered, the tightness in his chest spreading. He couldn't remember. Survival was his daily grind: kitchen heat, orders, and his father's disputes. He'd go home exhausted, too tired to think but too wired to sleep. There was no lightness in his days. No joy.

"I want that," Aidan murmured, almost to himself, his eyes still fixed on the photo.

Jazz looked where his eyes led, crossing her arms as a puzzled frown tugged at her lips. "You want what?"

"That," he said, nodding toward the wall. "Whatever they had back then. They look ... happy. Not just happy, but buzzing with life." He paused, his voice dipping softer, almost unsure. "I don't think I've ever felt that. That kind of ease. Like everything just fits."

"Can I be honest with you, hun?" Jazz studied him, her teasing tone fading.

"Hit me with it," Aidan responded.

"You won't find that here, Aidan, not in the kitchen, not at this bar. It's not going to just show up one day. You need to go fight for it."

She was right. That picture of his parents when they were young wasn't just a reminder of his loss—freedom, joy, the feeling that life was bigger than the walls of Murphy's Pub. Something had to change. The prospect of endless, slow burnout on this path was unbearable.

"I don't even know where to start," he admitted, running a hand through his hair.

Jazz's lips curved into a knowing smile as she leaned back in her chair. "Take a break. Go somewhere. Do something that doesn't involve the pub, family, or responsibilities. Even if it's just for a week."

The idea tugged at him, but hesitation tugged harder. "I wouldn't even know where to go. And ... going alone? I don't know, Jazz. I've never done anything like that."

"That's kind of the point," she said, her smirk sharpening. "It's just you, no one else to worry about. You might actually find that freedom you're talking about." She leaned forward, her voice soft but firm. "Go to the mountains. Go to the beach. Hell, go to Ireland. Anywhere that isn't here. Trust me, you'll figure it out once you let go of trying to plan every second."

"It's been years since I took a vacation." Aidan stared into his coffee, the steam curling up like the thoughts swirling in his head. The temptation to get away, to escape even for a little while, gnawed at him. He pictured quiet mornings far away, no bossing around, no fighting with his dad. Just space to breathe. To think. Maybe, just maybe, he could find a piece of that happiness he saw in the photo.

"I'll think about it," he said, though the words came out differently this time. They felt real, like the start of something.

Jazz grinned, lifting her coffee mug. "I'll take that as progress. Baby steps, Chef."

He tapped his mug against hers, letting out a light laugh. As the golden morning light continued to pour through the windows, casting the pub in its warm glow, Aidan let himself imagine, just for a moment, what it might feel like to step away truly. To be free.

Maybe, he thought, *I could find that feeling after all.*

Between plating orders and barking instructions, Aidan finally found a spare moment to slip into the narrow hallway behind the kitchen. His father and Declan were stacking boxes of fresh produce from the morning's delivery, their movements efficient but unhurried. The faint hum of the kitchen buzzed in the background, a steady rhythm Aidan knew as the soundtrack of his life.

"Da, Declan," Aidan said, wiping his hands on a towel as he stepped closer. His voice was steady, but the words felt heavier than expected. "Hey, I'm thinking about taking a couple of weeks off. Just to clear my head, maybe go somewhere for a bit. We can talk more after the rush, but I wanted to give you a heads-up."

Seamus turned toward Aidan, his expression unreadable, but something about his stance tensed. Declan straightened, curiosity sparking in his eyes. "A couple of weeks?" Seamus muttered, his voice gruff and skeptical. "Now?"

"Yeah, after this weekend," Aidan replied, keeping his tone casual but firm. "Let's talk after dinner, alright?"

Seamus's expression darkened, his lips pressing into a thin line. Aidan knew his dad's grunt meant trouble, but Aidan also knew he wouldn't argue ... yet. Declan quickly nodded, wiping sweat from his forehead with his hand.

"Alright, we'll talk about it later," he said, though there was something in his tone Aidan couldn't quite place. Approval? Worry? Maybe both.

Without waiting for a response, Aidan turned and headed back into the kitchen, already bracing himself for the conversation to come. He pushed through the rest of the dinner rush, the hours blurring into a whirlwind of heat, noise, and relentless motion. He tried to focus, but the persistent, if faint, lure of a proper break kept nagging at him.

When the last customers trickled out and the kitchen crew began the nightly cleanup, exhaustion tugged at every muscle in Aidan's body. He wiped his brow with his sleeve and leaned against the prep table, letting out a slow breath. *Another service is complete. Another grind survived. But tonight felt different. Tonight, something had to give.*

Seamus had already seated himself at one of the corner tables when Aidan and Declan joined him. The pub was empty now, the low clatter of dishes in the back the only sound breaking the quiet. An untouched pint sat in front of Seamus, his fingers drumming a steady rhythm against the table. His posture was rigid, tension radiating from him like a held breath. Aidan felt it too—wound tight in his own frame, an echo of the unease settling between them.

Aidan slid into the chair across from him while Declan leaned back in his seat, his usual simple grin replaced with something more serious.

"So," Seamus said, his tone clipped as he cast a quick glance at Aidan. "What's this about taking time off now? You've got a pub to run, and we've just come off a busy St. Patrick's Day. We don't exactly close up shop for personal vacations."

Aidan held his father's stare, steadying himself. "I'm not talking about leaving forever, Da. Just two weeks. I need to clear my head and figure some things out. Declan can handle the kitchen while I'm gone."

Seamus's fingers stilled against the tabletop before he leaned back, rubbing his jaw. "Two weeks?" he said, his voice heavy with skepticism.

Seamus's jaw tightened, and his fingers resumed tapping against the table. "You've been grinding hard; I'll give you that. And I've said before you needed a break. But two weeks? This isn't just about you clearing your head, lad. What happens if something goes wrong? If the kitchen gets slammed, or a customer has a complaint?"

Declan jumped in before Aidan could respond. "We'll figure it out," he said, his tone sharper now. "It's two weeks, Da, not two years. I've got it under control."

But Seamus didn't seem convinced. He shifted his attention back to Aidan, his voice dropping lower. "It's not just about the work," he muttered, the edge in his tone softening into something almost vulnerable. "You step away now, and what happens if things fall apart? This place ... It's already a fight to keep it going some days. And without you here ..." He stopped himself, exhaling sharply, his fingers tightening around the edge of the table. "What if it's too much?"

Aidan felt the weight of those words settle heavily in his chest. For years, he'd carried the unspoken expectation that Murphy's was his future. It wasn't just a job; it was a legacy, a duty. But hearing Seamus voice that fear made the burden even more suffocating.

"I'm not walking away for good, Da," Aidan said, his voice steady but tinged with frustration.

"Damn straight you're not," Seamus interjected, his voice low and sharp, the words laced with both defiance and fear. He gripped the table's edge, leaning forward with an intensity that bore down on Aidan. This isn't just a job, Aidan. It's your legacy. It's our family's name."

Unyielding, Aidan met his father's stare head-on. "It's only two weeks," he said, his tone firm but measured. "I just need time to clear my head. That's it."

Seamus rubbed a hand over his face, letting out a long sigh. He glanced from Aidan to Declan, ultimately fixing his focus on Declan, probing for the slightest sign of hesitation. But Declan didn't flinch. He held his ground, his confidence unshaken.

Finally, Seamus leaned back in his chair, his fingers tightening around the pint glass before him. "Fine," he said gruffly, though the reluctance in his tone was unmistakable. "Two weeks. But I'll be checking in, and if something goes wrong, I'll expect you back here."

Declan grinned, leaning back with a rare flash of pride. "I've got this. You'll barely notice he's gone."

Seamus shot him a skeptical look but didn't argue further. He stood, lifting his pint and draining half of it in one long drink before setting the glass down with a solid thud. "Well, don't waste time talking about it. We've still got a pub to clean."

As Seamus walked away, his footsteps heavy against the wooden floor, Aidan felt the tension in the room ease just slightly. He'd done it. He was going to step away—for two weeks, at least. It wasn't a complete escape, but it was a start. And for the first time in what felt like forever, he felt a flicker of relief.

Declan clapped him on the back, his grin widening. "You're really doing it, huh? Good for you, man. You deserve this."

Aidan gave him a small smile, but his mind was already turning. Jazz's voice echoed: *You won't find what you're looking for here.*

A thought tugged at him as he rose and glanced around the dimly lit pub. Perhaps he'd rediscover a part of himself.

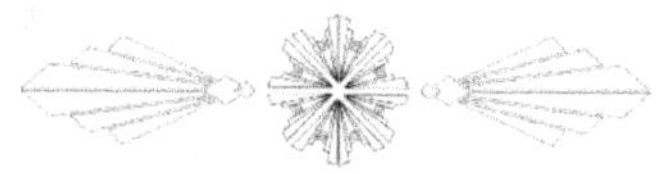

Monday morning dawned quietly, marking the start of Aidan's first week off in what felt like years. He sat at his small kitchen table, fingers curled around a mug of black coffee. The house was still. The absence of his usual Monday morning chaos felt both liberating and unsettling.

No rushing to the pub at dawn. Declan didn't ask where the inventory lists were. Just silence. And time.

So much time, he thought, staring into the dark swirl of coffee. He wasn't entirely sure what to do with it.

It had been a few days since he'd told Seamus and Declan he was stepping away for two weeks. His father had grumbled, as expected, reluctant to admit Murphy's could survive without Aidan. Declan had been firm, though, standing his ground and insisting he could handle the kitchen. In the end, Seamus had relented, albeit with skepticism that still weighed on Aidan. And now, for the first time in years, he was free. *Free to do what?*

His phone buzzed. A message from Jazz:

Jazz

Hope you're sleeping in, Chef. Don't think about stepping near that pub for the next two weeks! Enjoy the time off. Get away. You earned it.

Aidan smirked, typing back:

Setting the phone aside, he leaned back in his chair, letting the quiet seep in. With two entire weeks free, he was clueless how to spend it.

Jazz's words echoed in his head: *Get away.*

He sighed and opened his laptop, hesitating before pulling up a travel site. *Alright. Let's see what's out there.*

Scrolling through vacation options, he skimmed mountain cabins and beach rentals. They seemed ideal, peaceful, and picturesque, but neither felt right. They were just new boxes, trading one set of walls for another. What he needed wasn't rest; it was something bigger, something that would shake him out of this rut.

As doubt started creeping in, a brightly colored banner caught his eye: **Single Sailor Voyages: Escape the Ordinary! Set sail with other solo adventurers! New destinations, new companions, and the liberating expanse of the sea await!**

He blinked, staring at the ad. A cruise? The image showed people leaning over a ship's railing, the endless ocean stretching out behind them, their faces lit with laughter.

Clicking on the ad, he skimmed the itinerary. Six nights at sea. Stops at Elysian Isle, Jamaica, and Grand Cayman, with two full days of open water. The tagline read: **Sail solo, live connected.**

The words struck something deep inside him. Live connected. It wasn't simply a getaway; it was a departure from all that was familiar. New people, new places, and maybe even a new version of himself. He could almost feel the salt air on his skin and hear the hum of the ship beneath his feet. No orders to bark. No tension with Seamus. Just freedom.

But then hesitation clawed its way back. A cruise? Alone? It felt rash, irresponsible, and self-centered. *What if something goes wrong at the pub?* His thoughts raced with fear. *What if I hate it? Will I feel left out if everyone is in a couple or group?*

He sighed and clicked back to the primary site. Guilt twisted in his chest. Declan had promised he could handle things, but what if Dad was right? What if he was being irresponsible?

But his mind kept drifting back to the image of his parents on the Cliffs of Moher. They'd looked so alive, laughing into the wind, full of joy. More than just the photograph, the sentiment it expressed resonated. When had Aidan ever felt like that? When had he taken a chance purely for himself?

His fingers hovered over the "Book Now" button. The tagline glowed on the screen: **Escape the Ordinary.**

He took a deep breath. *This may be what I need. I may need to stop overthinking everything for once.*

Click.

The confirmation popped up almost immediately: **Reservation Confirmed. Six nights at sea. Departure: next weekend.**

Aidan stared at the screen, relief and nerves swirling in his chest. For once, he did something spontaneous, just for him. No expectations. No grind. Just the open sea.

He stood, stretching as he moved to the window. The neighborhood looked the same as it always did, but something about it felt smaller now. Quieter. Like a chapter, he was finally ready to leave behind.

He sipped the last of his coffee, letting the warmth settle in his chest alongside a growing sense of excitement. *This is it*, he thought, a small, genuine smile tugging at his lips. *This is how I figure things out.*

After ages, Aidan felt free. He felt something fresh.

Hope.

Five

Aidan stood at the foot of the gangway, his eyes wide as his breath caught in his throat. The sleek and gleaming Elysian Serenade towered above him, a pristine white colossus under the bright Miami sun. Despite its massive size, its elegant curves gave it an impossibly graceful appearance, as if designed to glide effortlessly across the ocean like a swan. Aidan craned his neck, trying to grasp its sheer scale. The ship seemed too big, too polished, too perfect.

Seeing it made his mind flicker to Murphy's Pub back home in Charlotte. He vividly imagined the worn tables and dim, warm lighting. Murphy's was a place of familiar chaos, where the air smelled of simmering stew, fresh bread, and just a hint of spilled beer. You could feel the history in every corner. Standing here now, Aidan could hardly believe the pub and this gleaming ship existed in the same world.

He hesitated at the gangway, feeling the salt-scented breeze's pull mingling with the excited passengers' chatter. Stepping forward, he felt as if he were crossing some invisible threshold into a world that was everything Murphy's was not. The soft hum of conversation followed him as he ascended, and when he stepped inside, the grand atrium unfolded before him like the opening act of a dream.

Aidan stopped in his tracks, his eyes adjusting to the brightness of the space. Glass skylights stretched high above him, flooding the atrium with golden light that seemed to shimmer and dance across the polished marble floors. Graceful spiral staircases shimmered with gold accents like jewelry in the light. From the ceiling, chandeliers scattered rainbows across the pearlescent walls, resembling frozen constellations. A romantic and refined warmth filled the space as blush pink and teal accents gently toned down the grandeur.

It was overwhelming, not just because of the grandeur, but because it felt so far removed from anything he had ever known. Murphy's felt like home, a place where everyone belonged. This ship was a glittering palace of endless possibilities. It seemed to ask you to look outward, to dream of horizons far beyond what you could see.

Aidan let out a small laugh, though it carried more nerves than humor. Back home, he was the boss. He gave orders, oversaw the kitchen, and ran the pub-like clockwork. Murphy's was predictable, solid, and entirely within his control. Here, though, he was just another face in the crowd. Nobody would ask him what to do or look to him for leadership. He wasn't sure if that thought was freeing or unsettling.

He ventured deeper into the atrium, drawn to a lounge with plush rose-colored chairs encircling small, gleaming tables. Travelers were already sinking into the seating, sipping champagne and cocktails as if this kind of luxury was second nature. Beyond them, massive windows framed the Miami skyline, its shimmering reflection rippling in the blue harbor water below. The sort of view that tugged at something deep inside him, restless and unspoken.

The room buzzed with a quiet, refined energy, every detail polished to perfection. Aidan thought again of Murphy's; the walls covered in old photos hung crooked, and shelves displayed mismatched beer steins alongside well-worn brass fixtures. There was nothing sleek about the pub. It was homey, lived-in, and unapologetically imperfect. Here, everything gleamed as though it had never been touched, as though it existed purely for display.

This ship was a different world altogether, and Aidan could feel the distance between himself and it in every step he took. He was not just a tourist in a new setting; he felt like an outsider stepping into a world that seemed designed for people who were nothing like him. The thought made him pause, his hand briefly brushing against the strap of his carry-on as if he were steadying himself.

For a moment, he looked back over his shoulder. He wasn't sure why, but it was almost instinctual, as though he expected to see the pub somehow trailing behind him. He thought of the cozy dimness of Murphy's, the smell of bread and stew filling the air, and the low, familiar hum of regulars laughing and arguing over their pints. Here, the golden light of the atrium and the soft scent of orchids made it clear how far away that world was, physically and emotionally.

Aidan inhaled deeply and faced forward again. The pub was behind him, and so was everything it represented. This was something entirely new, and he was here now. For better or worse, he had stepped into a space that had nothing to do with his family, his legacy, or the weight of keeping Murphy's alive. For the first time in years, nothing was tying him down.

Navigating the maze of passageways, Aidan found his stateroom—cabin 7517. The door was ajar, and inside, the low hum of music escaped the room.

He pushed the door open, immediately noticing the soft glow of natural light spilling across the room. His eyes bypassed the modest stateroom entirely, drawn straight to the open balcony door and the brilliant sliver of ocean visible beyond it. Without a second thought, Aidan unceremoniously dropped his bags on the floor and strode toward the balcony as if being pulled forward by a magnet.

The salty breeze hit him first, crisp and refreshing, carrying a faint tang of oil and harbor life. To his right, Miami sprawled into view beyond the aft of the ship. The mirrored skyline buildings glinted under the mid-afternoon sun, towering over the organized chaos of the port below. Cranes swept their mechanical arms across the docks, loading and unloading cargo with methodical precision. Additional cruise ships sat nose to tail in the channel, each buzzing with passengers eager to escape their routines. The Elysian Serenade wasn't the largest vessel in port, but its sleek lines and understated elegance made it stand apart.

Turning left, the world changed entirely. The open ocean stretched toward the horizon, a boundless canvas of deep blue that seemed to shimmer in perpetual motion. Calm waves reflected the sunlight in streaks of gold and silver, while the faintest whisper of its vastness sent a strange thrill through him. He gripped the railing and leaned forward, letting the moment sink in.

A small smile tugged at the corner of his lips. "I don't know if this is what Jazz envisioned," he murmured aloud to no one, "but wow. She was right. I needed this."

"Nice, huh?"

The voice came from nowhere, breaking his trance and jolting him slightly. Aidan spun around, his heart jumping, to see a figure leaning casually against the sliding doorframe to the balcony.

Tall and athletic, the man looked every bit like he belonged here—effortless and relaxed. Brody stood with one shoulder against the frame, a grin spreading across his face, his warm smile immediately disarming him. The afternoon light cast a faint glow over his dark skin, making him seem at ease in a way Aidan couldn't imagine for himself.

"Didn't mean to scare you," Brody said, straightening up. "Pretty wild view, huh?"

Aidan blinked, still catching up to the presence of someone else in the cabin. "Yeah, I didn't see you there," he replied, trying to play it off. "I was ... distracted."

"No worries, man." Brody flashed another amiable smile and stepped forward, extending a hand. "Brody Lawson. Looks like we're bunkmates for the week."

"Aidan. Aidan Murphy," he replied, shaking Brody's hand firmly.

Brody nodded, then turned and strolled back inside, dropping onto the bed he'd unpacked before Aidan arrived. He unzipped his duffel and pulled out a stack of shirts, tossing them casually onto the bed like he'd done this a dozen times before.

"So," Brody said without looking up, "first time cruising?"

Aidan leaned back against the small desk tucked into the corner, feeling the faint vibration of the ship beneath his feet. "Is it that obvious?"

Brody laughed, a deep, effortless sound. "Let's just say you've got that 'What the hell have I gotten myself into?' look. Don't worry —you'll get the hang of it. By day two, you'll be living the high life."

Aidan smirked and shook his head. "Yeah, well, this is not the kind of place I'm used to. Feels like I stepped into a whole other world."

"Welcome to the party, my man." Brody clapped him on the shoulder as he passed, grabbing another shirt from his bag. "This is my twelfth cruise, my third time doing one of these Mingle at Sea trips. They're always a blast. Perfect way to unwind, meet some cool people, live a little."

"Twelve cruises?" Aidan raised an eyebrow. "You're practically a professional."

Brody grinned, rolling up a pair of swim trunks and shoving them into a drawer. "What can I say? It's how I blow off steam between work stints. And trust me, there's no better place to meet fun people." He shot Aidan a knowing look, one that seemed full of promises Aidan wasn't quite ready to decipher. "You'll see."

Aidan wasn't so sure about that. Meeting new people wasn't exactly high on his list for this trip, but maybe Brody had a point.

"I don't know," Aidan said, glancing back toward the balcony. "I came here to get away from everything ... you know, clear my head. I'm not really looking for crazy."

Brody grinned as he pulled out a pair of brightly patterned board shorts and flung them onto the bed. "Sometimes a little crazy is exactly what you need. This ship's got a lot in store for you, man. You'll thank me later."

Aidan turned his attention back to the open balcony door. The faint murmur of the harbor was still audible over the hum of the ship's engines, but his eyes lingered on the horizon. For now, he was willing to let himself believe Brody might be right. He breathed in deeply, letting the view sink in. It had been a long time since he'd felt anything close to excitement, but now ... he could feel a flicker.

"Well," Aidan said while stepping away from the wall. "Here's to new experiences."

Brody grinned widely, raising an imaginary glass in the air. "Here's to that, my friend. Let's make the most of it."

As Aidan laughed, still trying to wrap his head around the enormity of it all, he asked, "Alright, so what exactly am I in for? You've done this a dozen times. Spill it. What kind of 'wild' are we talking about?"

Brody's smile broadened as he leaned onto the balcony railing. "Man, you've got no idea. These cruises are like summer camp for adults—booze, beaches, and zero real-world problems. Especially on Mingle at Sea. Trust me, this week's gonna change your life."

And for the first time in longer than he could remember, Aidan was willing to believe it just might.

"And the days at sea?" Aidan asked, trying to picture how the time would unfold. "What's the deal with those?"

"Ah, sea days," Brody said, stretching like a man who had perfected the art of doing absolutely nothing. "Those are all about kicking back. That infinity pool on the top deck? Absolute magic. There's also the gym, if that's your thing, spa treatments, games, dance classes, cooking demos, and, of course, the bars. Lots of bars. You're never more than ten feet from a drink on these ships."

Aidan turned to glance back at their sleek and modern cabin, so far removed from the worn wooden tables and vintage signs of Murphy's Pub. "It all sounds ... overwhelming, honestly."

Brody grinned, catching the hint of hesitation in his voice. "Look, man, I get it. You're out of your element. But that's the point, right? You came here to get away. Trust me, after a few drinks at the welcome mixer, you'll be glad you're here."

Aidan laughed, rubbing a hand through his hair. "Alright, I'll give it a shot. But I'm blaming you if I end up sunburned and covered in stingray slime."

Brody clapped him on the back, his laughter echoing across the cabin. "Deal. Now, speaking of mixers …" He glanced at his watch, his eyes widening. "We should probably get ready. The welcome party for the singles group starts in, like, twenty minutes. It's in the Topaz Lounge with free drinks, snacks, and icebreaker activities. It's a great way to meet some people before we set sail."

"Icebreakers?" Aidan repeated, rubbing the back of his neck. "Sounds … painful."

"It's not that bad, trust me," Brody said, rifling through his suitcase. "Think of it as free drinks and a chance to scope the scene. We're all here to chill, have fun, and meet new people. You'll fit right in."

Though Aidan wanted to scoff, a part of him, the part that had driven him to book the trip, was intrigued. Maybe Brody was right. Now was as good a time as any to break out of his comfort zone. After months of grinding away at the pub, the idea of free drinks, friendly conversation, and a week of freedom didn't sound half bad.

"Alright," Aidan said, moving toward his suitcase to pull out a clean shirt. "Let's see what this mixer's all about."

"Attaboy!" Brody grinned as he pulled a bright blue shirt over his head. "Just follow my lead, and you'll be golden."

As they left the cabin and made their way toward the Topaz Lounge, Aidan felt a flicker of something he hadn't felt in a long time. Excitement? Freedom? He couldn't place it, but something felt off, like a spark about to ignite.

Distant laughter and the soft clinking of glasses greeted them as they entered the ship's bright atrium. Polished marble floors reflected the soft glow of chandeliers while the air hummed with the buzz of conversation. With every pulse, the ship throbbed with possibility, feeling alive.

Aidan exhaled dramatically as a nervous smile emerged. He left Murphy's Pub, his family, and the rest of his life behind for a week. For the first time in a long time, the future felt like a blank page rather than an anchor.

Let's see where this goes, he thought, stepping toward the glowing entrance of the lounge.

Six

As the Elysian Serenade glided away from Miami, the Topaz Lounge was alive with conversation and the cheerful clinking of glasses. From the lounge's expansive windows, the majestic Miami skyline, with its skyscrapers and bright lights, appeared to diminish in size as dusk settled, painting the sky in soft lavender hues. The ship pressed onward into the vast expanse of open ocean, leaving behind the city's noise and Aidan's wearying routine.

"Here we go," Brody said, giving Aidan's shoulder a nudge as they neared the lounge entrance from the atrium. The indistinct murmur of conversation and the smooth strains of jazz spilled out into the hallway, mingling with the subtle hum of the ship beneath their feet.

Just outside the lounge's entryway, the Mingle at Sea team had set up a small table. A bright banner reading 'Welcome, Single Sailors!' draped across the front, and two smiling cruise hosts stood behind it, handing out colorful woven bracelets to passengers entering the mixer.

"Ah, the VIP treatment begins." Brody grinned as they approached the table.

One host, a woman with short blonde hair and a blue Mingle at Sea polo, greeted them cheerfully. "Welcome to the Mingle at Sea group! These bracelets will identify you as part of the singles group for all the exclusive events and activities during the cruise," she explained, holding up a pair of brightly woven bands.

The bracelets were simple but vibrant, a mix of teal and rose-pink threads that matched the cruise line's signature colors.

Brody accepted his with exaggerated enthusiasm, immediately sliding it onto his wrist. "Now, this is how you know you're in the club," he said, flashing the bracelet at Aidan.

The host handed Aidan his, and he slipped it over his wrist with far less fanfare, giving her a polite nod. "Thanks."

"Have fun in there," the host added with a wink before gesturing for the next group to proceed.

The warm golden light washed over them as they crossed into the lounge, giving the space an inviting glow. Plush velvet seating in deep rose tones lined the walls, and elegant windows framed the endless ocean beyond. The first stars reflected on the water's surface, adding to the room's romantic atmosphere. Aidan immediately noticed how carefully curated everything felt, from the gentle jazz drifting from the band in the corner to the faint fragrance of orchids and sea mist that lingered.

Mingle at Sea knew how to create the perfect environment for mingling. There was an easy, inclusive energy in the space that even Aidan, who wasn't exactly a social butterfly, couldn't help but feel.

"Alright, mate. Let's get this party started," Brody said, clapping Aidan on the back as they stepped deeper into the room. Small groups of singles had already gathered, chatting and laughing, their drinks clinking together in celebratory toasts. There was a giddy energy that came with the promise of adventure.

For Aidan, it was a strange mix of excitement and discomfort. Part of him felt out of place like he'd wandered into someone else's vacation. Meanwhile, a quieter, more inquisitive part anticipated the upcoming week.

"I'll take a Black Orchid Martini," Brody winked. The bartender nodded, mixing the drink with practiced flair.

"What about you?"

Aidan hesitated, glancing over the cocktail menu, most of which sounded far too elaborate for his taste. "Just a red ale for me," he said, feeling more comfortable sticking to what he knew.

Brody laughed, nudging him. "Keeping it simple, huh? Nothing wrong with that." As the bartender handed over their drinks, Brody held his martini up to the light, admiring the deep, inky purple liquid swirled with delicate floral notes. "You've gotta live a little, man. One of these days, I'm gonna get you to try something wild."

Aidan grinned, taking a sip of his ale. "Maybe one day, but today's not that day."

With their drinks in hand, the two wandered deeper into the lounge, mingling with the growing crowd. The chatter was easy, people exchanging stories about where they were from, what brought them on the cruise, and how they hoped to make the most of their time. Brody, as expected, dove right in, striking up conversations left and right, his natural charm on full display. Aidan, meanwhile, took a quieter approach, listening more than talking and trying to get a feel for the others around him.

A flicker of light caught his attention as Aidan stood near the edge of the room, sipping his beer and quietly observing the mingling crowd. The glass door to the promenade deck swung open, briefly reflecting the glow of the lounge as a woman stepped inside. His focus shifted her way, an invisible force seeming to guide him.

She moved with a composed grace, her heels clicking softly against the floor as she entered. Clad in a stunning black dress, the woman possessed an understated elegance that distinguished her. Soft waves of dark hair framed her shoulders, and a delicate bracelet added a touch of quiet class to her refined appearance.

Aidan lingered on her for a moment as she paused to give the room a once-over with an expression that didn't quite match the crowd's buoyant mood. Her polite smile seemed practiced, her warmth restrained, as though she was playing a role she didn't fully believe in. She surveyed the gathering, flitting between groups as if seeking something specific.

He couldn't help but wonder what she was thinking. Something about her drew him in, a quiet duality in her presence: poised yet restless, grounded yet guarded. She didn't strike him as someone who had come on this cruise looking for a carefree escape. No, there was more to her, something layered beneath the surface.

Aidan's curiosity simmered, the question settling in his chest: *Who is she?*

Before he could dwell on it further, a bubbly voice cut through the hum of conversation nearby.

"Hey, you two look like you're hiding out over here!"

Aidan turned to see a petite blonde bounding toward them, her sun-kissed skin glowing under the lounge's warm lighting. She practically radiated energy, her smile bright and disarming.

"Mind if I join?" she asked, her voice lilting and casual as she glanced between him and Brody.

Brody, ever the charmer, grinned and gestured broadly toward her. "Of course! The more the merrier. What's your name?"

"Paige," she said, bouncing slightly on her toes as though she couldn't contain her excitement. "You guys enjoying the mixer?"

"It's been solid so far," Brody said, holding up his fancy martini as though to toast. "Black Orchid Martini is a win. I'm Brody, by the way, and this here is Aidan."

Aidan gave her a polite nod, smiling faintly. "Nice to meet you."

"Likewise!" Paige chirped, flashing a grin so wide it was impossible not to smile back. "First Single Sailor Voyage for you guys?"

Brody grinned and shook his head. "For me? Not even close. I'm a seasoned vet at this point. But it's Aidan's first time, so I'm showing him the ropes."

Paige's eyes widened in exaggerated excitement, and she gave Aidan a playful nudge. "Well, welcome to the fun! No worries, we'll make sure you get everything."

Aidan's laughter bubbled up as her infectious energy relaxed the strain in his shoulders.

Before he could reply, Paige's attention darted to the other side of the room. Her expression lit up, and she stepped away from the group without missing a beat. "Oh, there's my roommate! Just a sec, I'm getting her to come here!"

Aidan watched Paige weave through the lounge, her colorful sundress swaying with each step. She took the hand of the woman he'd seen earlier, who had entered from the promenade. Paige pulled her back to the group with contagious determination, and Aidan couldn't help but laugh.

"Guys, this is my roommate, Harper," Paige said practically glowing with pride. "She's basically the classiest person here, so I figured you two should meet."

Despite a subtle smile, Harper's composure didn't waver. "Nice to meet you," she said, her voice smooth and calm. She glanced between Aidan and Brody, her attention settling on Aidan just a moment longer than expected.

Aidan cleared his throat, feeling an unexpected twist of nerves. "Uh, nice to meet you too," he said, doing his best not to sound awkward.

Brody, naturally, was smoother. "Harper, huh? Love the name. So, what brings you on this cruise?"

Harper gave Paige a quick, knowing smile. "Let's just say I needed a change of scenery."

Brody raised his martini in an exaggerated toast. "I can definitely relate to that. You've come to the right place—this is where all the action happens."

After a light laugh, Harper's attention returned to Aidan, who met her look with a nod.

"I think that's something we've all got in common," he said quietly, his voice steady.

For the first time, Harper's composed smile softened slightly, a hint of curiosity glimmering in her eyes.

Before the conversation could go much further, a soft chime echoed through the lounge, and the lights dimmed slightly. The room was hushed as the cruise's host, Maude Nereida, made her way to the small stage at the front of the room. Her presence commanded the space effortlessly, her sun-kissed skin and windswept hair giving her the air of someone who belonged to the sea.

"Good evening, everyone," Maude began, her voice warm and rich as she addressed the crowd. "Welcome aboard the Elysian Serenade—and more importantly, welcome to the start of what I hope will be a week full of adventure, laughter, and maybe even a little romance." She let the words hang for a beat, her dry humor earning a ripple of amused murmurs from the audience. "I'm Maude, your host for this journey here with Mingle at Sea, and I'll be guiding you through all the fun events we've got lined up. So get comfortable, get to know each other, and let's make this a week to remember."

The crowd clapped, and Maude gave a small wave before stepping off the stage, as the room buzzed back to life.

Aidan glanced over at Brody, who had already downed half his martini.

"Looks like things are about to get interesting," Brody said.

Aidan smiled faintly, his eyes flicking back to Harper, chatting quietly with Paige. Maybe Brody was right. Maybe things were about to get interesting.

Paige and Brody hit it off almost instantly, their conversation flowing like they'd known each other for years. Brody's effortless charm and quick wit met Paige's bubbly energy with a natural ease, the two of them already laughing about some shared joke Aidan hadn't entirely caught. As the two bantered and flirted, the atmosphere seemed to bubble with their chemistry. Aidan and Harper stood on the edges of the budding connection, observers of the show.

Aidan watched, amused, as Brody leaned in, his voice low but playful. He said something that made Paige toss her head back in laughter, her blonde hair catching the light. A fast friendship, or even something more intimate, was blossoming between the pair.

Beside him, Harper stood quietly, her expression calm, though there was a faint air of detachment about her as if she wasn't fully present. Her eyes were scanning the room, perhaps more out of habit than interest, but Aidan could sense she wasn't as comfortable as she appeared. He wasn't either, to be fair.

Feeling like a third wheel as Paige and Brody hit it off, Aidan turned to Harper, sensing her own detachment from the conversation. "Fancy getting another drink?" he asked, his tone light but genuine.

Harper's focus snapped back to him, as though he'd just jolted her from a deep reverie. She hesitated, studying him for a moment before giving a slight nod. Her smile was faint but polite. "Yeah, why not?"

Aidan gestured toward the bar, and they made their way through the clusters of singles mingling throughout the lounge. Interwoven conversations created a steady murmur, occasionally broken by a peal of laughter. As they weaved through the groups, Aidan stole a glance at Harper. Though outwardly calm, he sensed her subtle scanning of the room; she seemed to be searching for an exit.

When they reached the bar, the bartender greeted them with a friendly nod. "What'll it be?"

"Another red ale for me," Aidan said, his voice steady. He turned to Harper. "And for you?"

"Dry martini," she replied smoothly, her tone calm and measured, as though the choice was second nature. Aidan watched as she adjusted her posture slightly, standing tall with her shoulders squared. Rather than relaxing, it felt like a protective instinct, a way to stay in control in strange surroundings.

They waited silently at the bar, the gentle clink of glasses and soft jazz from the lounge band filling the air. The quiet wasn't awkward exactly, but Aidan felt the need to bridge it, even as he worked to find the right words.

"So," he began, rolling his beer glass lightly between his hands, "what brings you on this cruise?"

Harper exhaled quietly, as though she'd been asked a dozen times already. Her lips curved into a polite smile, her eyes dropping briefly to her hands before flicking back to his. "I needed to step away from work for a while. Clear my head, you know? Take a break."

Aidan nodded, her tone and posture reminding him of his own guarded answers to that same question earlier in the evening. He didn't push. "Yeah, same. Life at home was starting to feel like a grind. Figured some time away might help me figure a few things out."

Though casual, their glances held a searching intensity, hinting at a connection neither quite dared to explore fully. Aidan didn't press, and Harper seemed to appreciate that.

"Seems like we're all here for the same reason," Harper said after a moment, her voice soft and tinged with a wistfulness Aidan couldn't quite place. "Escape."

"Yeah," Aidan agreed, taking a sip of beer. The word sat heavily in his chest, not for its falsity, but its truth. "Something like that."

The bartender slid Harper's martini across the bar, and she picked it up with a quiet word of thanks. She took a measured sip, her fingers resting lightly on the glass as if it were something steady in an unsteady moment. Aidan glanced at her again. Her unease felt familiar, a feeling he knew only too well.

For a while, neither of them spoke. But the silence didn't bother Aidan; it felt like shared ground, a quiet recognition that they were both navigating this strange, new experience in their own way.

"I've never really done anything like this," Harper acknowledged in a whisper, her eyes quietly surveying the space around them. "I'm usually more … structured. This is kind of out of my element."

Aidan's light laugh gave way to a more genuine expression on his face. "Same here. I'm not exactly the 'cruise' type. Or the 'singles mixer' type, for that matter."

Harper tilted her head slightly, her lips curving into a small, genuine smile for the first time since they'd started talking. "But here we are," she said, her tone carrying a quiet acceptance.

"Here we are," Aidan echoed with a grin.

She took another sip of martini, her posture loosening just a fraction. "It's not so bad, though. Just … different."

"Yeah," Aidan agreed, his smile softening. "Different's not always a bad thing."

A quiet ease settled between them for the first time that evening. It wasn't the lively, rapid-fire banter Brody and Paige had struck up, but it didn't need to be. This was something quieter, something that didn't demand immediate answers. Harper seemed more at ease, too, her shoulders less rigid, and the faint tension in her posture gave way to something softer. It was a slight shift, but Aidan noticed it.

Before he could say anything more, a warm, confident voice cut through the low hum of conversation around them.

"Hello there. I hope you two are settling in."

Aidan and Harper turned toward the voice to see a woman standing beside them, her presence both understated and commanding. Maude Nereida. Aidan had heard her speak earlier during the welcome announcement, but her air of calm authority was even more striking up close. Her ocean-blue eyes sparkled with a knowing serenity like she'd seen every story play out on the sea and understood them all. She seemed entirely at home in this floating world.

"Hi, I'm Maude," she said softly, extending her hand first to Aidan, then to Harper. "I'm the host for the singles group, in case you didn't catch my little speech earlier."

Aidan shook her hand, noting how firm yet gentle her grip was. "Aidan," he said, then motioned to Harper. "And this is Harper."

Maude shifted her focus between them, a faint, knowing smile gracing her lips, as if she were one step ahead of them both. "It's a pleasure to meet you both. I hope you're finding your sea legs."

Though polite, Harper's returned smile didn't quite mask the flicker of curiosity, or maybe apprehension, in her eyes. "We're getting there. It's been ... a bit of an adjustment," she said, her voice composed but quieter than earlier.

"Understandable," Maude replied, her tone warm and soothing, almost like a lullaby. "These cruises can be a lot at first, but the sea has a way of helping people find what they're really looking for—even if they're not sure what that is yet."

Aidan raised an eyebrow, a hint of amusement tugging at the corner of his mouth. "Is that so?"

"Oh, absolutely," Maude said, her tone playful but layered with something deeper. "The sea has a rhythm, a way of drawing things out of us. Things we don't always expect. That's why Mingle at Sea exists. Solo travelers find themselves in good company here. Just remember to let the tide take you where it wants. You might be surprised where you end up."

Harper gave a gentle laugh, though she kept her focus on Maude, her face contemplative. It was as though she was weighing the older woman's words, trying to decide if they were simply metaphors or if there was some hidden truth beneath them. "Sounds ... like good advice," she said, quiet but sincere.

Maude nodded, her smile widening just a little, the kind that suggested she'd said all she needed to but knew the meaning would unfold in its own time. "It's worked for me so far," she said, her tone light but deliberate. "Well, I'll let you two enjoy the evening. If you need anything, don't hesitate to find me. I'll be around."

She gave them both a small wave and disappeared into the crowd, her presence leaving behind a kind of echo. Aidan watched her retreat, and when he glanced back at Harper, he found her still watching Maude, her lips pressed together in a contemplative line.

He took another sip of his ale, letting the warmth settle in his chest. "Do you think she knows something we don't?" he asked, a grin pulling at his lips.

Harper tilted her head slightly, her eyes narrowing just enough to suggest she was considering the question. Then, to his surprise, she gave a slight, playful smirk. "She definitely gives off that vibe. Maybe we should stick close to her if we want to figure it out."

"Maybe," Aidan replied, his grin widening to match hers. There was something lighter between them now, as though the moment they'd shared with Maude had subtly shifted the dynamic.

Harper turned back to him, her posture more relaxed, the slight guard she'd been carrying earlier nowhere to be seen. "Thanks for the drink, by the way," she said, her tone warmer than earlier.

"Anytime," Aidan said, his voice softening in response. He couldn't pinpoint when the tension dissipated, but he sensed a subtle yet significant release he hadn't felt before.

They said little else after that, but they didn't need to. The gentle hum of the ship beneath their feet and the faint roar of the ocean beyond the lounge filled the spaces between words, leaving room for something unspoken to grow. Aidan let the moment settle into his bones, the quiet satisfaction of being present.

Maybe Maude was right. Perhaps the tide really did know where it was going.

For the first time in a long while, Aidan felt himself let go of control, and it didn't scare him. It felt ... good.

Seven

The next afternoon, the Elysian Serenade was alive with activity. Passengers bustled from one event to another; their laughter and conversations carried on the salty breeze. Aidan stood at the edge of the deck, taking in the scene. He looked out over the crowd, even as his thoughts returned to the loose ends waiting in Murphy's kitchen. He couldn't help but notice the irony: he was on a relaxing cruise but felt just as tense as ever.

He checked his watch. It's time to head to Hestia's Hearth, the ship's gleaming cooking demo space. Brody had mentioned it would be a fun diversion, but Aidan saw it differently. It wasn't about learning something new. It was all about getting back to his cooking passion without his dad's pressure. Just a couple of hours of cooking for the sake of it, without expectations, without the weight of the restaurant.

He needed that.

Brody met him just outside the entrance, looking as carefree as ever, a grin already plastered across his face. "Ready to make some pasta, Murph?" Brody teased, giving Aidan a friendly nudge.

Aidan laughed and shook his head, replying, "You know I'm a professional chef, right?"

Brody's grin widened. "Doesn't mean you can't have a little fun with it. Besides, it's not like you've got a kitchen full of customers breathing down your neck right now."

Aidan smirked, tying on his apron. "True, but if this turns into a pasta disaster, don't blame me."

Brody laughed, holding up his hands in mock surrender. "No pressure, man. We're here to relax, remember? Worst case, you can show these people how a real chef works."

Aidan glanced around the sleek, state-of-the-art kitchen, the gleaming countertops under the lights, and the sea stretching beyond the floor-to-ceiling windows. It was a far cry from Murphy's warm, rustic vibe, but something about the pristine setup soothed him. No clanging of pots, no shouting of orders, no endless list of tasks. Just a simple cooking demo.

"So, think you'll ever start hosting cooking classes at Murphy's?" Brody asked as they found a station. "It could class up the joint a little?"

Aidan shot him a sideways glance. "Yeah, I can see that. Throw in a chandelier and mood lighting, and we'll be set."

Brody grinned, not missing a beat. "Go all out, you know? You've got the chef chops. Who wouldn't want to learn from a pro?"

"I'll stick to what I know," Aidan replied, adjusting his apron. "But for today, I'm fine making pasta with many tourists."

With an amused grin, Brody scanned the room. "Speaking of tourists ..." he said, lowering his voice. "Look who just walked in."

Aidan trailed his attention to the same spot, catching sight of Paige and Harper entering the room. Paige's enthusiasm was palpable, her apron already tied on with an exaggerated flourish. Harper trailed behind her, her expression more reserved, though there was something subtly uneasy in the way she held herself.

Before Aidan could comment, Paige beelined toward Brody with a wide grin. "Brody! You look like you need a partner!" she called out, abandoning Harper without a second thought.

Aidan shook his head, a wry grin tugging at his lips. *That was fast,* he thought to himself.

Harper stood alone, tightening her apron. *Guess we're both left behind,* Aidan thought, a flicker of amusement crossing his mind. He walked over to her, offering a small cordial smile. "Looks like we've both been left in the dust."

Harper turned, and for a fleeting moment, the walls around her expression crumbled. "Abandoned again, huh?"

"Seems to be a motif on this trip," Aidan said, letting out a mock heavy sigh. "It's gonna be a fight to keep those two separated."

Harper laughed low in her throat, her tension easing slightly. "Yeah, I think you're right."

"Looks like we'll have to make do," Aidan added, gesturing toward the kitchen station where their group was gathering for the pasta-making lesson.

The head chef clapped his hands together, his voice booming through the room with an exuberance that matched the bright lights overhead. "Buongiorno, tutti! Today, we make pasta from scratch—the true Italian way!" His thick accent and lively gestures immediately drew the room's attention as he explained the steps they would take to craft their fresh dough. The crowd, a mix of tourists and aspiring chefs, listened intently, eager to begin.

Aidan, meanwhile, barely registered the chef's instructions. He knew the drill, the steps of pasta-making etched into muscle memory from years in the kitchen. But here, for the first time in what felt like forever, he could move through the motions without the weight of the restaurant bearing down on him: just flour, eggs, dough, and a rare moment of peace.

He glanced at Harper beside him, catching the slight purse of her lips as she cracked an egg into the well of flour, her focus unshaken. She seemed lost in the task for a moment, her fingers moving through the ingredients with a quiet focus. But there was something weird, something he couldn't quite grasp. It wasn't the excitement he'd expected from someone learning to make pasta. No, there was something else.

"So," Aidan said casually after a few minutes, kneading the dough before him, "how's life?"

Even as he voiced the question, its significance landed heavily between them. Harper's hands stilled for a split second, her fingers lightly dusted with flour as she hesitated. The smile she gave him in return was thin, almost brittle, like it might crack if he pressed any further.

"You really want to know?" she asked, her tone light but lacking real levity. Her eyes flicked toward him, and for the first time, he could see how far from fine she was.

Aidan gave a slow nod, his voice warm with understanding. "That good, huh?"

Harper let out a small, bitter laugh, surprising herself. "Yeah," she mumbled, her hands resuming their work, kneading the dough as if it might help knead out the knots in her own thoughts. "Something like that."

For a moment, neither of them said anything. They stood in comfortable silence, the soft thuds of dough being worked and the chef's voice in the background filling the space between them. Aidan had always appreciated these quiet moments in the kitchen, where conversation didn't need to fill every pause.

As he glimpsed at Harper again, her expression softened, and he couldn't help but notice how methodically she worked. There was something therapeutic in the way she moved through the motions, as if focusing on the dough allowed her to block out everything else.

"You've done this before," Harper said, breaking the quiet. A quiet calm emanated from her, her voice a soft murmur as she studied his hands, her curiosity piqued by his skilled movements.

Aidan smirked, but there was something self-deprecating about it, a quiet admission in the curve of his lips. "You could say I've had some practice."

Harper kept kneading the pasta dough, her fingers pressing into it with practiced ease. Without pausing, she cast Aidan a sidelong glance, curiosity dancing in her eyes. "Professional pasta maker on the side?"

He shrugged, rolling his shoulders like the weight of the truth didn't sit so heavy. "Not quite. I run a restaurant back home. It's a family business, more or less. We don't do much pasta, but ... I've spent more time in kitchens than I care to admit."

The words came out casually, but Aidan felt the shift in the air the moment he said them. It was something about the way Harper's hands slowed, how her fingers hesitated over the dough.

"A restaurant?"

He nodded, keeping his tone light, though something inside him twisted. "Yeah. Irish place in Charlotte. It's been in the family for years. My dad built it from scratch. I've been running it with my brother for ... longer than I thought I would."

He didn't know why he added that last part. Perhaps speaking it out loud made it hit closer to home, or maybe, for the first time, he wasn't simply digesting the truth without resistance.

"And do you like it?"

Aidan looked at the window, his jaw tightening with unspoken tension. That was the question, wasn't it? He could've given the usual answer—the polite one, the easy one—but something about Harper made him want to be honest.

"I love cooking," he admitted finally, his voice quieter, steadier. "But the restaurant ... it's complicated. Family business comes with family expectations, you know?"

Harper nodded, and for a moment, a spark of understanding passed between them, unspoken but unmistakable. He didn't know her whole story, but he knew that look—the weight in her eyes, the kind that came from chasing something for so long only to wonder if you'd been running in the wrong direction.

"I get it," she whispered, rolling the dough beneath her palms. "I've spent the last several years chasing a career I thought would bring happiness." She paused, her lips pressing together like she was choosing her next words carefully. "And now? Well, I'm not so sure anymore."

Aidan studied her, the way she looked down at her work, as if trying to smooth out the uncertainty with every motion.

"Advertising, right?" he asked.

Harper sighed. "Yeah. Creative manager at an agency in New York. Big city, big job, big burnout."

Aidan smiled knowingly. "That's a lot of baggage to carry."

She let out a short laugh, but it lacked amusement. More like she was exhaling some of the weight of it.

He knew the feeling. The restless exhaustion. The gnawing sense that no matter how much effort you poured into something, it might never be enough—not for yourself, not for the people expecting you to succeed.

Harper kneaded the dough with renewed focus, her voice quieter now. "I thought if I worked hard enough, if I pushed myself, I'd get to this place where ... I don't know, everything would make sense. But now that I'm here ..."

"It's hard, isn't it?" Aidan murmured. "Realizing that what you thought you wanted isn't what you need."

She shook her head, a wry, almost tired smile tugging at her lips. "Yeah, something like that. I wanted to be the best ... make a name for myself." She hesitated, exhaling through her nose. "But now, all I feel is tired. Like I'm trying to hold on, but it doesn't even matter anymore."

Aidan's hands stilled, his chest tightening at the familiarity of her words. He could've said them himself.

"You're not alone in that," he said softly.

Harper turned to him then, and in her eyes, Aidan saw his own reflection—his own frustrations, his own quiet discontent. They barely knew each other, not really, but in that moment, they understood each other in a way that didn't need explaining.

"You ever think about walking?" Harper asked, her voice low, almost tentative.

Aidan exhaled sharply, somewhere between a sigh and a laugh. "Every damn day."

Their laughter was quiet, but something about it settled between them like an unspoken agreement. Neither of them had the answers, but at least, for now, they weren't alone in the uncertainty.

For the first time in a long while, Aidan felt like he could breathe. It wasn't a grand revelation, and it wasn't some life-altering epiphany—but it was something. A small, solid thing in the middle of all the doubt.

He glanced down at Harper's hands, at the smooth, even dough she'd been working. "Looks like you're pretty good at this," he said, nudging her elbow. "Maybe we open a pasta restaurant together."

Harper laughed, shaking her head. "One problem. I hate cooking."

Aidan's smile lingered, a hint of amusement in his voice. "That could be an issue."

Wiping her flour-covered hands on her apron, Harper smirked playfully. "Maybe someday I'll have to come and sample your cooking. You know, just to see if you live up to the hype."

Aidan's eyes sparkled with humor. "You're welcome anytime, and I promise, it'll be the best dish just for you."

"Better be," she teased lightly, a warmth creeping into her voice despite herself.

As they continued kneading dough and cutting fresh pasta, side by side, Aidan noticed the change in Harper. The tension visibly eased from her shoulders for the first time since they'd met, a small but noticeable change. He didn't know everything about her, but it didn't matter then.

Across the room, Paige and Brody were in their own world, laughing loudly as they tossed bits of flour at each other, smearing sauce on their aprons and making a complete mess of their station. Aidan couldn't help but laugh softly to himself, his eyes on Paige and Brody as their flirtation crackled with an almost tangible energy.

But it was different for Aidan and Harper. Lighter. Slower.

"They're certainly hitting it off," Harper observed with a mischievous lift of her lips, stealing a sideways glance at Aidan.

His eyes followed hers, and he couldn't help but grin. "Looks like a fun fling in the making, doesn't it?"

Harper nodded, though her smile faded. "Yeah, it does. Good for them, I guess. It's nice to see them so carefree."

Aidan glanced at her, sensing the subtle shift in her tone. "You don't sound too convinced."

She shrugged, her hands keeping busy with the pasta dough. "It's just ... I don't know. I used to think things like that were supposed to be simple. Fun. But they never turn out that way, do they?"

Aidan rolled out his dough, his movements calm and methodical, as though the conversation didn't surprise him. "Not often, no. Things get ... complicated."

"That's an understatement," Harper said with a short laugh, shaking her head. "It's funny. When I see Paige and Brody, I get this feeling that it's just a vacation thing. You know, something light that won't follow them home. But then I think about all the times I thought I was going to have something simple and ... well, it never worked out that way."

Aidan glanced at her, his expression thoughtful but not intrusive. "Yeah, I know what you mean. Simple's good in theory, but real life tends to mess it up."

Harper tilted her head slightly, a knowing smirk playing at her lips as she shot him a sideways glance. "Speaking from experience?"

Aidan let out a quiet sigh, leaning slightly against the counter. "You could say that."

And in that moment, they both fell into a comfortable silence, their hands busy with the motions of the class. They weren't alone, not really. Just two people sharing an understanding, working side by side.

"Had a relationship back home that started simple enough," Aidan said after a pause, his voice measured and steady. "We were both busy, so we didn't expect much. But the thing about busy lives is, eventually, someone starts wanting more, and when you can't give it ..."

"Things fall apart," Harper finished for him, her voice quieter now.

Aidan nodded, the truth of her words sitting heavy. "Yeah."

He noticed how Harper's hands stilled, her fingers pressing into the dough as if it held the answers to the questions swirling in her head. There was a vulnerability in the quiet between them, a shared understanding. Aidan hadn't expected to talk about his personal life here. Hell, he hadn't expected to talk about much of anything beyond pleasantries. But something about this felt ... safe. Like she wouldn't judge, because she already understood.

Harper bit her lip, focusing intently on the dough in front of her. Clearly, she wasn't ready to dive into her mess just yet, and Aidan wasn't the kind of guy to push. He recognized the profound impact of quiet contemplation, understanding its strength to surpass any amount of speech.

"What about you?" Aidan asked after a moment, keeping his tone gentle. "Any … complications?"

Harper gave a small, humorless laugh. "Complications is putting it mildly."

Aidan let the conversation drift, his hands rolling out the pasta dough in practiced, methodical movements. But his attention stayed on Harper, waiting. Not pressing, just patient. Something about her piqued his curiosity, making him want to learn more, not in a prying way, but in a way that felt … connected. Like whatever she had been through, he might understand it. Maybe all they required was understanding without prying.

After a beat, Harper broke the silence. "I was engaged once," she said, her voice careful, measured. She focused on the dough, smoothing it with more intent than necessary. "We were together for a while."

Aidan didn't react, didn't press her with questions. He just nodded, letting her set the pace. "Engaged, huh? That's … a big step."

"Yeah," Harper responded, her voice trailing off. There was a weight to the word, an unfinished story lurking behind it. She didn't go into details or explain whether she was still raw from the breakup only a few weeks ago or if she had moved on. Aidan sensed her reluctance to unpack everything there and then, and he understood.

"So, what happened?" Aidan asked, his voice soft and cautious. He wasn't trying to pry, just giving her room to talk if she felt like it.

Harper hesitated, her hands pressing into the dough harder than necessary. "Life happened. Work happened. I thought I could juggle everything. I thought … if I just worked hard enough, I could make it all fit. But in the end, I lost him." She gave a soft shrug, as if trying to brush off the deeper hurt beneath her words. "It's funny how you think you're doing the right thing, but when you look back ... you wonder if you missed the point entirely."

Aidan's eyes softened. He knew that feeling all too well. There was something in her words that resonated deeply, like an echo of his own thoughts, his own struggles. "I get that," he said finally, his voice quieter. "Trying to hold on to everything and ending up with nothing."

Harper glanced at him, her eyes searching his. "Yeah, exactly. It feels like that."

He nodded, folding his dough carefully. "It's hard to know when to let go. Or even what to let go of. I guess it's something we're all still figuring out."

She smiled at that, a small, genuine smile that eased their tension. "It's like that saying, 'You can have it all, just not all at once.' I'm still trying to learn that part."

Aidan nodded slowly in agreeance, a quiet warmth threading through him. "Same here. My father always says life's about balance, but the more I try to find it, the more unbalanced everything feels."

They fell into a comfortable silence again, working through the cooking class's motions but now sharing something beyond the ingredients. Aidan liked the quiet, easy connection; no need for endless chatter. It felt ... natural, like they were two people who understood something about the world that most people didn't.

Harper's attention drifted over to Paige and Brody, who were now dramatically taste-testing their sauce, spoon-feeding each other with exaggerated expressions. A streak of flour crossed Brody's cheek, and tomato sauce smeared Paige's apron, but neither seemed to care. They were in their own little world, oblivious to everyone else.

"They seem to be having fun," Harper mused, her tone thoughtful. "Makes me wonder if it's just a vacation thing, you know? Something that won't follow them home."

Aidan shifted his focus to match hers, catching sight of Brody and Paige enjoying each other's company as if it were second nature. "Maybe. But sometimes ... that's enough. It doesn't have to be anything more."

Harper tilted her head, considering his words. "You think?"

He shrugged, wiping his hands on a dish towel. "Yeah. I think not everything has to be serious to matter. Sometimes, a little fun and lightness are all you need. And if it ends when the cruise ends, well ... maybe that's okay, too."

Harper pondered his words, her expression relaxing as she considered the possibility. Perhaps he was right. Not every connection had to come with expectations or promises of forever. Some things are designed to be fleeting, offering support in the present before prompting you to move forward.

"I guess we'll see," she said. "Either way, they're making the most of it."

"Looks like it," Aidan agreed, his green eyes catching hers with a glint of humor. "Maybe we should take notes."

Harper laughed, feeling lighter than she had in days. "Maybe."

As they finished rolling out the pasta, Aidan watched as Harper's tension seemed to ease even more. There was something about the quiet rhythm of cooking, the shared conversation that demanded nothing more than honesty, that felt ... freeing. He didn't offer to fix things or offer clichés—he just listened.

Aidan noticed Harper glance out the window, watching the horizon stretch endlessly into the ocean. It seemed the burden of New York, her commitment, and her past were lifting a bit.

"Thanks for this," Harper said quietly, almost as an afterthought. "For ... listening. And not asking too many questions."

Aidan smiled, a soft, knowing smile. "Anytime. You've got my back for the next few days, right?"

Harper shook her head with a knowing smile. "If Paige and Brody keep going like this, I think we'll both need all the support we can get."

At the other work bench, their friends were in a world all their own, laughing hysterically as Brody pretended to drop a spoonful of sauce into Paige's hair. Harper rolled her eyes but couldn't help smiling.

"You're probably right. Looks like it's going to be an interesting week."

Harper held his stare; in that moment, the atmosphere softened, as if the weight they both carried had drifted off. "Yeah," she whispered, her smile lingering. "Interesting, for sure."

They returned to their cooking, their quiet connection deepening as the class continued. For the first time in a long time, Aidan didn't feel the tug of responsibility, the pull of the restaurant, or the endless expectations that came with it. Here, in this moment, on this ship, with someone who seemed to understand, he could just ... be.

He entertained the possibility that this week wouldn't be just an escape. Perhaps it has the potential to transform into something completely different from what he'd imagined.

Eight

Aidan let himself lean back in his chair, the smooth leather cushion creaking slightly beneath him, as he surveyed the faux wood paneling and dark decor accented with brass that filled the Sea Shanty.

The tang of spilled beer and fresh lemon polish mingled with the savory fragrance of fried appetizers drifting from the bar. The room was abuzz with chatter and laughter, the clinking of glasses weaving through the low hum of Irish folk music playing over the speakers. Antique-style lanterns cast uneven, flickering light, striving to evoke a sense of cozy warmth. Stained-glass windows, a jumble of greens and reds, adorned the space above the bar, adding a vibrant touch, their glow fragmented and uneven in the low light.

Aidan thought it was a good try, but it felt artificial. Gleaming brass, spotless floors, and unblemished wood paneling lacked the natural patina of time. He took a slow sip of his beer, letting its crisp, malty flavor settle on his tongue.

"Well, I guess they tried ..." he muttered under his breath, looking around the space. "At least they've got beer on tap. There's that."

Brody leaned back across from him at their small corner table and caught the smirk on Aidan's face. "What's that?" he asked, half-smiling like he knew a quip was coming.

Aidan shrugged, gesturing with his pint. "This place. The Sea Shanty. It's as if they just Googled 'Irish pub' and checked off every stereotype. Dark wood, Irish tunes, a few fake antiques on the wall. But it's missing something."

Brody rested his elbow on the table, his smile teasing. "Missing what?"

"The soul," Aidan responded, glancing around once more. "There's no grit. No history. I see their attempt, but the atmosphere they're creating isn't hitting the mark."

The words were out of his mouth before he realized how much they hit home. It wasn't just the makeshift pub; it was Murphy's back home, too. The pressure of keeping it running, of maintaining the legacy his father had built, was exhausting. As he struggled to meet everyone's expectations, the pub's soul, its essence, seemed to fade away. It had become impersonal, a routine he couldn't escape. Maybe the Sea Shanty had beer on tap, but it wasn't his place. And, lately, Murphy's didn't feel like his either.

He bit off the rest of that thought and forced a chuckle for levity. "But hey, at least they've got beer on tap. I'll take it."

Brody raised his glass, his grin easy and unwavering. "Here's to that."

Aidan clinked his glass with Brody's but held it a moment longer, pondering the unspoken. Maybe this cruise wasn't just about bailing for a while. Maybe it was really about figuring out why it had all gotten so hard in the first place. *I've been doing this far too long*, he thought. *I need to crawl my way back to the part of it I actually care about.*

The warm clink of their glasses melded with the general noise of the surrounding pub. For all its shortcomings, the Sea Shanty had a comforting feeling that Aidan couldn't quite shake. Maybe it was the wooden tables or the clattering of pint glasses, but even with its polished and varnished aesthetic, it was one of the few places where he felt he could finally sit back and just be. No kitchen. No expectations.

"Well, at the very least, they're keeping it interesting," Brody said, nodding toward the front of the room as a young woman with a clipboard stepped up to a microphone. Her voice rang out into the crowded space, filled with forced enthusiasm as she detailed the rules for the trivia game that was about to begin.

Aidan snorted, "Are you good at trivia?"

Brody smiled, tapping his temple. "I have a few random facts stored up here. But I wouldn't say I'm exactly an expert. How about you?"

Aidan shrugged. "I'm alright. But if they throw in pop culture, we're screwed."

"Good thing I'm here, then," said Brody with a wink. "You can handle the smart stuff. I'll take care of the fun facts."

With Brody's characteristic lack of creativity, they registered as 'Murphy's Law' and prepared for the trivia game to begin. The first few questions weren't too bad: easy geography, some history, a couple of general knowledge ones that Aidan and Brody breezed through.

But as the game wore on, the questions got obscure. Way obscure.

"What the heck is a 'bunyip'?" Aidan muttered, staring at the latest question on the screen and then looking over at Brody, who only shrugged.

Brody grinned. "I've got no clue. Some kind of space creature, maybe?"

Aidan shot him a look. "I thought you were the pop culture guy."

"I said 'fun facts,' man, not space opera deep cuts."

They hurriedly wrote their wild theory about a space monster, which they knew was wrong, and continued. The next few questions delved into random movies from the '80s, obscure sports trivia, and increasingly impossible astronomy facts.

"What was the name of the first man-made object to reach the moon's surface?" Aidan read aloud, glancing around the room.

He and Brody exchanged glances. "Uh ... Apollo something?" Brody ventured weakly.

Aidan groaned, rubbing his temples. "I think Apollo was the one that landed humans on the moon. There was something else before that ..."

"Well, I've got nothing," Brody said, writing Apollo 17, even though neither of them was sure. "How about we just enjoy the beer?"

"Good plan," said Aidan, laughing as he raised his glass.

It continued on through the night; lots of questions remained that were unanswerable, some of which even left the entire room scratching their heads. Never once did Brody give up that smiling demeanor, though, and kept things light, tossing in jokes at times when they were stumped.

One question asked, "Which country has the largest number of vending machines per capita?"

Brody leaned in further, an impish grin spreading across his face. "I bet it's Japan."

Aidan threw him a dubious look. "You sure?"

"Nope," Brody said, writing the answer down anyway. "But I'm going with my gut."

As the final scores were being tallied, both Aidan and Brody knew well enough that they hadn't exactly blown anyone away.

Silence settled over the pub as the host cleared her throat and began the closing announcements. "Alright, folks, the champions of this evening's trivia contest are ... Ship Happens!" A roar of applause erupted from a group near the bar, several of them cheering and high-fiving each other as they waved across the rest of the room.

"Coming in second, we have Trivia Newton John!" she continued, "And in third place ... Quiztal Clear!"

Yet another round of applause arced through the crowd, but Aidan and Brody exchanged a knowing look. They both knew they hadn't remotely placed in the top three.

Brody heaved his arms up into the air in a mock-celebratory manner. "And we won nothing! Success!"

"At least we didn't come in dead last," Aidan responded.

Brody raised his glass, unruffled by their defeat. "Exactly. It's about the fun, not the win, right?"

They clinked glasses again, both laughing at their less-than-stellar performance in trivia. On a larger scale, it didn't matter. Tonight wasn't about winning; it was about having fun, kicking back, and enjoying themselves in the freedom of being far from their regular lives.

"So, how do you think the whole restaurant talk is going to go when you get back?" Brody asked, his tone a little more serious now, though his characteristic smile still came through easily.

Aidan sighed, reclining in his seat. "Honestly? No clue. He's not exactly big on change, yeah? But the more I think about it, the more I'm just … burned out, y'know?"

Brody nodded, taking a sip of his drink. "Yeah, dude, I hear you. Running a spot like Murphy's has got to be pretty intense. You've got all the pressures of keeping it afloat, getting things running right, dealing with your dad. It's just a lot."

Aidan stared into his beer, the foam settling around the edges of the glass. "It is. I love cooking, but the restaurant? It's all-consuming. And I don't know if I want that for the rest of my life."

Brody gave him a sympathetic look, leaning forward slightly. "You ever think about just … stepping back for a while? Letting your brother take the reins?"

Aidan let out a dry laugh. "Declan? He's great in the kitchen, but him running the place? I don't think that would go over well with my dad. He's … well, let's just say he's a bit of a control freak."

"Yeah, I can see that," Brody said, nodding reflectively. "But at some point, you gotta take care of yourself, too, you know?"

Aidan exhaled a deep sigh, knowing that Brody was right. He had been carrying the restaurant on his shoulders for so long, he wasn't even sure how to set it down. Perhaps this journey was a beginning, a chance to pause, reflect, and determine what comes next.

Before he could answer, the voice of the trivia host boomed across the room again, thanking everyone who had participated and wishing all a good night. The pub emptied after the trivia, but Aidan and Brody stayed at their table, relishing the evening's camaraderie, laughter, and friendly competition. It wasn't about the trivia itself. It had nothing to do with the bar. The moment was all that mattered, a unique chance to surrender to the present and simply be.

Aidan raised his glass once more. "To not winning."

Brody grinned, raising his own glass to meet Aidan's. "To not winning."

Their glasses clinked again, the sound a small but satisfying punctuation to the night. For Aidan, it was another reminder of why he'd come on this cruise in the first place: to escape, to reflect, and maybe, just maybe, to find a bit of clarity about the life waiting for him back home.

Brody grinned as he took another sip of his beer. "And to not giving a damn about it."

For a long moment, they sat there, soaking in the lively atmosphere of the Sea Shanty around them. Pockets of passengers were still laughing, clinking glasses, and celebrating their trivia victories. The moment provided a pleasant respite from the weighty thoughts that had been burdening Aidan since their departure. He could let his guard down here, at least a little. With Brody, everything felt lighter, easier. No pressure, no expectations. Just a good time.

But as he looked across at his friend, Aidan couldn't shake the feeling that there had to be more to Brody than the laid-back, carefree guy he portrayed. They'd discussed Murphy's, Aidan's life back home, but Brody hadn't said much about his own. Now, with the trivia game over and a couple of beers already down, Aidan figured it was time to turn the conversation around and find out just what was going on in the enigmatic mind of his friend.

"So," Aidan started, easing back into his chair. "We've been talking about me and the pub all night. What about you? You're always so easygoing, but you've gotta have something keeping you grounded back home."

For a moment, Brody's eyes widened with surprise, but then he quickly broke into a grin. "Ah, man, I wouldn't say I'm grounded. I try not to take things too seriously. Just keep things light, you know?"

Aidan grinned, but didn't let it go. "Come on. No one is that laid back all the time. What's a day like when you're not out here cruisin' and meetin' new people?"

Brody took a sip of his beer before responding, "Alright, alright, you got me. I do have a life back home, same as everybody else. Nothing too wild, though. I live near Atlanta, just outside the city. My family's been there forever."

"Family business, eh?" Aidan asked, dredging the memory out of his mind from somewhere. Brody had once mentioned something about it.

"Yep. HVAC," Brody said, nodding. "I'm co-vice president of the family business. My brother and I run the show these days, though my folks are still involved. They're planning to retire soon ... leave the whole thing to us."

Aidan whistled low, impressed. "So, you're in charge, huh? Must be a lot of responsibility."

Brody shrugged, his grin softening somewhat. "Yeah, but it's not like I'm getting my hands dirty. I mostly deal with customers, manage the front end of things, make sure the business is running smoothly. It's stable, pays the bills, and gives me the flexibility to do stuff like this." He gestured to the bar, the cruise, the whole carefree vibe that seemed to define him.

"Doesn't sound so bad," said Aidan, though he detected a hint of reserve in Brody's tone. "Despite being customer-facing, any business will, inevitably, have some degree of difficulty, don't you think?"

Brody shrugged, leaning forward to prop his elbows on the table, and nodded. "Yeah, it does. I mean, I like it well enough. It's not my passion, you know? Not like football was." A fire danced in his eyes for a second, that familiar spark whenever he talked about his college football days. "But it's fine. I've accepted it. The HVAC thing isn't glamorous, but it's steady. And honestly, I love the balance it gives me. I'm not always desk-chained or totally out in the field. It's flexible."

Aidan took another sip, pondering that. Unlike Aidan, who sometimes seemed engrossed in Murphy's, Brody didn't appear trapped in the family business. There was an acceptance in his tone like he'd made peace with where he'd landed. It wasn't necessarily what he had dreamed of, sure, but he wasn't fighting it, either.

"Doesn't sound like you're too concerned about the future," Aidan said, a trace of envy in his tone at the acceptance in Brody's voice.

Brody grinned, that carefree charm slipping back into place. "I try not to be. Life's too short to stress over what you can't control. The way I see it, the HVAC business keeps me comfortable, gives me enough money to enjoy life, and lets me do stuff like this. So, why rock the boat, right?"

The words sank in, and Aidan nodded slowly. It wasn't a bad way to put it. Brody really didn't sound saddled with hope or obligation—not in ways that seemed to burden him. Yet there was still something submerged, something Brody wasn't sharing. Still, Aidan wasn't one to push too much. He knew how hard it could be to speak about the things gnawing away at you.

"So, no regrets about not pursuing football?" he asked after a moment, backpedaling into safer dialogue.

Brody laughed, a bit of wistfulness seeping into his tone. "Nah, man. I mean, I loved playing. Still do, when I can. But I wasn't going to go pro, and I knew that. It just wasn't in the cards for me. Sure, it stung for a while, but you learn to pivot. Now I get to talk about it on the radio from time to time, so that's something."

"You do broadcasting?" Aidan asked, astonished.

"Just a part-time gig," Brody said casually, lifting his shoulders in a shrug. "I do some college football analysis for a local station. I enjoy it because I can stay involved with the sport without the physical demands. It's a win-win situation, really."

Aidan nodded, a weird sense of respect washing over him for the way Brody had adapted. He might've let go of his football dreams, but he hadn't completely walked away. He'd found a way to stay near the thing he loved, even if it wasn't the way he'd originally planned. There was something admirable in that.

"You ever think about going full-time with that?" he asked. "The broadcasting, I mean."

Brody was silent for a moment, then shook his head. "I don't know. I like it as a side gig, something I can do when the season's on. But full-time? I think that might take the fun out of it. Right now, it's just something I enjoy—no pressure, no big expectations. I can walk away whenever I want, and that's the way I like it."

Aidan couldn't help but smile at that. There again was that casual, free-spirited approach to life that seemed to define Brody. He wasn't chasing anything too hard, wasn't looking for something to fill a void or prove a point. He was just ... living. Enjoying the ride, wherever it took him.

"I wish I could share your optimism," Aidan admitted after a pause. It feels like I'm forever juggling what I want with what's expected of me. "Don't get me wrong, I like the pub, but sometimes I feel like it's the only thing I do."

Brody nodded, his face softening. "Yeah, I get that. Sometimes family business feels like a trap, even when it isn't. But hey, maybe that's what this cruise is for, right? Shake things up a bit. Get some perspective."

Aidan smiled, knowing it was a well-intentioned sentiment. "Perhaps. It's certainly making me think about some things differently."

The noise of the Sea Shanty buzzed around them, but for once, Aidan felt he wasn't drowning in it. Sharing stories with Brody provided a sense of grounding during this trip, something genuine beneath the surface.

"Here's to shaking it up," Brody said, flashing a grin as he raised his glass.

"To stirring things up," Aidan replied, clinking his glass against Brody's.

Aidan felt as though he might finally make his life work with what he wanted, as opposed to his father's expectations. If Brody could, why not him?

Nine

On the morning after, the Elysian Serenade moored close to Elysian Isle, a secluded Bahamian island, a private refuge for the cruise line's exclusive clientele. As the ship came to a gentle stop, the tropical paradise unfolded before Aidan like something out of a dream. From the deck, he could see the entire shoreline: soft white sand that sparkled in the sunlight surrounding a lush green interior. Tall palms swayed lazily in the breeze, their fronds casting shifting shadows on the shore. The turquoise water glinted in the early light, stretching endlessly until sea and sky blurred into one.

From here, it seemed pristine, like a postcard come to life. Aidan couldn't see any high-rise hotels or busy roads, just nature. The sea was so clear that even from the ship, he could spot dark silhouettes of fish darting around the shallow coral reefs near the shore.

He inhaled deeply, filling his lungs with the salty, sun-warmed air. A strange mix of anticipation and serenity washed over him. Though remote, the place had a certain appeal, the kind that made him envision being stranded there for days, weeks even. This was the ultimate refuge, a haven for complete disconnection from the hustle and bustle of life.

The island wasn't large. From the ship, he could see both ends tapering into rocky outcroppings where waves crashed rhythmically in white-capped sprays. Little beach cabanas lined the edges of the sand, their straw roofs adding to the rustic charm. The crew had already set coral and teal umbrellas up, their soft pops of color dotting the shoreline. Hammocks strung between palm trees swayed invitingly, practically begging for someone to melt into them with a drink in hand.

"I wouldn't complain about being marooned here," Aidan muttered to himself.

Brody sidled up beside him, his attention riveted on the island. "If we're stuck here, I dibs the first hammock," he teased. "This place looks like heaven."

"Yeah," Aidan said, still staring out at the view. "It sure does."

The plan for the day was to go ashore with Harper and Paige. A spark of anticipation coursed through Aidan at the thought. It wasn't just the island, although that was a draw, but the opportunity to spend more time with Harper. There was a pull there, subtle but undeniable. Maybe it was just a vacation thing, a fleeting connection that would dissolve when the cruise ended. But a part of him wanted to see where it might lead.

The gangway was already down, and passengers were starting to disembark onto the tenders that would ferry them to the island. The energy on deck was electric: families chattering excitedly about their plans for the day, kids bouncing with glee at the idea of playing in the waves, couples eyeing cabanas as if already staking a claim to their little piece of paradise.

Aidan and Brody navigated the bustling crowd, eventually spotting Harper and Paige near the pool. They stood with beach bags slung over their shoulders, both wearing wide-brimmed straw hats that shielded their faces from the tropical sun. Upon seeing them, Paige waved with great excitement, her smile as dazzling as the rising sun. Her hot pink bikini, revealing and vibrant, was a perfect match for her lively energy. The sheer cover-up hung loosely around her waist, barely providing a pretense of modesty. The fabric barely concealed the shape of her fit legs and the outlines of her cheeks, peeking out from under her thong bikini bottoms. Her confidence was innate and relaxed like she commanded the ship, a casual adjustment of her sunglasses emphasizing her self-assurance.

Compared to Paige's showy display, Harper was the picture of simplicity. In comparison, her ensemble was more subdued, with a navy tube-top bikini and worn-in jean shorts hanging low on her waist. Despite its simplicity and practicality, the outfit looked completely natural on Harper, as if she had chosen it without effort yet still managed to achieve a perfect look. The soft denim of her shorts hugged her hips perfectly, hinting at her form without being too revealing. Despite the shadow cast by her straw hat, Aidan could clearly see the curve of her smile and the blush on her cheeks, a testament to the morning sun.

His eyes lingered on Harper for a fleeting instant. Even though Aidan hadn't known Paige long, her boldness was obvious, but Harper was different. Her quiet self-assurance spoke volumes, needing no outward declaration. There was something about the way she held herself, calm and grounded, that drew him in. She wasn't trying to stand out, but that somehow made her even more alluring.

He shifted his focus back to Paige, who toyed with her sunglasses and tossed them a bright smile, evidently enjoying the attention. She had a magnetism, loud and bright, that was impossible to ignore. And yet, it was Harper who held his focus. Aidan found himself wondering what was beneath that quiet exterior, what thoughts lingered behind those steady eyes.

You're staring, he realized, breaking his focus and forcing himself to glance away. But the thought stayed with him—that sometimes the loudest person in the room wasn't the one who left the biggest impression.

"Ready for the beach?" Paige called out, her voice brimming with excitement as she waved them over. She adjusted her hat, tilting it back just enough to reveal a dazzling smile.

Brody's face lit up as he walked. "As long as there's a hammock with my name on it, I'm ready."

A soft laugh escaped Aidan's lips as he walked behind his cruise mate. "Yeah, this looks like the kind of place you'd thrive."

Paige released a giggle as she placed a hand on her hip. "You mean paradise? Because that's exactly what this is."

Meanwhile, Harper stood quietly beside her, adjusting the strap of her bag on her shoulder as her soft smile grew a fraction wider. While her voice was quiet, her impact was undeniable. She didn't need to compete with Paige's energy, and she didn't seem interested in trying. Aidan was impressed by her quiet confidence, which spoke volumes without needing words.

As the group started making their way toward the gangway for the tender boats, Aidan let his thoughts drift. Paige was a force of nature, her energy and confidence radiating from her. Harper, though ... Harper was different. Her presence was subtle but undeniable, slowly drawing you in. And for reasons he didn't fully understand yet, he wanted to know more.

The four boarded one of the tender boats, joining the steady stream of passengers heading to shore. The gentle breeze off the water carried the sound of laughter and chatter as they approached the island. As they arrived at the beach, Aidan felt the sand beneath his feet, impossibly soft, warm but not scorching, perfectly kissed by the sun.

With the sun high in the sky, casting a golden glow over the island, the rhythm of beach life enveloped them. The soft sand squished between their toes as they found a spot beneath one of the coral-and-teal umbrellas. The breeze rustled the palm fronds above, carrying the faint scent of saltwater and coconut sunscreen.

Paige was in her element, animatedly recounting a wild road trip she'd once taken through California. She spoke with dramatic hand gestures, her voice rising and falling with each twist of her story. Brody, naturally, jumped in with his own tale of a 'way more adventurous' cross-country escapade, sparking playful banter between the two.

Conversation flowed around them, easy and full of energy, coaxing relaxed smiles from Harper and Aidan. Harper didn't speak much, but the way she leaned in, her lips twitching at particularly funny remarks, showed her enjoyment. Aidan, for his part, found himself laughing more freely than he had in months, maybe longer. There was something about this place, these people, that was slowly chipping away at the tension he'd held for too long.

As Paige launched into another story, Harper leaned back in her lounge chair, tilting her face up to catch the sun. Aidan glanced over, catching the serene expression on her face. She looked at ease, like she belonged here in this moment, away from the noise of everyday life. The possibility that she, like him, had embarked on this journey to escape the ordinary and discover something fresh struck him.

And for the first time in what felt like forever, Aidan felt that same ease settling over him. He began to feel like the beach, the company, and the laughter were exactly what he needed.

"You know," Brody said with a big grin, kicking back in his chair, "we could just stay here. Open a tiki bar. I could mix drinks, Aidan can handle the food. Harper, you'd bring the refined charm, and Paige ... well, you'd be in charge of entertainment."

Paige burst out laughing and flicked a bit of sand in his direction. "Please, like I wouldn't be running the show."

Harper smiled wryly, tipping her hat up. "Not sure refined charm fits the aesthetic, but I'll take the compliment."

Brody winked. "Without a doubt, you'd be the most stylish person on the island."

They were in the middle of their playful conversation about Brody's possible tiki bar when they noticed someone approaching from the distance. Squinting against the sun, Aidan noticed a man who resembled a rock star from a vintage photo: lean, scruffy, sporting a faded band shirt and a swagger that was both relaxed and confident. His hair was slicked back, and he carried a volleyball under one arm as if it were an extension of himself.

"Hey, I know you guys," the man said, tugging on a lazy smile as he neared them. He cast a cursory glance at Harper and Paige before zeroing in on Aidan and Brody. "You're part of the singles group, right?"

Aidan nodded, placing him now. Steve's enthusiasm for the group is, to put it mildly, quite pronounced. Steve had been hitting every event so far, behaving as though he were the unofficial host of the whole thing. If there was an afterparty or impromptu gathering, Steve was almost always at the center of it.

"That's us," Brody said, sitting up and flashing his natural grin. "What's up?"

Steve spun the volleyball in his hand. "Getting a game of beach volleyball together. We've got a pretty good crew so far, but we could use a few more. You guys in?" His eyes darted briefly to Harper and Paige before settling back on Brody and Aidan.

Brody's face lit up immediately. "Volleyball? Hell yeah, I'm in." He playfully nudged Harper's bare arm. "You down?"

Harper hesitated, her eyes darting briefly to Aidan before she offered a nonchalant shrug. "Why not? It's been a while, but I'm game."

Aidan relaxed in his chair, "Think I'll sit this one out."

Paige grinned and chimed in, "Me too. Somebody's got to hold the fort down."

Steve nodded, looking satisfied. "Alright then, you two stay put. Brody, Harper, let's go show these people how it's done."

Harper followed Brody's lead, adjusting her hat and getting ready as he stood and brushed sand off his legs. Brody threw a wink in Aidan's direction. "Don't you worry, man. I'll carry the team."

Aidan laughed. "That's what I'm afraid of."

With Steve leading the way, Brody and Harper walked down the beach to the makeshift volleyball court, leaving Aidan and Paige alone in the comfortable quiet of their little patch of sand. Paige stretched out in her chair, the sun glinting off the water and reflecting in her shades while Aidan settled back in his.

"Well, at least they look like they're about to have fun," Paige said with a soft chuckle that easily broke the silence.

Aidan smiled faintly. "Yeah, Brody's as happy as a lark. Give him a ball and some sand, and he's set."

Paige adjusted her hat, tipping it back so she could look at him more directly. Your roommate is a good guy.

"Yes, he is," Aidan agreed, his tone contemplative. "He's got that laid-back thing down. You'd wonder if anything ever riles him."

"Oh, I'm sure things bother him," Paige replied with a knowing smile. "He's just good at not letting it show. I think that's part of his charm."

Aidan considered that for a moment, his eyes drifting back toward the volleyball game. Brody was diving for the ball already, laughing as he hit the sand. It was hard not to admire the way Brody seemed to roll easily with whatever came his way, like life was just one big game.

"So, you?" Paige asked softly, her tone curious but non-intrusive. "You don't really strike me as the type to dive into games of beach volleyball."

Aidan huffed, shaking his head. "Nah, not really. I mean, it's fun and all, but I'm more of a spectator when it comes to stuff like this, I guess."

Paige smiled, a flicker of amusement dancing about her expression. "Harper said you're more of the grounded, serious type."

That caught Aidan's attention, and he leaned toward Paige slightly. "She said that, huh?"

Paige nodded, her eyes sparkling with mischief. "She didn't mean it as an insult. Don't worry." I think she likes that about you."

Aidan raised an eyebrow. "Oh yeah? And what exactly did she say?"

Paige leaned in, deliberating just how much to reveal. Then she shrugged and continued, "Let's just say Harper thinks you're … interesting. She's not the kind of person to hand out compliments freely, but I can tell she's into you. Even if she won't admit it yet."

Aidan blinked, surprised by the casualness of Paige's words. "Really?" he echoed, unsure of what to do with the information. A quiet sense of joy filled him despite his attempts to deny it.

Paige burst out laughing. "Don't look so shocked. She's had her eye on you since day one."

Aidan leaned back in his chair, curiosity mingling with something else. Something that felt a little too much like hope. He hadn't come on this cruise looking for anything romantic, but now that Paige had said it out loud, he couldn't help but wonder if there might actually be something there.

"You two seem like such opposites," Paige offered her words softly, her look steady as she watched him. "But sometimes opposites work, you know? I feel like Harper needs someone who can make her feel … grounded. And you could probably use someone to shake things up."

"I don't know about that," Aidan responded.

"Trust me," Paige said, her voice dipping into a rare moment of seriousness. "You two could be good for each other."

Aidan shifted his focus back to the volleyball game. Harper was mid-laugh as she made a halfhearted attempt to hit the ball, her movements unhurried but still full of life. Brody, ever the showman, was dramatically diving for the ball, rallying the team like a one-man pep squad. But it wasn't Brody and his antics that held Aidan's attention—it was Harper. Her smile caught him off guard, warm and unguarded in a way that softened the edges of her typically polished demeanor.

"Perhaps," Aidan said softly, almost to himself. The word slipped out with little thought, and yet it lingered like an acknowledgment of something he wasn't quite ready to name.

He reclined in his chair, his eyes wandering once more to the game unfolding down the beach. Brody was hamming it up as usual, drawing laughter from the small group gathered to watch. Harper, though, was different. She moved with a natural grace that surprised Aidan—effortless yet grounded. There was a quiet determination in her that balanced out the lightheartedness of her laughter. She wasn't trying to stand out, but somehow, she always did.

Aidan's breath caught slightly when Harper dove into the sand to save a point, her dark hair spilling loose as she brushed it back from her face, laughing unabashedly as her teammates cheered. She was completely present, radiating happiness and untouchable freedom that was captivating.

"Enjoying the view?" Paige's voice broke through his thoughts, playful yet pointed.

Aidan blinked, his focus snapping back to the present. Paige leaned against the counter, arms crossed, her smirk widening as she caught him mid-stare.

His fair skin betrayed him as warmth crept up his neck, but he forced a casual shrug, hoping to disguise the guilty smile hovering on his lips. "Just watching the game," he said, a little too quickly.

Paige smirked, clearly unconvinced. "Uh-huh. Sure." She turned her attention back to Harper, then leaned closer to Aidan, lowering her voice. "You aren't as subtle as you think you are."

Aidan shook his head and took a slow sip of his drink, as if dismissing her comment, but his thoughts had already returned to Harper. Paige's words echoed in his mind, making him wonder if she'd noticed something he hadn't quite been willing to admit to himself yet.

Maybe there was more to this trip than he'd anticipated.

Ten

Amidst the bustling conversations in the dining room, Aidan found himself drawn to the distinct rhythm of his table: Brody's booming voice, Paige's quick responses, and Harper's occasional quiet laugh, which felt reassuring in the chaos. The smell of lemon chicken and garlic butter lingered, but Aidan hardly noticed. Time after time, he found his focus returning to Harper, tracking the subtle twitch of her smile and the idle way she twirled the wineglass' stem in her fingers. The ship's gentle sway was comforting, though it felt faint compared to the energy Brody radiated.

"Alright, we're hitting up the comedy club," Brody declared, shoving back his chair with an exaggerated flourish. He grinned at Aidan, his smirk widening. "You two coming, or do you have more ... refined plans for the evening?" His tone dripped with playful insinuation, just in case his teasing wasn't clear enough.

Aidan felt Harper's eyes on him. "I think we'll pass," she said lightly.

He shrugged, meeting Brody's grin with a faint smirk. "Comedy's not really my thing tonight."

"Suit yourselves," Paige said, already tugging Brody's sleeve. "Have fun, you two!" She winked, her playful energy lingering like static as she and Brody disappeared into the crowd.

The table fell into a quiet stillness once they left, the distant murmur of the dining room fading to white noise. Aidan let out a breath, leaning back in his chair and studying Harper. For a moment, she seemed lost in thought, her fingers tracing lazy patterns on the tablecloth.

"So," he said, breaking the silence, his voice low, steady. "What now?"

Harper paused, considering. "Actually," she said, almost shyly, "there's an art gallery on board I've wanted to check out. Care to join me?"

Aidan blinked, feeling a bit out of his depth. Art wasn't something that interested him, at least not the type found in galleries. But there was something about the way Harper's eyes lit up, the subtle energy that crept into her voice, that made him curious.

"Sure," he said, pushing his chair back. "Lead the way."

As they stepped inside the ship's onboard gallery, Aidan immediately felt the shift in Harper. The space was sleek and modern, with polished floors that echoed their footsteps. Vibrant, abstract pieces hung on the walls, their bold colors popping against the minimalist backdrop. Aidan wasn't much of an art guy, but even he could appreciate the effort that had gone into curating the space.

But Harper? She was in her element. Her entire demeanor changed as soon as they crossed the threshold. Gone was the quiet, somewhat reserved woman he'd been getting to know. In her place was someone alive with enthusiasm, her eyes scanning the paintings with an energy he hadn't seen from her before.

Her focus shifted to a large canvas, a riot of scorching reds and shadowy purples. "Look at the way the brushstrokes flow," she murmured, more to herself than to him. "It's so intense ... like you can feel the emotion in every movement."

Aidan stepped beside her, staring at the painting, trying to see it through her eyes. The swirling colors formed a chaotic pattern, clearly abstract, but he couldn't understand its meaning. "What's it supposed to be?" he asked, frowning slightly.

Harper smiled, her eyes gleaming with excitement. "It's not about what it's supposed to be. It's about how it makes you feel. Observe how the colors clash but also complement each other. It's like the artist is telling a story with no need to spell it out. You feel it here," she said, placing her hand on Aidan's chest above his heart before tapping the side of his head, "Not here."

"I don't know if I'm wired that way," he said.

"Perhaps not, at least not right now," Harper said, giving him a playful smile. "You're capable of embracing new things, and with my help, you can unlock your full potential."

They moved through the gallery, Harper taking the lead, guiding him from one piece to the next. As they walked, she talked about brushstrokes and composition, about the stories behind the paintings and the emotions they evoked. Harper's passion for art was clear, and Aidan found himself drawn to her enthusiasm more than the paintings themselves. There was something magnetic about the way she spoke, how her eyes lit up when she explained the subtleties of a piece, the way she saw depth in places he hadn't even thought to look.

"So, you really love this stuff, huh?" Aidan asked as they paused in front of a piece that was all sharp lines and stark contrasts of black and white.

"I do," Harper admitted, her voice softer now. "Art's always been my escape. When life gets too loud, too overwhelming ... I come back to this." She gestured to the painting in front of them. "It reminds me that there's more to life than deadlines and schedules. There's beauty in the chaos, too."

Aidan nodded, letting her words sink in. "I get that," he said. "It's like cooking for me, I guess. When I'm in the kitchen, it's the one place where everything makes sense. But lately ... it hasn't felt like that."

Harper studied him. "Why not?"

Aidan hesitated, then shrugged. "Too many expectations. It used to be about the food, about the process. Now it feels like it's just ... work. I don't know. It's hard to explain."

Harper nodded, her expression thoughtful. "It sounds like maybe you need to find the passion again."

"Maybe," Aidan conceded, questioning the disappearance of his passion and its potential return. Observing Harper's delight at the paintings, he felt a flicker of hope, a reminder that life offered more than his monotonous routine.

They continued through the gallery, their conversation flowing easily, a quiet understanding settling between them. It wasn't clear when it occurred, but Aidan started to transform, not just in his feelings for Harper but in his view of himself. Watching her in her element, seeing her passion for art, it struck him that maybe he'd been stifling his own creative side, just as she had been pushing down this part of herself.

"Thanks for bringing me here," Aidan said as they reached the end of the gallery. "I never thought I'd say this, but ... I actually enjoyed it."

Harper smiled, and there was something peaceful in her expression, something unguarded. "You're welcome. I'm glad you came."

After their tour of the gallery, Aidan and Harper made their way to El Corazón, one of the ship's liveliest bars. The rhythmic pulse of Latin music floated through the air as they entered the warm, vibrant space. Deep reds and tropical greens enhanced the bar's ambiance, with murals of palm trees and golden beaches lining the walls, adding to the festive atmosphere. Colorful lights twinkled above the bar, casting a warm, lively glow over the room.

Aidan turned slowly, absorbing the vibrant atmosphere. "Well, this is a change of pace," he said, his voice light as the soft beat of conga drums pulsed in the background.

Harper smiled. "El Corazón is one of my favorite spots on the ship. It's got good vibes and even better mojitos."

Aidan tapped his fingers against the bar, considering the options. "Guess I'll have to switch things up, then." He'd been drinking beer most of the cruise, but tonight felt different. Tonight, he wanted something with a little more kick, a little more flavor. Something that matched the energy between him and Harper.

They slid up to the counter, and Aidan signaled to the bartender. "Two mojitos," he said, flashing a grin. "Seems like the right choice."

Harper smiled at him from the side, a little impressed by the switch from his usual. "Good call," she said, a playful glint in her eye. "A mojito's hard to beat."

The bartender placed their drinks in front of them, the ice clinking softly against the glass. The sharp scent of mint drifted up, cool and inviting. Aidan took a slow sip, the tangy lime and subtle sweetness dancing over his tongue, chased by the crisp chill of mint.

"Not bad," he admitted, smiling at her over the rim of his glass. "Good choice."

Harper sipped her mojito, her eyes scanning the room, clearly enjoying the change in the atmosphere. They both sat in a comfortable silence for a few moments, the lively hum of the bar filling the space between them. Aidan looked at her over his drink, reflecting on their time in the gallery.

"You know," he began, "I never thought I'd be the kind of guy to get into art. But watching you in that gallery, I don't know ... you've got a genuine passion for it. You made me see things I wouldn't have noticed otherwise."

Harper smiled, a soft flush rising to her cheeks. "I guess I can get a little carried away when I talk about art," she admitted, her tone humble. "It's always been my escape, my way of making sense of things."

"Well, you're a good teacher," Aidan replied, meeting her eyes. "You've got that kind of passion people don't see every day. It's ... infectious."

Harper's eyes settled as there was a spark of something unspoken between them, a connection deeper than just casual conversation. "Thanks," she said, more sincere. "That means a lot."

Before the moment could stretch too long, the music shifted gears, a lively salsa beat swelling through the speakers. Harper perked up at the sound, her body instinctively moving to the rhythm. She turned to Aidan, her eyes dancing with mischief.

"You know how to salsa?" she asked, swaying her hips slightly and lifting a hand as if inviting Aidan to join.

Aidan blinked, surprised. "Not exactly," he admitted with a sheepish grin. "But I've got two feet, and I can try to follow your lead."

Harper laughed, her smile wide and bright. "Come on, then. Let's see what you've got."

She grabbed his hand, pulling him off the barstool and onto the small dance floor, where a few couples were already swaying to the music. The room was alive with energy, the rhythmic sound of the maracas and trumpets.

Aidan took her hand, feeling the warmth of her fingers in his, as she showed him the basic steps.

"It's easy," she said, her voice light with amusement. "Just follow me."

He did his best to mimic her movements, stepping forward, then back, moving in time with the music. Harper's hips swayed effortlessly to the beat, her movements fluid and graceful, while Aidan tried to keep up. He wasn't a natural by any means, but Harper's laughter and the way her smile never left her face made the experience worth it.

"Not bad," Harper teased as they moved in sync. "You're getting the hang of it."

Aidan adjusted his footing, his shirt sticking slightly to his back as he fought to match the rhythm. "Just trying not to step on your toes," he admitted, flashing a lopsided grin, oblivious to the heat creeping up his neck.

Their dancing unveiled a shift in their relationship, a shared feeling of relaxed joy that was previously unknown. The music and laughter from other couples dancing swirled around them, but for Aidan, the world narrowed to Harper—to the feel of her hand in his, the sound of her laughter, and the way she looked at him, her eyes sparkling in the soft, colored lights of the bar.

Eleven

Aidan stood in his cabin, leaning against the sliding door leading to the balcony, the cool night air wafted in with a hint of salt from the ocean below. He had left the door cracked open to enjoy the breeze, though his mind was anything but calm. He was still feeling the afterglow of the evening, a blend of art, mojitos, and dancing at El Corazón with Harper.

It was strange how quickly the rhythm of the night had gotten under his skin, especially her. She was all he could think about now. Harper's enthusiasm in the art gallery, her effortless explanation of the abstract shapes and vibrant colors, it was truly inspiring. He'd never been the type to appreciate art like that, but with her, it felt different. She'd opened up a part of herself, and in doing so, Aidan had found himself opening up too, more than he'd intended.

But then, there was the other side of his thoughts. This was just a six-day cruise. Six days, and then it was back to his life at Murphy's Pub. Back to the grind, the family business, and everything that came with it. A small, gnawing voice in the back of his head reminded him not to get too comfortable. Nothing here was built to endure.

He let out a soft sigh and rubbed the back of his neck, trying to shake off the tension as he pulled off his shirt, leaving him in just a plain white tee and athletic shorts. He watched the vastness just beyond the balcony, the sound of the waves crashing against the ship's hull soothing, but not quite enough to settle the internal conflict.

Suddenly, there was a knock at the door. *At this time of night?* He frowned and moved toward it, opening it slowly.

There, standing in the hallway, was Harper. She remained in the jeans and tank top she'd worn during their evening together. Now she was carrying her heels in one hand and her eyes carrying a mix of hesitation and something else ... hope?

Aidan blinked in surprise, then smiled. "Hey," he greeted, his voice warm but tinged with curiosity. "What's up?"

Harper shifted on her feet, glancing back down the hallway before turning back to him. "Uh, Paige and Brody ..." She gestured vaguely toward her cabin. "They're, um, a little busy. And by 'a little,' I mean ... really busy. I can't get into my room. Do you think I can crash here tonight?"

Aidan sighed, rubbing his temples as if bracing himself. But, without hesitation, he stepped aside and gestured for her to come in. "Sure, you can stay here. Sounds like Brody won't be needing his bed tonight."

Harper smiled as she stepped into the room, glancing around before turning back to Aidan.

"Thanks," she said softly. "I, uh, didn't exactly plan on ending up here, but ... desperate times, you know?"

Aidan nodded a little too fast, shifting his stance as if unsure what to do with himself. "No worries. Make yourself at home."

Harper shifted awkwardly, glancing down at her jeans and tank top. She bit her lip. "Actually, do you think I could borrow a shirt or something to sleep in? My pajamas are ... well ... you know."

Aidan grinned, moving toward the small closet and pulling out a soft, worn T-shirt. "Yeah, of course. Here, this should work."

Harper took the shirt with a grateful smile, the tension in her shoulders visibly relaxing. "Thanks." She glanced toward the bathroom. "I'll just, um, change real quick."

Aidan nodded casually as Harper disappeared into the small bathroom. While she changed, he moved to the balcony, quietly closing the door and drawing the drapes. The room felt smaller now, more intimate, and as he straightened up the bed, he couldn't help but think of how close they'd gotten tonight—closer than he'd expected. His thoughts drifted again, lingering on Harper.

Then he heard the bathroom door click open to reveal Harper, now dressed in his shirt.

Aidan's breath caught for just a moment. The sight of her in his oversized shirt stirred something unexpected. The soft fabric draped casually over her chest, hugging her frame in all the right ways. As she walked, the shirt rode up slightly, revealing long, smooth legs that seemed to stretch endlessly.

"Looks better on you," Aidan said, his voice teasing, though he felt anything but casual inside. He couldn't help but notice how the shirt clung gently to her form, highlighting her curves in a way that was impossible to ignore. Harper smiled, her eyes meeting his with a spark of something playful yet unspoken.

She glided across the room, and he observed her in silence, drinking in every curve. Just before she reached the other bed, he caught sight of her black lace underwear framing the curves of her buttocks, peeking out from beneath the fabric as the shirt swayed with her movements. He struggled to resist the pull of temptation.

Wow.

Harper settled onto the bed with a relaxed posture, folding her legs beneath her, and the intimacy of the moment heightened. Aidan shifted subtly, trying to focus his thoughts and contain himself. The pull between them was undeniable, but he was reluctant to risk damaging the comfortable relationship they had built.

The room felt suddenly too quiet after the closeness they had shared earlier. Aidan's mind buzzed with possibilities, but he fought back the urge to overstep their undefined boundaries. This wasn't just about attraction. There was something deeper forming between them, and he wasn't sure where it would lead. For now, he was determined to take it slow, to let the moment be enough without complicating it.

"Hey," Harper said, her voice hesitant but playful. "You mind if we ... I don't know, maybe cuddle? Just for a little while. No funny business. It's just ... been a long day."

Aidan blinked in surprise at her suggestion, tilting his head as if to make sure he'd heard her right. But her tone was sincere, and he couldn't help but smile. "Cuddle, huh?" He scooted over on his bed, patting the space beside him. "Sure, I think I can handle that. Boundaries included."

A soft laugh escaped Harper's lips as she rose, her bare feet making barely a sound on the carpet as she walked toward him. The warmth of her body was immediately felt as she slid into the bed beside him. The twin bed left barely any space for them. Without thinking, Aidan's arm found its way around her, and they both just rested, listening to the soothing ocean sounds.

In the soft glow of the cabin, Aidan rested against the headboard with Harper in his arms. His hand gently stroked the small of her back, offering a comforting, almost absentminded gesture. With each breath she took, he felt her presence against his chest, erasing the outside world. This quiet moment, this fleeting intimacy, was a temporary escape from the harsh realities awaiting them back on land.

Harper broke the momentary silence with a small grin, looking up at him through her lashes. "Bet you didn't expect to get me into bed tonight," she quipped, her voice light and teasing.

Aidan gave her a light squeeze, the warmth of his voice matching the moment. "Yeah, not exactly how I saw the night going, but I'm not complaining."

They both laughed softly, the tension between them easing as they settled more comfortably into each other's arms. It felt effortlessly natural. Despite the unexpectedness of the situation, it felt right.

After a few moments, Aidan spoke again, his voice low and almost thoughtful. "So ... Paige and Brody. Do you think that's gonna flame out after the cruise? Or do they actually stand a chance?"

Harper tilted her head, peering toward the door, no doubt imagining the whirlwind of energy that was Paige and Brody in their own little world. "Hard to say. They're definitely having fun now, but it's all pretty fast. Could be just a cruise fling, you know?"

Aidan nodded in agreement. "Yeah, it feels like that. But who knows? Stranger things have happened."

The conversation shifted naturally, flowing into a more serious space as the two of them settled into something deeper. "Long-distance is hard," Aidan added, his tone more reflective now. "Even if they did try to make it work, once the cruise is over, they're in completely different places. It's tough to keep something going when you're not in the same world."

Harper's expression softened as her fingers absentmindedly traced small circles on his chest. "It doesn't even have to be long distance," she murmured, her voice quiet but full of meaning. "You could be sitting right next to someone and feel you're miles away. Like you're not even speaking the same language anymore."

Aidan nodded, understanding more than he wanted to admit. He thought about the distance he'd felt with his own family lately, especially with the weight of Murphy's Pub pressing down on him. The struggle wasn't always about physical space; sometimes the hardest part was bridging the emotional gap.

They lay in silence for a while, both lost in their own thoughts. Aidan could tell there was more to Harper's story, something she wasn't quite ready to share, and he respected that. He had his own walls up, too. For now, the quiet companionship between them was enough.

"This is nice," Harper whispered suddenly, breaking the silence.

Aidan tilted his head slightly, looking down at her. "What's that?"

"This," she whispered, glancing up at him with a gentle smile. "Just ... being here. Being in the moment. It's nice to have someone to really connect with on this cruise. Even if it's just for now. Even if it's just a fleeting wave."

"Yeah," he agreed quietly. "It is nice. Sometimes, a genuine connection is all that matters, even if it's temporary."

There was a pause, a shift in the air between them. Harper's smile faded slightly, replaced by something more vulnerable, more uncertain. She hesitated, her voice barely above a whisper when she spoke again.

"Aidan," she whispered, her tone soft, unsure.

"Yeah?" he responded, his own voice low and growing sleepier by the minute.

A beat of silence followed before Harper finally spoke, "Do you want to kiss me?"

Aidan hadn't expected the question, but the moment Harper asked if he wanted to kiss her, something clicked inside him. Her vulnerability, the quiet way she posed it, struck a chord. He didn't answer with words, just gently tilted her chin up, his fingers brushing the soft skin of her jaw. As he leaned in, everything seemed to slow down as the air between them thickened with anticipation.

When their lips met, it was tentative at first, like testing unknown waters. But the second he felt the warmth of her mouth against his, it deepened, drawing him in. There was nothing rushed about the slow, deliberate kiss. Her hand found its way to his chest, and he pulled her closer, feeling the rise and fall of her breath. Their lips moving together felt intimate, going beyond mere physical attraction, like a door opening to a previously unseen part of themselves, a part neither had shown before.

Aidan's pulse quickened, the kiss growing more intense, more urgent, as if both of them were grasping for something just beyond reach. Then, as they finally broke apart, he gasped for breath, his heart racing. Looking at Harper, her face flushed, he felt a strong desire to stay in that moment, right beside her. For the first time in a long while, something felt right.

They nestled back into each other's arms, the warmth of their bodies filling the space between them. Aidan felt a deep sense of calm settle over him as he held her close, his hand gently stroking her back again in a soothing rhythm.

"Goodnight," Harper whispered, her voice barely audible, the exhaustion from the day finally catching up to her.

Aidan squeezed her gently, his voice soft as he replied, "Goodnight, Harper."

As they nestled back into each other's arms, the warmth of Harper against him brought Aidan a quiet sense of peace he hadn't realized he craved. The noise of his internal struggle, the constant tug of responsibility and doubt, subsided, replaced by the calm rhythm of their breathing in the darkness.

He didn't know what tomorrow held or what this connection between them really meant, but in that moment, none of it mattered. As Harper leaned against him, Aidan experienced a rare feeling of contentment in the quiet of the night.

And for now, that was enough.

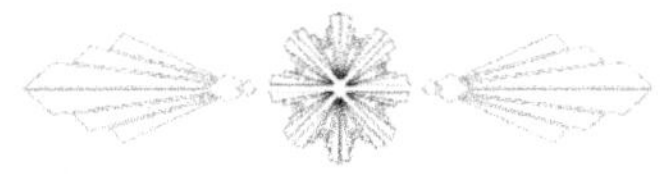

Aidan woke to the soft sound of the ocean outside and the warm weight of Harper still curled against his side. For a moment, he stayed perfectly still, letting the peaceful rhythm of her breathing ground him. A flood of memories overwhelming ... the art, the mojitos, the dancing, and Harper showing up at his door, wanting to stay. Her presence felt both natural and slightly surreal, like a fleeting dream he didn't want to wake from.

The click of the cabin door unlocking shattered the calm.

Aidan stiffened as Brody barged in, his signature wide grin leading the way. "Morning, lovebirds!" he announced loudly, clearly reveling in the moment. He raised a hand to his eyes in mock modesty. "Everyone decent in here, or should I come back later?"

Harper stirred, stretching under the covers before letting out a throaty laugh. "Decent?" she teased, her voice husky with sleep. "Not exactly. Unless lacy underwear counts." Her lips curved into a slow, mischievous smile as she snuggled the blanket higher, her eyes sparkling with amusement.

Brody froze mid-step, his hand still shielding his eyes. "Do you really want me to answer that?" he quipped as he retreated toward the bathroom. "I'll give you two some space, anyway. Take your time, my lady. I'll just be in here, definitely not picturing anything, I swear." The door clicked shut behind him.

Harper stretched, her hair slightly tousled and lips curling lazily. "Guess I should get dressed and head back before Paige sends out a search party," she said, though there was a trace of reluctance in her voice.

Aidan sat up, swinging his legs over the edge of the bed. "I should probably give you some privacy," he said, standing and turning his back to her without hesitation.

"Oh, come on," Harper said, her tone laced with teasing heat as she sat up, letting the blanket fall slightly down her bare shoulders.

"You've already seen me in a bikini, Aidan. My underwear isn't all that different, but I'd say it's a bit more ... captivating.

"Still," Aidan replied, crossing his arms and staring firmly at the balcony door. "I'm trying to be a gentleman here."

"Hmm." Her voice dipped slightly, amused. "You know, the whole 'gentleman' act is kind of undercut when you make it such a big deal. It's cute, though." She shifted under the covers, the faint rustle of fabric making Aidan's pulse quicken. "Kinda makes me wonder if you're afraid you'll like what you'll see too much."

Aidan shifted his stance, suddenly hyperaware of the shirt hitting the floor beside him, but he kept his eyes forward. "Nice try. I'm not looking."

"Oh, really?" Her tone was downright sinful now, playful but laced with suggestion. "So, you're just going to stand there and pretend you're not curious? After all, I did mention the lace."

Aidan snorted, his jaw tightening as he stood firmly by the balcony door. "Not happening. You're not gonna crack me."

The silence stretched for a moment, thick with Harper's unspoken challenge. He felt the weight of her stare, pressing on him, tempting him to give in. It wasn't just teasing anymore; she was testing him, and he wasn't sure he could win.

Her voice came again, soft and sweet, with a note of wicked amusement beneath it. "Okay, it's safe now. You can turn around."

Aidan exhaled and turned, ready to prove he could stay unshaken. The moment his eyes landed on her, he froze.

Harper had lifted the shirt high, revealing her bare chest. Her grin widened as she gave her breasts a little jiggle, the motion both ridiculous and completely mesmerizing. Her laughter bubbled up as she watched his reaction, her eyes shining with mischief. She looked completely unrestrained, free in a way that left him speechless. Aidan couldn't look away. This wasn't just teasing anymore. There was something wild and untamed in her boldness, a side of her he hadn't seen before, and it struck him like a wave he hadn't braced for.

"See?" Harper said, her voice light, as though she hadn't just turned his brain inside out. "Not so scary, right?" She tilted her head, her grin softening but never fading. "Consider it a little reward for being such a gentleman last night."

Aidan felt the heat rush to his face. His breath caught somewhere between a gasp and a laugh. "Harper?!" he managed, his voice cracking as her name stumbled out of his mouth.

She dropped the shirt with a shrug, letting it fall back into place like nothing had happened. Taking a slow step forward, she crossed her arms, her stance effortlessly self-assured. The ease in her movements, the way she stood there watching him squirm, sent his pulse hammering in his chest.

"Relax, Aidan," she said breezily, tossing her hair back over her shoulder. "You deserved it. And, honestly ..." She stepped closer, closing the space between them until she was near enough for him to catch the faint, floral scent of her. Her voice dropped to a whisper against his ear, her words curling around him like a secret. "I kind of enjoyed watching you squirm."

She smiled, and for just a moment, Aidan thought he saw something deeper flicker in her eyes, something that wasn't just teasing. Then she pulled back, grabbing her heels from the floor and turning toward the door like nothing out of the ordinary had happened.

"Brody!" she called, her voice light and carefree again. "You're good to come out now!"

Aidan stood rooted to the spot, struggling to keep his thoughts in order. His pulse thundered in his ears as she stepped to the door. Her movements were graceful, filled with the kind of unfiltered energy he was starting to realize he couldn't ignore. She turned back one last time, her lips curling into a smirk as she glanced at him over her shoulder.

"See you around, gentleman," she said, her voice soft but deliberate as if she had just left him with more questions than answers. Before he could find the words to respond, she disappeared into the hallway, leaving him alone with the echoes of her laughter.

The room felt ten degrees warmer as Aidan sank back onto the bed, running a hand down his face, his pulse hammering in his ears.

Brody stepped out of the bathroom, his grin creeping back into place as he leaned casually against the doorframe. "Alright, spill. What the hell just happened here?"

Aidan shook his head, trying to play it cool. "Nothing happened."

"Uh-huh." Brody crossed his arms, his smirk skeptical. "So you're telling me Harper just walked out of here looking all ... well, Harper, and you two just, what, braided each other's hair and talked about your feelings?"

Aidan groaned at the question. "She asked to cuddle, so we cuddled. That's it. She said, 'no funny business,' and I respected that."

Brody stared at him for a beat, then burst out laughing, doubling over as he clutched his stomach. "You cuddled?! Oh my God, you're killing me, man. Harper asked you to cuddle? That's like going to a steakhouse and ordering the breadsticks."

Aidan shot him a look. "What's that supposed to mean?"

"It means," Brody said, still laughing, "she was waving all the green lights in sight, traffic lights, Christmas lights. And you?"

Aidan shook his head, though he couldn't help the small smile tugging at his lips. "She said cuddling was the limit. I wasn't gonna push her."

Brody slapped a hand against the wall, grinning ear to ear. "You're too damn pure for this world, Aidan. But let me guess—she tested you, didn't she? Flashed you the high beams?"

Aidan blinked, his mouth opening and closing. "How did you ...?"

"Oh, come on, dude!" Brody said knowingly. "I can see it all over your face. And let me guess, you still didn't make a move after that, did you?"

Aidan groaned again, burying his face in his hands. "I don't kiss and tell, Brody."

Brody clapped him on the shoulder, shaking his head with a laugh. "No need, man. You're an open book. I have just one request: Don't let her keep you in the friend zone indefinitely. A guy can only be a gentleman for so long."

Aidan didn't reply, but Brody's words lingered long after the laughter died down. Even as a gentleman, he couldn't help but wonder if Harper's 'reward' had a hidden meaning beyond just playful mischief and what it truly meant for their future.

Aidan's eyes drifted to the shirt on the floor, the one Harper had borrowed last night. It was a simple item, but now it felt charged with meaning as if it carried a piece of her spirit. Memories of her laugh, her teasing smirk, and the way she'd fit so naturally in his arms came rushing back.

He picked up the shirt, running his fingers over the soft fabric before draping it over the chair.

Three days left, he thought, already anticipating the next time he'd see her. Let's make them count.

Twelve

The days had blurred together, a sun-drenched haze of island hopping, laughter, and lazy afternoons. Since that night, when Harper had stayed with him, things between them had shifted into an easy, comfortable rhythm. She'd grown more relaxed around him, their playful banter laced with quiet intimacy. Despite the lack of anything serious, a clear and growing bond linked them, drawing them closer with each passing day.

Jamaica had been a whirlwind of colorful markets and lively reggae music, and now they were in Grand Cayman, their final island stop before a sea day would bring them back to Miami. Aidan savored these moments more than he'd expected. The sun, the sea, and Harper by his side, with no distractions or work stress, created a grounding simplicity. It was a rare peace he hadn't realized he'd been missing.

Around lunchtime, as the four of them relaxed at a small beach-front café, Paige leaned casually into Brody's side, her smile more mischievous than anything else. "I've got a bit of a headache," she said, though her grin betrayed her. "We're just going to head back to the ship early. Maybe rest up a little. You two okay here?"

Harper let out a soft hum, clearly unimpressed by the blatant excuse, but didn't press the issue. "Sure," she replied, her look at Paige clearly indicated that she understood the subtext.

Brody smirked as he stood, tossing Aidan a quick wink. "See you later, man," he said, already guiding Paige toward the path that led back to the ship.

As they disappeared from view, Aidan turned back to Harper, the midday sun casting a golden glow across the beach. The mood between them felt easy like they had all the time in the world. He gestured toward a small bar a few steps away, its thatched roof offering a bit of shade from the Caribbean heat. "How about another round of cocktails before we head back?"

Harper smiled, nodding. "Why not?"

They made their way to the bar, where a friendly server quickly brought over two icy mojitos, garnished with fresh mint. Aidan leaned back in his chair, the cool drink refreshing against the lingering heat of the day. He watched Harper for a moment—the way her eyes sparkled when she laughed, the way the sea breeze tousled her hair just so. There was a quiet intensity between them now, a deepening connection he hadn't quite expected but welcomed, nonetheless.

"So," he began, his voice casual though carrying a hint of something deeper, "I was thinking ..."

Harper tilted her head slightly, the rim of her glass resting against her lips. "Oh? About what?"

Aidan glanced out to the sea for a moment, as if gathering his thoughts, before turning back to her. "Would you like to have dinner with me tonight? Like ... a date?"

Harper blinked, clearly caught off guard. They'd spent so much time together these past few days that the idea of a formal date hadn't even crossed her mind. Theirs had been an unspoken closeness, something that felt natural and unhurried, so the thought of a more intentional evening together made her heart skip. "Like ... a date date?" she asked, a small smile tugging at the corner of her lips.

Aidan grinned, his boyish charm breaking through. "Yeah, like a date. It's a formal night on the ship, so I thought ... it might be nice. We could check out that Greek restaurant. I've heard good things."

Harper took another sip of her drink, playing it cool, even though a flutter of excitement had already started in her chest. "That sounds ... really nice, actually," she admitted. "I'd love to."

"Great," Aidan said, his smile widening, a sense of warmth spreading through him. "I'll pick you up around seven? We can take our time and enjoy it."

Harper nodded, feeling a lightness she hadn't felt in a long time. "It's a date, then."

The easy banter between them, the shared stories of adventures, and the comfortable warmth of their shared space all built a sense of ease around Aidan. Something real. And as the afternoon sun began its slow descent toward the horizon, he couldn't help but look forward to what the night might bring.

As they finished their drinks, Aidan couldn't shake the feeling that today had been different. The tranquil day, with cocktails by the water, simple conversation, and Harper beside him, had brought a feeling to life. Something he hadn't realized he was missing. They headed toward the tenders, the boat that would take them back to the ship, and as they boarded, he felt an unexpected nervous energy building inside. It wasn't the typical pre-date jitters; it was something deeper, more unsettling.

Only a handful of other passengers were on the boat, making it feel uncrowded. Harper found a seat near the back, and Aidan slid in beside her, the space between them disappearing as she naturally leaned into him. Her body fit perfectly against his as if they'd been doing this for longer than just a few days. Without thinking, Aidan slipped his arm around her shoulders, pulling her close. It felt easy, natural, like the most comfortable thing in the world.

But it was also terrifying.

He hadn't expected this. Sure, he'd signed up for the cruise to relax, to escape the grind of the restaurant and the weight of everything back home. He'd expected some fun, maybe a fling, but not this. Not the slow, quiet connection that had been building between him and Harper. The feeling was pleasant, incredibly pleasant, but it also ignited a more profound emotion within him. A kind of longing he hadn't let himself feel in a long time. The kind that made him wonder if he was ready to let someone in again.

As the boat pulled away from the dock, Aidan pressed a soft kiss to the crown of Harper's head. His lips lingered there longer than necessary, the warmth of her melting into him. For a fleeting moment, he surrendered to the feeling, his breath hitching as he recognized the undeniable comfort and rightness of holding her.

Harper leaned in even closer, letting out a soft, contented sigh. The sound stirred something protective in him, something that made him want to keep this feeling going for as long as possible. But that only made him more aware of how fleeting it all was. They had a couple of days left on this cruise, and then ... what? They'd return to their separate lives, worlds apart.

Aidan swallowed the thought as the tender boat bumped lightly against the dock. It was too soon to think about that. Too soon to overthink everything, like he always did.

As the other passengers rose, Harper and Aidan pulled apart, sharing a quiet smile. Neither of them said anything, but the connection between them hung, as palpable as the warm Caribbean breeze. He cherished the moment, reluctant to let go of the silent understanding they'd established. But they had to part, at least for a little while, to prepare for the evening ahead.

"So," Aidan said, his voice light, though something deeper tugged at the edges, "I'll see you tonight?"

Harper nodded, her smile widening, and there was that flutter again. "Seven o'clock," she confirmed. "I'll be ready."

He watched her walk away, her silhouette disappearing into the flow of passengers heading back to their cabins. His heart pounded a little harder than it should've, and a thousand thoughts raced through his head.

Wow.

Aidan lingered for a moment longer, shaking his head with a soft grin. Tonight was going to be ... something.

As he walked back toward his cabin, a subtle rush of anticipation coursed through him. The time spent with Harper had been relaxed and easy, but it left him strangely energized. He hadn't expected to feel this much, this quickly, and the thought hit harder than he cared to admit. But as he turned the corner to his room, his mood shifted.

Hanging on the doorknob was a 'Do Not Disturb' sign.

Aidan stopped, narrowing his eyes with an amused sigh. Of course, he thought. Paige and Brody were still "curing" her so-called headache. A grin tugged at his lips as he shook his head, silently giving Brody credit for his impeccable timing.

With his cabin temporarily out of reach, Aidan considered his options. He could wander the ship, grab a bite, or maybe spend some time at one of the lounges. But as his reflection caught his eye in a polished mirror nearby, another idea took hold. A fresh haircut and a shave would help him feel a little sharper. *Why not clean up before dinner with Harper?*

It was formal night, after all.

Deciding on the ship's barbershop, Aidan welcomed the unexpected downtime. As he walked through the ship, his thoughts drifted. The past few days had been surprising in more ways than one. The speed and intensity of his connection with Harper surprised him. Her intelligence and quiet grace had drawn him in, but it was the unspoken bond between them that stirred something deeper. That both thrilled and unnerved him.

As he reached the barbershop, the barber gave him a nod and motioned toward the waiting area. "Got about thirty minutes until I can fit you in, bud," the man said with a polite smile.

"No problem," Aidan replied, taking a seat.

He settled into one of the leather chairs, enveloped by the smell of shaving cream and aftershave. It had been a while since he'd had time to sit and reflect like this without the demands of the restaurant pulling him in every direction. He leaned back, closing his eyes for a moment, letting the quiet hum of the ship surround him.

The more he thought about Harper, the more conflicted he felt. He intended this vacation to be a respite from his home life, not an opportunity to open up emotionally. But with Harper, things had shifted. She'd slipped past the walls he'd carefully built, and now he wondered what it all meant. What would happen after the cruise? She lived in New York. He had Murphy's Pub to run in Charlotte. Different cities, different lives. And yet, here they were, tangled up in something that felt ... real.

"Wow," he muttered to himself, running a hand through his hair. What had started as a casual connection was turning into something more complicated than he'd expected.

As he sat there, lost in thought, a familiar voice broke through his reverie. "Aidan! Fancy seeing you here."

He looked up to see Maude strolling by, her sun-kissed skin and ever-present calm demeanor making her instantly recognizable. Her smile was knowing, the kind that suggested she was always ahead of the game, privy to secrets you weren't.

Aidan straightened up in his chair, offering her a grin. "Maude, hey. Just waiting for a haircut."

She stopped, tilting her head with a knowing look. "Getting spruced up for formal night? Or is this more for Harper?"

Aidan smiled back at her, suddenly feeling exposed under her unwavering scrutiny. "Something like that," he admitted.

Maude's smile widened. "Mind if I join you for a moment?"

Aidan nodded, and she gracefully sat beside him. Neither spoke for several moments, but Maude's presence was steady, like the ocean itself. Aidan couldn't help but wonder. How does she do it? Always knowing, always sensing. Seafaring magic? Witchcraft? Or just years of reading people? Whatever it was, Maude had a way of pulling thoughts from him he wasn't ready to confront.

"So," she said softly, eyes twinkling, "what's weighing on you, Aidan?"

His eyes met hers before drifting back to the barber's mirror, where his reflection seemed almost unfamiliar. Harper. The future. This cruise. Maybe she'd have some wisdom he needed.

Whatever this magic was, he could use it right now.

Thirteen

"So," she said softly, eyes twinkling, "what's weighing on you, Aidan?"

Aidan leaned back in his chair, his mind swirling with everything he hadn't said until now. It wasn't like him to open up easily, but with Maude, the words just tumbled out. "There's less than thirty-six hours left on this cruise, and I thought by now I'd have it all figured out." He sighed, rubbing the back of his neck. "My future, my family, the restaurant ... and now ... Harper."

Maude listened with unbroken focus; the kind of calm scrutiny that made you feel truly seen. She said nothing, just waited letting the silence coax him further.

"I came on this trip to get away, to clear my head," Aidan continued. "Murphy's Pub ... it's been my whole life, you know? My dad's life, too. There's a lot riding on it. And I thought by stepping away for a few days, I'd find some clarity. But the closer we get to the end of this cruise, the more lost I feel."

He paused, glancing at her and biting his lip. "And then there's Harper. God, I didn't expect any of this ... I mean, it's been great but also ... terrifying. It's not like we're living in the same world. She's got her life in New York, and I've got Murphy's back in Charlotte. The idea of running away to the city with her? It's ridiculous, right?"

Maude's eyes softened, her mouth curling into a small, understanding smile. She was familiar with individuals grappling with conflicting emotions, torn between their feelings and what they knew was morally correct. "It's crossed your mind though, hasn't it?"

Aidan exhaled, running a hand through his hair as he nodded. "Yeah, it has. But what am I supposed to do? I can't abandon everything back home. I can't just leave my family behind for ... something that might not last beyond the next two nights."

Maude finally spoke, her voice gentle but laced with the wisdom that only comes from years of watching people struggle with the same heartache, the same choices. "Aidan, life rarely gives us all the answers when we want them. It's not meant to be solved in a few days or even a lifetime. The best we can do is live in the moment, make the choices that feel right now, and trust that the rest will unfold in time."

She let that sink in before continuing. "The future? Family, career, and love are all unpredictable areas of life. But the beauty of the moment is that you don't have to have all the answers right now. You just need to be open to the possibilities. And if those possibilities lead you to New York ... or back to Charlotte ... or somewhere else entirely, then so be it."

Aidan absorbed her words, feeling the weight of his worries shift, if only a little. Maybe she was right. Maybe he didn't have to figure it all out in the next thirty-six hours. He glanced at Maude, grateful for her insight but still uncertain about what the future would hold.

The barber called his name, interrupting the moment. Aidan stood, giving Maude a small smile before heading toward the chair.

As he passed her, Maude touched his arm gently. "Remember, Aidan ... the tide always knows where it's going, even if we don't."

It took Aidan a pause to register what she had just said. *The tide always knows where it's going, even if we don't.*

He blinked, the words tumbling around in his mind, their simplicity carrying more weight the longer he thought about them. Before he could process it fully, Aidan turned back, half expecting to see Maude still sitting there, ready to offer more of her cryptic, sea-worn wisdom.

But she was gone.

He looked around, scanning the small waiting area and the hall beyond, but there was no sign of her. It was as if she had vanished into thin air. Aidan stood there bewildered. *Maybe she really is a wizard,* he mused, shaking his head slightly.

Leaning back in the barber's chair, Aidan let the words play over again in his mind. The tide, always knowing its course, even when he didn't. It was so Maude to say something like that—just vague enough to sound profound, but somehow, exactly what he needed to hear. Maybe life didn't need to make perfect sense. Maybe, like the tide, it would pull him in the right direction when the time came.

He settled into the barber's seat as his mind drifted back to Harper, the cruise, and everything that still lay ahead.

After finishing up at the barbershop, Aidan made his way back to his cabin. The 'Do Not Disturb' sign was no longer in place. Good, he thought. He didn't feel like wandering the ship anymore, not with the formal dinner looming and his head still full of Maude's cryptic advice. Time to get ready.

As he opened the door and stepped inside, he saw Brody standing by the mirror, his hair gelled up, hands busy as he meticulously tried to get it just right. Brody had already showered and was standing in just a pair of shorts, looking like he was getting ready for something much more glamorous than dinner on a cruise ship.

"Trouble helping Paige with that 'headache' earlier?" Aidan asked, throwing a playful smirk his way.

Brody turned, grinning, but there was a mischievous glint in his eye. "Let's just say the remedy worked wonders." He laughed, running a hand through his hair to fluff it just a bit more. "Though I'd call it less of a 'headache' cure and more ... preventive care."

Aidan chuckled, rolling his eyes. He grabbed some clothes from his drawer and tossed them on the bed before heading toward the bathroom. But before he could get too far, Brody spoke up again.

"You alright, man? You seem like you've got a lot on your mind." Brody looked at him in the mirror, brow furrowed. It was clear he'd noticed the shift in Aidan's demeanor over the past couple of days.

Aidan shrugged, brushing it off with a nonchalant wave of his hand. "Just tired, I guess. Long day."

Brody gave him a knowing look but didn't press further. "Alright, man. But if you need to talk, you know where to find me."

"Yeah, thanks," Aidan said, his voice trailing off as he headed for the shower. He turned on the water, letting the steam fill the small bathroom, and stepped inside.

As the hot water poured over him, he leaned against the wall, eyes closed, trying to clear his mind. But it just filled with more questions. Harper. Maude's words. The future waiting for him back home.

And there it was again, that creeping sense of uncertainty. He tried to resist, but the tide's relentless force was pulling him in an unknown direction.

As Aidan stood under the hot stream of the shower, something clicked. Out of nowhere, Maude's words came rushing back to him with clarity—*The tide always knows where it's going, even if we don't.* It wasn't some vague, cryptic line anymore; it actually made sense. Maybe he didn't need to figure everything out right now. Maybe the future could wait for the future.

A wave of determination surged through him. Screw it, he thought. Tonight, he was going to have the best night ever with Harper. Forget about Murphy's Pub, forget about the family pressure, and forget about whatever might or might not happen after this cruise. Tonight, he was going to live in the moment.

By the time he stepped out of the shower, towel wrapped around his waist, his entire mood had shifted. His mind, once clouded with indecision and self-doubt, was now clear. The thought of Harper waiting for him sent a spark through his chest, making him grin.

Brody, still fixing his hair in front of the mirror, glanced at him and tilted his head slightly. "What's with the grin? You rub one out in there or something?"

Aidan laughed, shaking his head as he grabbed his suit from the closet. "Yeah, that's it. A quick fix and all's right with the world again."

Brody smirked. "Hey, whatever works, man. But seriously, you were all mopey earlier, and now you're practically beaming. What's going on?"

"I just realized something," Aidan said, slipping into his nearly all-black suit. "I've been overthinking everything, and it's time to stop. Tonight's about having a good time. No more worrying about tomorrow."

Brody nodded, though he still wore a playful grin. "So, you're just gonna have the time of your life with Harper and let the rest take care of itself, huh?"

"Pretty much." Aidan adjusted his black tie, which had the faintest hint of emerald green woven through it, a subtle nod to his Irish roots and a bit of good luck. This was the most he'd cleaned up the entire cruise, and honestly, he couldn't even remember the last time he'd dressed up this nicely. Maybe some long-forgotten wedding or special occasion, but these days, he was always in his chef's coat, always thinking about the restaurant. Tonight, though, he looked sharp, and it felt good.

Brody gave Aidan an exaggerated once-over let out an appreciative whistle. "Damn, Murph. Looking slick. That's probably the cleanest I've ever seen you. You're sure this isn't some secret proposal or something?"

Aidan laughed, shaking his head. "No proposals, I promise. Just a good night."

"Well, good luck, man." Brody paused, his tone turning more sincere for just a second. "And, uh, in true wingman fashion, I'll be staying over at Paige's place tonight. You know, to give you and Harper some space." He winked, his grin widening.

Aidan rolled his eyes, knowing exactly what that meant. "Yeah, sure. Thanks for the *sacrifice*. Pretty sure you're just in it for your own pleasure-filled night."

"Hey, a win-win situation if I ever saw one," Brody said with a laugh, grabbing his jacket off the bed. "But seriously, have a great time tonight. You deserve it."

Aidan smiled, feeling more ready for this night than he'd been for anything in a long time. "Thanks, man."

Brody slapped him on the back as he headed toward the door. "Knock her dead. Or, you know, don't—whatever works."

With a last grin, Aidan watched Brody leave before turning back to the mirror. He felt good for the first time in ages, genuinely good. Tonight wasn't about the future or the past. It was about now. And that was more than enough.

Time to meet Harper.

Fourteen

Aidan waited in the atrium, letting the ambiance sink in as he tried to tame the wild beat of his heart. Around him, guests milled about in elegant evening wear, their laughter and murmured conversations filling the space with an air of anticipation. He reached for the vodka shot he'd ordered, the glass cool and smooth in his hand. He downed it in one quick motion, savoring the warmth that slid down his throat, grounding him. It didn't fully calm his nerves, but it sharpened his senses, making him more attuned to the moment. Tonight, he told himself, would be different.

He wasn't seeking solutions; he craved experiences, wanting to embrace the energy of the night.

As he set the glass down, he noticed a familiar figure at the bar. Maude, draped in her usual aura of wisdom and mystery, was watching him with a smile that held a hint of mischief. She raised her glass to him, and then, with a gentle wink, she seemed to remind him to stop overthinking, to let himself go. He gave her a nod, an unspoken promise that he'd try. She seemed to have peeled back his hesitation, revealing the part of him that craved nothing more than to simply exist, to embrace the fleeting magic of this evening. With a deep breath, he refocused on the stairs, and that's when she came into view.

The atrium could have held a thousand passengers that night, but Aidan wouldn't have paid attention.

Aidan's breath caught as Harper appeared at the top of the crystal-lined staircase, a vision of elegance that left him rooted in place. Shimmering subtly in the light, the deep sapphire blue dress captured the chandelier's gleam like the sea at twilight. The fabric flowed gracefully over her curves, creating a sensual silhouette that was both sophisticated and alluring. The gown, secured by a single strap, revealed a tempting curve of her breast, sending a jolt through him. Trailing down her back, the fabric revealed her spine before pooling at her hips, clinging to her form in a captivating manner.

His focus dipped to the high slit on her dress, parting with every stride and offering glimpses of her elegantly tapered leg. A quiet confidence marked her movements, each step measured and flowing, a casual elegance that seemed to fit perfectly in a magazine spread. Completely mesmerized, Aidan watched, his eyes locked on the gentle sway of her hips, the irresistible curve of her waist, and the elegant arch of her neck. Her beauty was stunning, but her presence was hypnotic. The dress, like a liquid reflection of the sea they sailed on, shimmered with starlight and clung to her form, transforming her into something almost mythical.

Her scent was another thing. The subtle, warm fragrance of vanilla, a deeper spice, and a hint of jasmine drifted toward him as she approached. The scent wrapped around him, filling his lungs with a heady, intoxicating aroma that made his pulse beat faster. It was enchanting, seductive, an invisible pull that left him helpless to do anything but drink her in with every one of his senses.

His world shifted as she reached the last stair and their eyes locked.

She looked at him just as fiercely, a slight, knowing smile touching her lips, as if sensing how deeply she affected him. Heart pounding, he took a step forward and extended his hand, the gesture instinctive, reverent, as if she were someone to be treasured. Her touch sent a jolt of electricity through him, a warm and tingling sensation that settled deep in his chest. The feel of her skin against his was both comforting and exhilarating, a reminder that this wasn't a dream, that she was here, with him, in this moment.

Her smile was delicate and radiant as Aidan felt everything else disappear, leaving only her and the intensity of their connection. There was a spark in her eyes, a warmth that pulled him in, wrapped around him, and made him feel like he was exactly where he was supposed to be. For the first time in a long time, Aidan felt alive, fully present, caught in a moment that he never wanted to end.

Aidan's pulse quickened as Harper stepped down from the final stair, her hand still in his. She stole the breath from his lungs, but the warmth in her smile and the mischief in her eyes brought him back to solid ground—proof that even in the midst of all this grandeur, they remained two souls sharing something true. He managed to find his voice, though it came out quieter than he intended.

"You look … incredible," he whispered, his voice full of wonder. Words seemed insufficient to express the awe she inspired in him with her breathtaking appearance.

Harper's smile widened, her eyes twinkling as she gave him an appreciative once-over. "You look pretty slick yourself, Mr. Fresh Shave," she teased, letting her fingertips trail along his jawline. "What's the occasion? Special date?"

Aidan grinned, his hand still holding hers, and there was a playful glint in his emerald-green eyes. "Maybe. Figured I should clean up if I wanted to keep up with you tonight." He leaned in slightly, his voice dropping to a murmur, "Didn't want you thinking I only looked good in an apron."

Her laughter was like a cozy fire on a cold night, filling him with a sense of contentment. "Oh, I don't know," she replied, her voice soft and teasing, "I think you might look good in only an apron." The words hung between them, charged and daring, and she felt a thrill at the way his eyes darkened and his expression quirked into a surprised but delighted smile.

"Is that so?" he asked, rubbing his jaw as if considering the idea, though the amusement in his voice gave him away. The corner of his mouth lifted in that crooked, irresistible grin she was beginning to adore. "Guess I'll have to find an excuse to make that happen sometime."

She tilted her head, feigning innocence, though the sparkle in her eyes was anything but. "Just say the word. I'll bring the apron."

Aidan chuckled, his heart thudding a little harder. Her quick wit and fearless flirtation had him completely captivated, pulling him further into her presence. Still holding her hand, he gave it a gentle squeeze, silently marveling at how this woman could make him feel both exhilarated and at ease at the same time.

Aidan didn't feel the need to speak as they left the atrium, Harper's hand resting comfortably in his. The gentle heat of her hand, a comforting beacon in the cool ship's interior, pulled him onward toward their evening rendezvous.

The scent of rosemary, oregano, and olive oil met them at the entrance, mingling with the tangy salt air drifting in from the open deck. Aidan felt himself transported, as though he'd stepped out of the structured elegance of the cruise and into something more intimate, more timeless. White stone walls draped with ivy framed the cozy space, and golden lanterns cast a flickering warmth over the tables, decorated with delicate bouquets of olive branches and jasmine. A soft melody of bouzouki music hummed through the air, blending with the rhythmic clinking of glasses and the occasional call, "Opa!" from a nearby table where a waiter ignited a sizzling plate of saganaki. The atmosphere wrapped around them, inviting them to linger.

Their table was near a window, offering an unobstructed view of the sea stretching endlessly under the night sky, a silvery path reflected across the water. As Aidan pulled out Harper's chair, he noticed how the moonlight caught the shimmer in her dress, making her look almost ethereal. He settled into his seat, shifting his attention from the horizon back to Harper, feeling a surprising wave of contentment as they both reached for their wine. The deep ruby hue of the Agiorgitiko swirled in their glasses, catching the golden glow of the lanterns. When she lifted hers to toast, he was ready.

"To new adventures," she said, her voice soft yet filled with something deeper.

"To new adventures," he echoed, his expression steady over the rim of his glass. That indescribable warmth rose within him, one that had stealthily grown over time, startling him with its strength.

The staff moved gracefully through the restaurant, setting down plates brimming with roasted lamb, creamy moussaka, and horiatiki salad glistening with plump Kalamata olives and crumbles of feta. The warm scent of freshly baked pita and the sharp citrus of lemon drizzled over grilled octopus filled the space, each dish a reminder of Greece's rich culinary tradition. Aidan savored the first bite, the layers of cinnamon-laced béchamel in the moussaka melting on his tongue, the slow-cooked richness felt familiar yet new.

With each course, their conversation flowed effortlessly. Aidan found himself talking about his family's restaurant, the words spilling out naturally. He described his childhood spent in the kitchen, the clattering of pots and the comforting smell of simmering stews, the way his parents had built the place from scratch before he was even born.

"Cooking's in my blood, I guess," he admitted, a note of nostalgia coloring his voice. "I was practically raised with a wooden spoon in one hand and a ladle in the other. The restaurant has always felt … natural, you know? Like it was what I was meant to do."

Harper listened attentively, a thoughtful expression settling over her. "You make it sound like a fairytale," she said, her tone almost wistful. "A life where you know exactly where you belong."

Aidan shrugged, glancing out the window for a moment, watching the gentle waves catch the moonlight. "Maybe … but somewhere along the way, it started to feel like a job. Like I was just … going through the motions, meeting expectations." He let out a sigh, running a hand through his hair. "I guess I lost the spark somewhere, forgot what it felt like to cook for the joy of it."

"I know what you mean," she murmured. "I used to dream about a big-city life, working with high-profile clients, building my career in the creative world. But sometimes … I wonder if the dream I had isn't the life I actually want. Somewhere along the way, it started feeling more like a cage than a dream."

Empathy stirred within Aidan as he recognized the disappointment of chasing a dream that turned out differently than expected. "I think a lot of us feel that way," he said, his voice quieter now, almost reflective. "It's like we get so focused on chasing this vision of success, we forget why we wanted it in the first place."

They fell into a comfortable silence, sharing a moment of mutual understanding. The candlelight cast a soft glow over their table, the gentle strains of a Greek love ballad playing in the background, and Aidan felt … lighter. It was as though the weight of all his unresolved questions and buried doubts had been momentarily lifted.

Ambrosia's warmth and the shimmering sea created an atmosphere that encouraged openness, allowing them to share their thoughts freely, unburdened by expectations.

When they finished their meal, Aidan set his napkin down and leaned in, his smile easy and genuine. "What do you say we take a walk? Get a little fresh air."

Harper's cheeks flushed, her eyes bright with the lingering excitement of the evening. "I'd like that," she replied.

The promenade stretched before them, softly illuminated by flickering lanterns that cast warm pools of golden light across the polished deck. Above them, the night sky unfurled in a blanket of stars, reflections of the ship's lights shimmering faintly on the dark, endless sea. The world beyond the ship seemed to melt away, leaving only the two of them suspended in this perfect, secluded moment. With each step, Harper's arm brushed against his, her warmth steady and grounding, even as his heart raced.

The lantern light caught the elegant drape of her dress, the fabric shimmering like water under moonlight. A high slit revealed the graceful line of her leg, her movements exuding effortless confidence. She was radiant, the kind of beauty that made him feel both mesmerized and at ease. He hadn't expected to feel this pull, this quiet but undeniable connection, but here it was—impossible to ignore.

They walked without speaking, yet she'd steal the occasional glance at him, her tender smile rousing a deep sensation in his chest. Aidan didn't rush to speak, savoring the rare comfort of being fully present. This bond, both exhilarating and soothing, felt like piecing together a forgotten part of himself.

Harper stopped at the railing, looking out over the vast stretch of ocean that disappeared into the horizon. Aidan leaned beside her, their arms touching as they both took in the stillness of the night. The rhythmic sound of waves against the hull, mingling with the faint scent of gardenias. For a heartbeat, Aidan closed his eyes, letting himself sink into the serenity of her presence.

"So," Harper said, breaking the silence with a mischievous glint in her eye, "how's life?"

Aidan chuckled, recognizing the playful reference. "Life," he murmured, "at least right now, feels pretty damn perfect."

She smiled back at his response, an expression that left his hear a flutter. Standing there, with the stars above and the sea stretching endlessly around them, he wanted to freeze time. He wanted more nights like this—simple, warm, and filled with her laughter.

"Think we could just … stay here forever?" she whispered, half-joking, though there was a pensive note in her tone.

Aidan reached over, covering her hand with his. "I'd be fine with that," he said. "Let's not worry about tomorrow."

Harper stayed quiet, turning her focus back to the distant skyline. When she spoke again, her voice was quieter. "Do you ever think about leaving it all behind? Just … walking away and starting over?"

The question caught him off guard. He leaned on the railing, letting the waves fill the pause as he considered her words. "Yeah," he admitted, after a beat. "But there's always something that holds me back—responsibility, family, guilt." He exhaled slowly, his voice dropping. "I guess I've always been the one to hold the line, you know? Even when it feels like it's crushing me."

Harper's lips curved into a faint smile, though her eyes remained thoughtful. "I get that," she murmured, her attention falling to the rippling water. "For me, it's fear. Fear of what I'd lose if I left. Fear of what I might not find if I did." She paused, brushing her fingers along the railing. "Sometimes I wonder if the dream I've been chasing all these years is even mine. Or if it's just something I thought I wanted because it looked good on paper."

Aidan turned toward her, struck by the raw honesty of her words. "So, what keeps you from walking away?"

She sighed, her shoulders lifting in a subtle shrug. "I keep hoping it'll get better. That I'll find a way to make it work." She looked back at him, her eyes searching his. "But some days, it feels like I'm just … surviving. You ever feel like that?"

Aidan's throat tightened. "Yeah," he said quietly. "I know that feeling."

The weight of their unspoken doubts and shared struggles hung between them, but it didn't feel heavy. Instead, there was comfort in knowing they weren't alone. Aidan looked back toward the horizon, the vast, unending sea awakening in him dreams of possibilities previously unconsidered.

"Do you think we'll ever figure it out? What we really want?" Harper asked.

"Maybe," he said. "Or maybe we just have to stop trying so hard to figure it out and let ourselves be happy where we are."

Her smile widened, warm and genuine, and it lit up something inside him. "That's not a bad idea," she said, her voice barely above a whisper.

The intimacy of lingered, unspoken truths weaving between them as the waves continued their steady rhythm. Aidan felt a quiet peace settle over him, a rare reprieve from the storm of doubts and responsibilities that usually consumed him. Harper's presence, her honesty, was an anchor in the chaos.

Drawn by the pull of their connection, Aidan leaned closer, his hand brushing lightly against hers as though testing the fragile thread of their shared vulnerability. She locked eyes with him—steady, open—and in that quiet moment, his answer emerged. Slowly, he leaned down, his lips meeting hers in a kiss that was gentle, almost reverent at first. But as her arms slipped around his neck, pulling him closer, he let himself get lost in the fire simmering between them. The world around them faded to nothing, leaving only the warmth of her body against his, the taste of her lips, the quiet intensity of a kiss that said everything he hadn't dared put into words.

When they finally pulled back, breathless and smiling, he saw her with fresh eyes, realizing this night had fundamentally altered him.

As they parted, their breaths still shallow, Aidan looked at Harper with an undercurrent of intensity—an unspoken mix of awe and fervent desire that lay just beneath the surface. He traced gentle circles on her waist with his thumb, unwilling to let go, savoring the warmth radiating between them. Harper's eyes dropped, and for a moment, her lips parted as though she was about to say something but was searching for the right words.

"This ..." she whispered, her lip caught between her teeth as she wrestled with her nerves. "This feels—"

But before she could finish, he captured her lips again, unable to resist. This kiss was more insistent, even as he felt her melt against him, lost in the surge of passion that seemed to flow between them effortlessly, naturally. When they finally broke apart, their foreheads rested together, the quiet thrum of the ship and the distant sound of waves against the hull the only witnesses to their stolen moment.

After a beat, Aidan leaned closer, his voice an indistinct murmur against her ear. "Brody mentioned he'd be staying with Paige tonight." His eyes held hers, simmering with a barely contained intensity that spoke volumes. "So ... if you'd like, you're welcome to come back to my cabin."

Without hesitation, Harper answered him, her eyes gleaming with anticipation as she drew him in for another passionate, all-consuming kiss. Her hands slipped into his hair, fingers tangling as she pressed herself against him, every touch a spark that only heightened his desire. When they finally pulled away, she looked up at him and said, "Why are we still standing here?" Her voice was laced with playful impatience.

The words were all the encouragement he needed. Without hesitation, they turned and began weaving through the ship's corridors, moving in sync, each step charged with purpose. The distance between them and his cabin felt like miles. Every glance they stole at each other adding fuel to the fire. Aidan's pulse raced, his mind clouded with anticipation, each door they passed stretched his desire until it was almost unbearable.

Every brush of her shoulder against his, every shared look, felt like electricity crackling through him. The warmth building inside him was nearly molten, a visceral pull that sharpened his senses. He couldn't stop himself from imagining what awaited them in the quiet privacy of his room—her laughter, the soft sighs, the intimacy that was so close, just a few doors away now. The entire ship seemed to fade into the background, leaving only the thrill of their shared urgency.

They turned another corner, and the hallway stretched out ahead, his cabin just a few strides away. Aidan's mind was a mix of exhilaration and nervous energy, a realization that tonight would be a night he'd remember long after the ship docked. He locked eyes with Harper and in that split second the world outside ceased to matter.

As they stepped into the quiet sanctuary of Aidan's cabin, the door clicked shut behind them, sealing them off from the rest of the world. Aidan turned to hang the 'Do Not Disturb' sign on the handle, a subtle assurance that this moment would be theirs alone, uninterrupted. When he faced Harper again, the look in her eyes was electric, her expression filled with a mixture of anticipation and daring. She reached for his tie, fingers curling around the fabric, and pulled him close, her lips meeting his with a passion that stole his breath.

Their kiss deepened, both of them giving in to the pent-up desire that had been building over days. Their movements were almost instinctive as Aidan's hands reached for her waist, leading them toward the bed. Harper's hands were already busy, sliding his jacket off his shoulders and letting it drop to the floor, her fingers nimble as they tugged at his tie. She loosened the knot, her lips still fervent against his, and then slipped it from his collar and cast it across the room.

As their kisses grew more fervent, Aidan's fingers sought the zipper at the side of her dress, his touch slow and careful as he drew it down, feeling the fabric begin to loosen around her curves. But Harper's impatience flared, and she took over, swiftly finishing the zipper and allowing the dress to slip, though it clung to her frame for a tantalizing moment longer. Her hands moved to the buttons of his shirt, but they resisted her eager fingers. With a small, frustrated laugh, she tugged a little harder, popping the first button.

Aidan brushed his lips against hers, his voice husky. "It's okay," he murmured, a hint of mischief in his eyes. "I never wear this shirt anyway."

Seemingly, that was the only push Harper needed. Catching his eye, she smirked mischievously and, with a swift, forceful pull, sent the rest of the buttons careening away. As his shirt fell open, exposing his chest, he basked in the freedom of the night, consumed by her touch, her scent, and her presence.

As his shirt fell away, Harper instinctively moved back, lifting her arm to release the strap securing her dress. The sapphire material shimmered for a fleeting second before falling to the floor in a luxurious cascade, revealing a delicate black thong that accentuated, rather than obscured, her beauty. Aidan stared, speechless, at the sight, a quiet awe enveloping him.

Harper sat on the bed's edge, her eyes burning into his with smoldering passion. With a gentle tilt of her head and a slow, enticing smile, she waited, her glance drawing him in and inviting him closer. Aidan took a breath, feeling the pulse of anticipation thrumming through him, and stepped toward her, ready to let the night carry them wherever it wanted.

With a beckoning gesture and a soft, alluring voice, she urged him nearer. "Are you just going to stand there?"

In the dim light of the cabin, Aidan drew in a slow breath, his pulse kicking up as he tried to steady himself. Harper's voice, low and effortlessly captivating, made his pulse jump, stirring something deep and restless within him. It was rare, this boyish rush of excitement—a sensation he hadn't felt in years. This wasn't just a fleeting encounter; it was something he hadn't quite expected, something that felt both exhilarating and daunting.

His hands remained steady as he reached for his belt buckle, yet his heart raced with anticipation. His belt loosened, sending his trousers tumbling to the floor.

Harper's eyes widened as she gasped, her hand flying to her mouth—first in shock, then in growing amusement. Silence stretched between them for half a second before she let out a bright, delighted laugh, the sound breaking the tension like a popped balloon.

Aidan glanced down at his own unicorn-print boxers, then back up at her, and suddenly, he was laughing too. The ridiculousness of the moment wrapped around them both, melting away any nerves.

Harper clutched her stomach, shaking her head as she tried to catch her breath, and Aidan could only grin, warmth rushing up his spine as he gave an exaggerated shrug.

"Not what I was expecting," she murmured, her voice laced with teasing.

"What? They're my lucky undies," he said, a faint blush coloring his cheeks as he grinned, letting his playful side break through the tension.

Harper hummed as if considering, then slowly lifted a single finger, curling it toward herself in a beckoning motion. "Well then," she purred, amusement dancing in her eyes. "Come prove it."

Aidan swallowed, heat rising in his chest as his confidence grew. Though she smiled playfully, there was no mistaking the intensity in her gaze. Moving toward her, he climbed onto the bed, the mattress dipping under their combined weight as he leaned over her, letting his hands slide along her curves. Their laughter faded, replaced by a deeper connection, as his lips found her neck. With a deliberate slowness, he kissed his way down, relishing the sighs, the arch of her back, and the way her hands moved through his hair.

As Aidan followed the graceful line of her collarbone and the soft curve of her breasts with his lips, his initial nerves dissolved, replaced by a natural rhythm that felt both instinctive and intimate. His fingers brushed her skin with a tenderness that surprised even him, a reverence he hadn't known he'd been holding back. Each touch, each kiss, felt like an exploration, a journey he was savoring more than he'd expected.

Harper's hands wove through Aidan's hair, her fingers curling with a mix of urgency and tenderness, gently urging him downward. Her touch was both a command and a reassurance, sending a thrilling heat coursing through him. He could feel her pulse quickening beneath his lips, the soft flutter of her breaths coming in uneven waves. Every quiet gasp, trembling exhale, and shift of her body, wrapped around him, binding him to her in a way that felt undeniable.

His lips traced a path along her form, worshipful in their movements, brushing over the soft curve of her waist and lingering at her hip. The smooth warmth of her skin against his mouth sent a shiver through him, igniting a desire that felt as inevitable as the tide. As he reached the tender skin of her inner thigh, he felt her muscles tense beneath his touch, her anticipation heightening the charge in the air. The world outside the room faded into irrelevance, leaving only the two of them cocooned in an intimacy that felt as timeless as the sea beyond the cabin walls.

His hand hesitated as it reached the edge of her thong, the lace a delicate barrier against the heat radiating from the apex of her desire. He paused, breathing deeply, savoring the heady anticipation between them. It was almost tangible, a shared rhythm of longing that neither needed to voice. With a deliberate slowness, he slid his fingers beneath the fabric, easing it away and baring the heart of her. The silky heat of her skin beneath his fingertips sent a shudder through him. It wasn't just desire—it was something deeper, something that consumed him entirely.

Aidan lowered himself further, his breath teasing over the swollen folds of her arousal, his lips brushing the delicate, glistening petals of her slit with infinite care. He felt her thighs quiver beneath his palms, her body responding instinctively to his touch, and it was enough to make his pulse thunder in his ears. His tongue slid forward, tasting her, savoring the intoxicating sweetness of her slick heat. Slowly, he traced a path through her lips, his tongue swirling around the sensitive bud nestled at the apex of her desire. He circled her swollen nub with precision, his movements tender yet deliberate, as though he were learning her in a language only they could understand.

Harper's back arched beneath him, her breath catching as her fingers tightened in his hair, her grip firm yet trembling. He felt her body flutter against his tongue, the subtle pulses of pleasure echoing through her as her soft moans filled the room, a symphony that spurred him on. Each time he pressed against the gem of her desire, a new wave of warmth and wetness greeted him, and he found himself completely enraptured by her. Her body was a canvas of reactions, each sound a whispered confession of trust and surrender—until an unrestrained squeal slipped free, startling, unfiltered, and utterly intoxicating.

But then her hands tugged at him, guiding him back up, pulling him from between her legs with a need that matched his own. He lifted himself, pressing kisses along the soft curve of her stomach, the swell of her bosom, until their lips met again in a kiss that was both searing and tender. Her skin was flushed, her breasts rising and falling with her quickened breaths, and her eyes met his with an intensity that left him undone.

Harper's hands moved down, her touch deliberate as her fingers grazed over the hard length of his shaft, the sensation drawing a low, guttural sound from deep in his throat. Her grip was firm yet teasing as she guided him, her touch sending a fresh wave of heat coursing through his body. He felt her adjust beneath him, the warmth of her slick entrance pressing against the head, and for a moment, he froze, overwhelmed by the sheer intimacy.

Meeting his gaze, her lips parted in a gentle whisper, "Aidan ..." It wasn't a plea, but an invitation—a quiet assurance that this was right, that this was theirs.

With a steady hand, she guided him into her, the heat of her canal enveloping him inch by inch, her slickness making the movement achingly smooth. Aidan let out a sharp breath as her body fluttered around him, the tight warmth drawing him deeper, his girth stretching her in a way that was both exhilarating and humbling. He paused, letting her adjust, feeling the way her body molded to him, perfectly, as if they were two pieces of the same puzzle.

The sensations threatened to overwhelm him—the wet heat of her, the soft sighs that escaped her lips, the way her curves pressed against him, grounding him even as his pulse raced. Her hands slid along his shoulders, pulling him closer, and he dipped his head to kiss her again, their lips meeting in a union as intimate as their bodies. The tenderness of her touch, the way her fingers brushed against the nape of his neck, sent a shiver down his spine, anchoring him to her.

As he began to move, slow and deliberate, he was acutely aware of every detail—the way her breath hitched with each thrust, the way her body responded to his, her warmth and wetness pulling him deeper into a rhythm that felt both primal and transcendent.

Each movement was a conversation, a shared language of pleasure and connection that needed no words.

And then, with a final, desperate thrust, he unraveled, surrendering to her—completely.

Fifteen

The morning sun broke through the thin curtains of Aidan's cabin, casting a golden light across the quiet chaos left from the night before. The blankets lay rumpled at the foot of the bed, and on the floor beside them, Harper's sapphire dress was a silken pool, glittering faintly in the morning light. Shoes, a shirt, a tie, and an array of clothes trailed from the door to the bed, evidence of their hurried journey to one another.

Aidan's eyes drifted open slowly, and he blinked, disoriented. But then, with a small, calm breath, he remembered. He reveled in the warmth of Harper's body against his own; her sleep-filled breaths caressing his collarbone. His arm lay protectively around her, fingers brushing the small of her back. Even in sleep, she looked peaceful and radiant, her hair spilling over his shoulder like the last traces of the night.

With a deep breath, Aidan held her close, allowing himself to be consumed by the comforting warmth of her presence, a feeling he hadn't known he was missing. His fingers skimmed along her shoulder, marveling at her nearness. In that quiet morning, he felt like they were on their own for a second, without the pressures of home. Here, there was no family restaurant, no deadlines, no expectations. Just the two of them.

But the thought lingered like a shadow, filling him with a sense of dread he couldn't ignore. Tomorrow morning, it would all be over. They would step off this ship, this cocoon of shared moments and ocean sunsets, and return to lives that seemed worlds apart. He had spent these days savoring the present, diving headlong into each moment, but he could already feel the weight of reality bearing down on him, urging him to think about the "what now" he'd tried so hard to avoid.

With a soft sigh, he felt her nudge closer. Harper shifted, her teeth catching her lower lip as she looked up at him, her gaze tired yet unmistakably attentive. She studied him, a slight smile touching her lips, but it quickly faded as she caught the distant look in his eyes.

"You've got that look," she murmured, her voice gentle with a morning haze.

He blinked, trying to ease the tension in his expression, but he knew he couldn't hide from her. Not now. He ran a hand through his hair, glancing down as if the mess of blankets could somehow offer him clarity.

"Just ... thinking about tomorrow," he admitted, his voice low. "About the end of this ... all of this."

Adjusting her position onto her side, she propped herself up on one elbow, allowing their eyes to connect more intimately. "That was bound to come up eventually, wasn't it?" Though her voice was soft, there was a trace of sadness in it—a comprehension as constant as the look in her eyes.

Aidan nodded, swallowing as he tried to put his jumbled thoughts into words. "I've been trying not to think about it," he confessed. "Just wanted to enjoy this, to let go for once and live in the moment. And it's been amazing. More than I expected." He paused, looking at her carefully, knowing the next words would open the door to the questions he had been quietly burying. "But I can't help but wonder … where does it go from here?"

Harper nodded slowly, glancing down as her fingers traced the edges of the sheets. "You're right. It's been incredible." She locked eyes with him again, her look searching his with a blend of empathy and mutual uncertainty. "But it's … complicated, isn't it?" Her words lingered, heavy with all the realities they'd sidestepped until now. "I have my life in New York, and you … you have Charlotte. The restaurant, your family …"

He noticed the shift in her voice, that quiet trace of melancholy as she spoke of his family. He knew she understood the weight of his responsibilities; she had her own burdens, her own deadlines and demands pulling her in a hundred directions back in New York.

"Yeah," he murmured. "I'm not ready to leave the restaurant or my family. But I also don't want to go back to that feeling of being … trapped."

She nodded, her hand gliding down his arm in a slow, deliberate motion, steadying him even as her words cracked open thoughts he hadn't let himself consider.

"I get it, Aidan. Maybe that's why we both needed this cruise, you know? To get away and figure out what we really want."

He studied her face, the sadness in her expression, and the echo of his own fear flickered in her eyes. "So ... what do we do?" His voice was quiet, edged with a reluctance to say goodbye, to give up the spark he'd felt in these days with her.

She looked down thoughtfully as if weighing her words carefully. "I don't know," she whispered, almost to herself. "But maybe we don't have to figure it all out right now. Maybe ..." She hesitated, then looked up, a small, uncertain smile tugging at her lips. "Maybe we just make the most of today. We have, what, twenty-four hours left on this ship?"

The relief that washed over him was almost overwhelming like a tide pulling back to reveal calm, clear waters. Aidan return her smile, his hand instinctively finding hers beneath the tangled blankets. "Twenty-four hours," he repeated, nodding. "If this is all we get, let's make it count."

Harper's fingers began to move in slow, lazy patterns across his chest, the tips tracing deliberate paths over the ridges of his muscles. Her touch was like a spark, sending faint currents of heat coursing through him, building anticipation with every stroke. He couldn't help but tense beneath her hand, his breathing quickening as her fingertips dipped lower, sliding across the line of his stomach.

Her touch was a contradiction—soft yet commanding, steady yet full of promise. When her fingers brushed against the sensitive flesh of his shaft, the energy shifted, heavy with unspoken desire. His erection responded immediately, swelling beneath her delicate touch, the warmth of her palm igniting a fire that spread through his core. A sharp breath hitched in his throat, his control fraying as he fought to contain the groan rising within him.

"Let's not waste any time," she whispered, her voice husky and brimming with intent. She moved with effortless grace, straddling him, her thighs framing his hips as her weight pressed lightly against him. The curve of her waist, the swell of her hips, and the way her skin glowed in the morning light stole the air from his lungs. He could feel her slickness brushing against his shaft as she adjusted herself, her warmth teasing him with an intimacy that made his pulse thrum wildly.

She leaned in, her hair whispering across his skin as her lips pressed against him. Each kiss was slow and purposeful, her mouth leaving a trail of heat in its wake. Her lips moved down his chest, pausing briefly over his heart as if she were savoring the steady rhythm beneath. Aidan exhaled shakily, his body surrendering to her every touch. Her kisses wove a quiet melody, a rhythm that sank into him, pulling him deeper into a world where nothing existed but her.

As her mouth traveled lower, he could feel the tension building within him, a delicious pressure coiling tightly in his core. Her lips hovered over the sensitive skin of his stomach, and his muscles twitched involuntarily beneath her touch. When she finally reached his length, she paused for a moment, her breath warm against him, sending a shiver down his spine.

The first touch of her lips against his shaft was enough to make him momentarily forget how to breathe. Her mouth was soft and warm, her movements deliberate yet unhurried. The sensation of her lips sliding over his flesh was exquisite, a perfect blend of pleasure and worship that left him utterly undone. As her tongue traced the sensitive ridge of his head, his hips bucked instinctively, a low groan escaping him before he could stop it.

Aidan clenched his fists at his sides, his body taut as he fought to hold back the tide of his own arousal. The rhythmic pull of her mouth, the way her lips enveloped him with each glide, threatened to consume him completely. He was drowning in the warmth of her, the wet, fluttering movements of her tongue sent jolts of pleasure through him that made it almost impossible to think.

Her hands gripped his thighs, a tether anchoring him as pleasure coiled tighter as his body fought to hold the edge at bay. He closed his eyes, letting himself sink into the sensations, the heat, the pressure, the soft rhythm of her mouth that mirrored the rise and fall of a distant wave. It was as if she were conducting an orchestra, her movements the melody, his body the instrument responding to her every touch.

She pulled back at last, her lips still glistening and her eyes fixed on his, and in that moment, Aidan was flooded with awe. She looked ethereal, her cheeks flushed, her hair slightly tousled, and her lips curved into a small, knowing smile. He couldn't help but reach for her, his hands sliding up the soft curve of her waist to anchor her against him.

She shifted again, her movements fluid and unhurried, and he felt the heat of her center press against his length. Harper's fingers slid between them, guiding him to her entrance with a confidence that made his breath hitch. The slick warmth enveloped him slowly, inch by inch, her body molding around his girth with a tight, perfect fit that sent sparks shooting through him.

Aidan bit his lip, his hands gripping her hips as he tried to hold himself steady, the exquisite pressure almost too much to bear. She paused, her body adjusting to his, and the stillness between them was electric, their breaths mingling in the quiet intimacy.

When she began to move, her hips rolling in slow, methodical circles, Aidan's resolve threatened to shatter. The way her body enveloped him, slick and warm, her walls fluttering around his length, sent waves of pleasure radiating through him. He couldn't help but moan softly, his hands sliding down to cup her ass, his fingers pressing into the soft curves as he guided her movements.

Each rise and fall of her hips was a note in their shared sonata, a crescendo building with every thrust. The sound of their breaths mingling, the soft gasp of her voice as she moved, and the gentle creak of the bed beneath them created a harmony that filled the room. Aidan felt himself teetering on the edge, his body straining against the overwhelming pleasure, but he held on, determined to savor every moment, every movement, every sigh.

As their rhythm quickened, he leaned forward, his lips finding hers in a kiss that was both tender and desperate. The taste of her, the way her hands tangled in his hair and her body pressed so perfectly against his, left him breathless. He could feel the tension in her body, the way her thighs trembled against his, and he knew she was close, her own climax building like the final, triumphant note of their song.

Aidan let himself get lost in her, in the warmth of her curves, the softness of her skin, the intoxicating way she moved against him. When she finally cried out, her body tightening around his as she reached her peak, the sight and feel of her release pushed him over the edge. A tidal wave of heat and light consumed him as he followed her into bliss, his body shuddering with the force of his climax.

For a moment, there was nothing but the sound of their breathing, the steady rise and fall of their chests as they clung to each other in the aftermath. Aidan closed his eyes, his forehead resting against hers, and he let out a soft, contented sigh. The world outside the cabin didn't matter; all that mattered was this moment, the quiet, unspoken connection between them that felt as natural as the rhythm of the ocean.

As they lay together, their bodies still entwined, Aidan traced slow circles along her back, his touch light and reverential. He didn't speak—there was no need. Everything he felt, every unspoken thought, was written in the way his hands moved over her skin, memorizing her, savoring her, holding her close as if to keep time from slipping away.

The quiet hum of the ship in the background, the faint sway of the sea beneath them, only added to the sense of timelessness. Yet here time felt suspended—a delicate melody stretched between them, waiting to be played just a little longer.

The morning light seeped through the curtains, illuminating the rumpled bed and the trail of clothes strewn across the floor. Aidan lay still, Harper curled against him, her warm, steady breaths brushing his collarbone. For a moment, the world outside didn't exist. With every gentle stroke on her shoulder, the burden of the restaurant, Charlotte, and the upcoming decisions faded, replaced by a sense of contentment in her proximity.

But reality lingered at the edges, impossible to ignore. Tomorrow, the ship would dock. The bubble they'd built, filled with sunsets, laughter, and peaceful moments, was on the verge of bursting. The thought tightened his chest, but he pushed it aside, determined to stay here, in this fleeting moment.

Aidan lay still as Harper's laugh broke the morning quiet. "If I stay here any longer, I might melt into the bed," she teased, stretching in a way that made the sunlight dance across her skin.

"Would that be so bad?" Aidan propped himself up, smirking. "I could just tell Brody you've retired to become part of the mattress."

Harper swatted his arm, her eyes sparkling. "Oh, sure. That'll go over well." She motioned at the pile of clothes on the floor and laughed. "Yeah, not exactly breakfast attire."

Aidan climbed out of bed and rifled through his drawer. "Here," he said, tossing her a faded blue T-shirt and gym shorts.

Harper slipped into the oversized shirt, tying a knot at the side with an exaggerated flourish. "Move over, Paris Fashion Week," she quipped, striking a pose that made Aidan laugh despite the weight pressing at his chest. She looked ridiculous and stunning all at once. How was it possible that even in his old gym shorts, she managed to take his breath away?

"How do you make my laundry-day leftovers look runway-ready?" he admired.

He held onto the quiet, but the bubble of their cabin felt fragile, too perfect to last. Tomorrow's sunrise would mark a return to their separate journeys, tearing them apart from the shared moments they cherished.

Harper slipped her hand into his, snapping him out of his thoughts. "Come on, Chef," she said playfully, tugging him toward the door. "Let's get some breakfast before Brody organizes a search party."

As they walked through the ship's corridors, her hand still in his, he found himself grateful for even the small, ordinary moments like this. The bustle of the morning swirled around them, other passengers chatting over coffee or loading their plates at the buffet, but Aidan's focus stayed on Harper, her presence anchoring him.

They spotted Brody and Paige sitting near a window, the sunlight casting warm halos over their heads as they waved them over. Aidan couldn't help but grin as they approached, Harper's fingers still laced through his.

"Well, well, well," Brody said, crossing his arms with an exaggerated grin. "Wasn't sure if the two of you were going to come up for air."

Aidan rolled his eyes, but a grin broke through his feigned exasperation. "Good morning to you, too," he replied, grabbing a chair as Harper's laughter danced between them while she slipped into the seat beside him. Brody only smirked more, tossing Aidan a wink.

Paige, shaking her head at Brody's antics, turned to Harper. "Is that Aidan's shirt?"

Harper laughed, adjusting the knotted fabric at her waist. "Turns out his wardrobe has a little versatility," she said with a shrug, her eyes meeting Aidan's with a lighthearted glint.

They settled into simple conversation, the four of them catching up on last night's adventures. While sharing stories and laughter over breakfast, But even as Aidan smiled, a lingering thought settled in his chest—how was he supposed to let go of something that felt like it had only just started?

As Harper laughed at something Brody said, Aidan watched her, his coffee forgotten. The way her eyes sparkled, reflecting the light within her, made him want to memorize every detail. The slight tilt of her head, the way her voice softened as if revealing a secret, was like a melody playing in his heart. Tomorrow, this would be gone. Soon, the laughter, their easy camaraderie, and the way she fit so seamlessly beside him would all fade into a cherished memory.

Harper turned to him, her hand brushing his under the table. "You're quiet," she said softly, her smile full of warmth.

"Just taking it all in," he replied, giving her hand a gentle squeeze. And he was. Every laugh, every look, every second.

As the conversation continued, he found himself caught up in the memory of their week together, each day a new layer to a story he wasn't ready to end. He studied Harper's face, watching the way her eyes sparkled when she laughed, the way her fingers brushed absently against his on the table. A pang of dread coiled in his chest, realizing how quickly the clock was ticking toward their last goodbye. He wanted to ask her what came next, but held back, not wanting to dim the lightness of this last day.

Under the table, his fingers tightened around hers, a silent pledge to hold on to this unpredictable chapter of their lives, a shared experience that had surprised him with its transformative power, no matter what tomorrow might bring.

"So, one last day together?" he asked, trying to push aside the looming farewell and focus on the here and now.

Harper's fingers tightened around his. "One last day," she agreed. "Let's make it count."

As breakfast wound down, Brody leaned back with a grin. "Alright, we can't just let this end tomorrow and never see each other again. Promise me we'll stay in touch, alright? If nothing else, we're booking another cruise together one day."

Paige nodded eagerly, raising her coffee cup like a toast. "Absolutely! It's tough to find both good friends and great travel buddies. We can't let this go."

Harper's eyes lit up as she looked from Paige to Aidan and Brody. "Agreed. We'll need another adventure to look forward to."

Aidan smiled, but the weight of goodbye hung in his chest. Meeting her eyes, he allowed himself to be enveloped by the warmth in them, feeling the flood of memories from their week together—the laughter, the sunsets, the candid talks, and the spark that had grown between them. He didn't want it to end, and the thought of returning to life without her by his side filled him with an ache he hadn't expected.

But today wasn't over yet. They had one last day and night to enjoy together, one more day to make memories before they'd all part ways.

As they pushed their chairs back and stood up, Aidan moved beside Harper, wrapping his arm around her waist as they fell in step with Brody and Paige. She slipped her hand into his back pocket, giving him a playful squeeze that made him chuckle.

"You're thinking too much," in a quiet murmur, she spoke, her eyes both steady and warmly attentive.

Aidan met her eyes, feeling the weight lift. She was right; questions could wait for later. But one thing he did know; he wasn't going to waste a single moment they had left.

"You're right," he said, letting his grip around her tighten slightly. "Let's make the most of today."

With their arms wrapped around each other, they set off together, laughter drifting behind them as they prepared to enjoy every minute.

Sixteen

Aidan moved around the cabin, shoving shirts into his suitcase with more care than he needed to, drifting over each last item like it might hold the answers he hadn't yet found. The morning's gray light filtering through the balcony, the throng of messages, and his packed bags all forced him to face the reality of the day ahead. And yet, the room still held a faint, undeniable trace of Harper.

The room lay untouched, a quiet mess of tangled sheets and scattered pillows. A glass of water sat forgotten on the desk, alongside a crumpled napkin and a pen teetering near the edge. The room, like Aidan, felt rooted in the past few days, resistant to embracing the present.

He swore he could still catch the faint, warm scent of her shampoo on the bed, a surviving reminder of the morning they'd spent together just twenty-four hours ago. He could still see her there, teasing him, stretching in the golden light, her laughter soft and unguarded. It had felt effortless, the perfection he'd tried to savor while it lasted.

Last night, though, had been different. Their goodnight was quiet, a calculated effort to minimize the morning's hurt. But as he stared at the unmade bed now, it felt impossible not to think of her. She hadn't just left a scent behind; she'd left herself embedded in his thoughts, impossible to ignore.

Brody, too, was moving about the room, though with none of Aidan's hesitation, tossing things haphazardly into his suitcase as if he could hardly wait to leap into whatever awaited him next. Brody's laughter, light and careless, echoed in the small cabin as he stumbled on an old sock left under the bed. It was a relief, honestly, the natural rhythm of Brody's motions and jokes. Brody noticed him idling by the closet for too long and shot him a pointed look.

"All this time thinking about Harper, and you're barely even sentimental about saying goodbye to your favorite roommate? I'm hurt."

Aidan laughed, feeling a bit of the tension ease out of him. "Trust me, you'll be missed." No one else is going to leave their dirty socks around for me to trip over."

Brody grinned. "You're welcome. Anyway, you're the one moping like it's your last day of summer camp. And here I thought you'd be ready to get back to reality."

Aidan shrugged, his face falling into a thoughtful frown as he flicked his phone back on. A few texts from Declan, one from his mom, and more than a few missed calls from the restaurant flashed across the screen, and he felt that familiar tug, the heavy responsibility of life, waiting for him back home. He cleared his throat, not looking up. "Well, maybe I'm not in any rush this time."

He hadn't exactly come here looking for life-altering revelations, but that's how it felt. It all felt unreal like he was watching someone else live his life. The easy way he'd laughed with Harper, the quiet glances they'd shared over morning coffee on the deck, the deeper conversations that had unfurled as the days wore on … it was a kind of lightness he'd nearly forgotten was possible. There was a depth and authenticity to his feelings for her that was unlike anything he'd known before.

Brody sat down on the bed, clearly picking up on Aidan's unspoken struggle. "You know, this cruise has been pretty damn great," he said, stretching out casually. "I mean, Paige and I … talk about a fire. I wasn't looking for anything serious, but man … she's … she's different, you know. I guess I'm lucky she's only a couple of hours away. Maybe we'll see where this goes."

Aidan smiled at that, feeling a flicker of something bittersweet. From the moment they met, Brody and Paige's relationship was a blazing inferno, burning with passion and intensity. There had been no hesitation, no second-guessing, just an immediate connection that had burned hot and bright. They'd been everywhere together, always laughing, always with their arms wrapped around each other, disappearing from dinner parties and reappearing hours later, looking equally radiant and exhausted. For Brody, the cruise had been a whirlwind romance, an adventure he seemed more than ready to continue back home.

And then there was Aidan and Harper. There had been no instant spark, no headlong rush into romance. With Harper, things had moved slowly, unfolding layer by layer, like a story he'd waited his whole life to read. Their nights together had started with long, meandering conversations, with stolen glances across crowded dinner tables, with hands that found each other only after the long, lingering moments had done their work. They had unknowingly creat-ed something, like waves slowly eroding stone until only the gentle, steady rhythm of trust remained. But now, with the cruise ending, he was wondering if the slowness of their connection, the deep-rooted warmth of it, meant it would stay here, in these memories, unable to follow them back into real life.

Brody watched him, as if sensing Aidan's thoughts. "So, what's going on with you and Harper? You two seemed, you know ... solid."

Aidan ran a hand through his hair, not sure how to put it into words. "Honestly? I don't know. Being with her was ... everything I didn't realize I needed. And now, it just feels like a wonderful memory I'll look back on. She's got her life in New York, and I've got the restaurant in Charlotte. I'd be crazy to think there's anything more than what we've had here." He shook his head, laughing softly at himself. "It's like I've been telling myself all week to keep it simple, to enjoy it while it lasts. But here I am, wishing for more anyway."

With a nod, Brody's look mingled genuine empathy with a playful spark in his eyes. "Look, man, whatever happens, I'm cheering for you two. I mean, yeah, she's a big-city girl, and you're Mr. Murphy's Pub. But things have a way of working out when they're supposed to." He hesitated, then shrugged. "You two had something different. It wasn't all fireworks, you know? It was real."

Aidan knew Brody was right, even if it only made things harder. Her presence lingered in his mind, an inescapable melody he couldn't help but replay. He hadn't meant for her to take up space in his life, but somehow, she'd found a way in and stayed. But what were the chances they could ever really make it work? Their lives were a world apart, shaped by different paths, different expectations. Maybe it was best, he thought, to let the memory of her stay here, on this ship, as a perfect, unblemished part of him.

Brody snapped him out of his thoughts with a laugh, holding up a scrap of black lace he'd just uncovered from under the bed. "Well, well. You lose something here, Aidan? Didn't think lace thongs were part of your wardrobe."

Aidan grinned, reaching for it and tucking it into the side pocket of his suitcase. "Actually, I'd been wondering where those had gone. But they're definitely Harper's. Guess I'll just have to hope I run into her later to hand these off."

Brody laughed, shaking his head as he finished zipping his own bag. "Man, I can't tell if you're heartbroken or holding on for dear life."

Aidan forced a laugh, too, trying to shake off the ache remaining in his chest. "Maybe a bit of both. I'll get over it, though. I have to." But even as he said it, the words felt hollow.

Brody stretched, then turned to him, attempting a sage tone. "Well, you know, like that tide stuff Maude was saying. 'Something, something, the tide watches over everything ... something, you're always where you are meant to be,' or whatever she said."

Aidan let out a sigh of amusement, squeezing Brody's shoulder. "You're really on fire with these quotes. Maude would be proud."

"Maybe," Brody said with a grin. "But hey, all I'm saying is, if anyone can figure it out, you can." He picked up his suitcase, his usual easygoing confidence intact. "Come on, man. Let's get one last look at the ocean."

Aidan followed him, a pang of finality pressing down as he knew he was leaving more behind than just a beautiful view.

Aidan and Brody made their way down the hallway toward the exit, following the slow-moving crowd as they navigated the gangway. Outside, the early morning sunlight poured through the terminal windows. The end of the journey brought a mix of excitement and reluctance for Aidan.

With every step, he could still feel Harper, her laughter echoing in his thoughts, her touch lingering on his skin. The ship's scent clung to him, a drifting mixture of sunblock, coffee, and the salty air that whispered of faraway shores. It felt like the final notes of a song he hadn't wanted to end.

Brody walked beside him, slinging his bag over his shoulder with the kind of effortless motion that usually meant he wasn't dwelling on things. But in the quiet that stretched between them, the finality of it all hung in the air. As they stepped onto solid ground, the ship behind them, the weight of everything they'd shared remained.

In the terminal, the crowd dispersed as passengers met family and friends, while others joined the lines for customs or waited for their bags to arrive on the conveyor. Aidan and Brody found an unoccupied bench, dropping their bags beside them as they sat in silence, absorbing the quiet realization that their time on the ship had officially ended.

"Well, guess this is it," Brody said, giving Aidan a clap on the shoulder. "Been one hell of a week, huh?"

"You can say that again." They shared a knowing grin, both men appreciating the wild turns the cruise had taken them on.

Brody's grin widened. "You know, don't think you're getting rid of me just yet. We need to plan another cruise, thanks to our resident travel expert. Can't just let a week like this be a one-off."

"True," Aidan agreed, a smile tugging at the corner of his mouth. "And I'll be watching my mailbox for a wedding invite, too."

Brody scoffed, though there was a glimmer of something in his eye. "Yeah, don't hold your breath. But hey, don't run off too far. Paige is already talking about a reunion trip."

They exchanged a quick hug, and Aidan clapped Brody on the back. "Take care, man. For real, keep me posted."

Brody nodded. "You, too. Say hi to that pub of yours for me." With one last smile, Brody grabbed his bag and headed off, disappearing into the sea of people.

Aidan watched him go, a pang of nostalgia already settling in. Brody's lighthearted nature had been a perfect match for the cruise's carefree rhythm, and he realized saying goodbye felt like closing a chapter he wasn't quite ready to finish. A part of him wanted to turn back, to head up to the top deck and delay leaving for just a little while longer.

But, he reminded himself, that wasn't how things worked. His time aboard the ship, with its long sunny days and starry nights, was destined to end. Still, he couldn't help but feel the weight of it now, the ending sitting heavy in his chest.

As he grabbed his suitcase, Aidan made his way toward the exit of the terminal. That's when he spotted her.

Across the bustling space, Harper was stepping out of the baggage claim area, her hand raised to flag down a cab waiting just outside. She was wearing jeans and the blue T-shirt he'd lent her the day before, the same knot tied casually at her waist. Her silhouette, bathed in the morning light, wearing his shirt, a comforting reminder of their last shared dawn, ignited a flame of warmth and longing within him.

The room buzzed with unfamiliar faces, yet her presence was like a beacon, radiating the quiet power of their shared history, a silent echo of unspoken memories.

She turned, and their eyes met across the crowded terminal. She lifted her hand, blowing him a playful kiss, her smile soft and knowing. It was a small, simple gesture, yet it struck him with an intensity that threatened to knock him off his feet. Then, with one last wave, she slipped into the cab and disappeared from view.

He stood there, watching as the cab pulled away, running a hand over his face as reality settled in. This was the ending he'd braced for, the quiet shift from presence to absence. They had made memories worth keeping, but now they belonged to the past, waiting to be carefully folded away like the pages of an old, well-loved book.

Aidan turned, a strange feeling of gratitude and loss in his gut. What he'd had with Harper wasn't just a casual fling; it was a quiet, unexpected connection that had somehow shown him a part of himself he'd almost forgotten. He wanted to hold on to it, to keep that feeling alive. But he knew it was time to get back to reality, to face the life he'd left behind in Charlotte. The Murphy family pub, the kitchen, his family ... they needed him. And he couldn't ignore that pull, as much as he wanted to stay in the warmth of the past week's memories.

Just as he was about to head out of the terminal, his phone buzzed in his pocket. Glancing down, he saw a message from Declan.

Declan

> Hey ... back soon? Da has been riding me all week. Think he wants you here for the dinner rush tonight.

Aidan felt a wry smile cross his face. The familiar tug of responsibility washed over him in an instant. His vacation was officially over. He tucked his phone back in his pocket, feeling the echoes of the restaurant's demands return, the rhythm of the kitchen creeping back into his mind.

But as he stepped outside, suitcase in hand, he let himself pause, breathing in the sea's scent one last time. He could almost hear Maude's voice echoing in his mind, her cryptic advice about the tides, and trusting the journey.

He didn't know if he'd ever see Harper again or if this trip would just be a sweet memory he'd look back on whenever he felt the need to escape. It was undeniable, though, that this week had altered him. He felt it in the way he'd woken up this morning, the way he'd laughed with Brody, and even now, in the way he was seeing his life waiting for him back home.

It was time to get back to work, to face whatever awaited him in Charlotte with a little more purpose. Perhaps he'd carry a piece of this experience, a reminder that life held more than just his daily routine. Maybe the unexpected tide had pulled him somewhere new, offering a glimpse of something valuable, worth cherishing.

Seventeen

Clanging metal, shouting voices, and sizzling hot oil filled the chaotic kitchen at Murphy's Pub. The relentless flow of orders kept coming, adding to the ever-growing pile of tickets that were already overflowing from the pass. Driven by instinct, Aidan's hands moved with practiced speed, executing a familiar rhythm that felt like second nature. He tossed a handful of chopped onions onto the griddle with a sharp, practiced motion, smelling caramelizing sweetness cutting through the humid air.

Aidan shouted across the line to Declan, who was flipping a mountain of burgers with practiced ease, sweat dotting his brow. Jazz, the bartender, was at the window with a drink order, grinning as she yelled through to him, "If you don't hurry, we're gonna have a revolt out there!" Her voice carried the teasing sensation that only came from years of camaraderie in the trenches of dinner rushes.

Although the pace was unrelenting, Aidan felt a growing unease beneath the high energy. The Philly Cheesesteak Shepherd's Pie special, his latest experiment, had been an unexpected hit. It was a bold and whimsical fusion of two comfort food worlds, like a playful duet between two unlikely partners, resulting in a surprisingly harmonious and satisfying dish. The idea of adding the dish to the menu made him uneasy, given his father's unwavering commitment to Murphy's established cuisine. But in the cruise's wake and Harper, a change came over him. For the first time in years, he'd dared to believe in his own instincts because shaking things up could bring something good.

Each time the dish went out, Aidan couldn't help but feel a surge of satisfaction. Witnessing the delighted expressions of his patrons as they savored his creation validated his decision to pursue passion. The Philly Pie had quickly gained popularity, with people coming in and requesting it by name after just a few days. While the victory was minor, it resonated deeply on a personal level.

He allowed himself a brief smile as he pulled the next order together. Harper's words, a call to action, urged him to embrace courage and risk it all. She hadn't been talking about food, but it didn't matter. She'd awakened something, reminding him that sometimes the best things in life came from leaving safety behind and following your gut.

His happiness was abruptly destroyed, replaced by a sense of unease. And everything went downhill as Seamus entered the kitchen. Instinctively, Aidan stiffened his shoulders, the familiar weight of Seamus's disapproval already bearing down on him. He barely had time to set a new skillet on the burner before his father's voice sliced through the din like a cleaver.

"What is that ... that thing doing on the menu, Aidan?" Seamus's eyes flicked to the tray of Philly-inspired shepherd's pies waiting to go out, his face twisting in visible disdain. "This ... this Americanized monstrosity is being served in my restaurant?"

Aidan kept his tone steady, tamping down his frustration. "Da, it's been a hit. People love it. They've been coming in just for it since I added it." He kept stirring, hoping to defuse his father's glare with calm reasoning.

Seamus shook his head, the frown deepening. "Hit or not, it doesn't belong on this menu. Murphy's Pub serves Irish food, son. Authentic Irish dishes. Not some bastardized cheesesteak mess."

Aidan swallowed the words that threatened to spill out. This wasn't the first time he'd clashed with his dad over the menu. Seamus had always insisted on sticking to tradition, and while Aidan respected that, he couldn't help but feel boxed in by it. They were arguing about the menu again. Aidan wanted to add new dishes, but Seamus was all about keeping things traditional.

"Look, Da, it's just a special. It's not replacing anything, and it's bringing people in the door," Aidan replied, trying to keep his tone steady as he flipped a skillet full of onions.

But Seamus wasn't having it. His fists tightened, his voice rising above the clamor of the kitchen. "I don't care if it's bringing in every damn person in Charlotte! This isn't some ... food truck or burger joint. It's Murphy's! You know as well as I do what that name stands for." He swept a hand through the air, dismissing the tray of shepherd's pie as if it were an insult in itself.

Aidan could feel the stares of the line cooks and prep staff around him, all trying to work while keeping an ear on the father-son standoff. He clenched his jaw, choosing his words carefully. "I thought ... I thought maybe it was time we tried to bring something fresh in, Da. That's all. Something that keeps things interesting."

"Interesting?" Seamus echoed, his voice a sneer. "You think any-one comes here looking for interesting, Aidan? They come here for tradition. For what we've been doing since I opened this place. Not whatever you've cobbled together to look like the damn American Dream."

Aidan braced himself, trying not to let the tension spill over. This was what he'd been struggling with, the push-and-pull between honoring the past and creating something of his own. He'd hoped, even after years of this, that maybe his dad would see things differently, that Seamus would understand the need to evolve.

"Fine," Seamus snapped, slamming a fist on the counter. "You can run this ... whatever it is for tonight, and then it's gone. Tomorrow, we're back to the real menu. I won't have this place turned into a fast-food circus."

He shot Aidan one last glare before spinning on his heel, storming back through the swinging doors into the front of the pub.

Aidan watched him go. Every muscle tensed as he resisted the urge to throw the skillet he was holding. The adrenaline of the dinner rush mixed with a sudden wave of frustration and resentment. *This isn't some food truck or burger joint,* Seamus' words kept ringing in his ears. Maybe that was the problem. Maybe the legacy Seamus was so dead set on protecting was suffocating Aidan's chance to build something of his own.

The tickets kept coming, and Aidan forced himself to snap back into work mode, moving with a practiced efficiency even as his mind spun. The irony was obvious; here he was, back in the place he'd grown up in, back in the role that had defined him for so long, yet it felt stifling in a way he could hardly ignore.

Jazz came by, glancing over her shoulder to make sure Seamus was nowhere in sight. "Philly Shepherd's Pie, huh?" she said with a grin, handing over a drink ticket. "People out there are raving about it, by the way. I think you've got a hit on your hands, Aidan."

Aidan forced a smile, nodding as he pulled the next order up. "Yeah, well, don't tell Da. Apparently, it's blasphemy to the 'Murphy's legacy.'"

She laughed, yet her eyes took on a soft, gentle glow. "Hey, you've got some pretty loyal fans out there tonight. You're doing something right, even if the old man doesn't see it." She patted his shoulder before heading back to the bar.

Aidan worked through the rest of the night on autopilot, letting his hands do the familiar work while his mind wandered. It was like he'd slipped back into a routine he'd tried so hard to step away from, one that felt increasingly at odds with who he was becoming.

As the dinner service slowed, the frantic clanging and sizzling in the kitchen simmered down to a steady hum. Aidan wiped his hands on his apron, his mind still buzzing from his battle with Seamus and the busy night. He started prepping for cleanup when Jazz popped her head through the pass window, her eyes sparkling with mischief.

"Hey, Chef," she called, her voice just loud enough to be heard over the kitchen noise. "There's someone out here asking to see you."

Aidan glanced up, curious. "Who is it?"

Jazz shrugged with a grin. "Some girl who says she knows you."

For one wild second, his heart leaped, Harper? Could it really be her? The idea surged through him before he could stop it, his pulse quickening at the thought of seeing her again, of hearing her voice cut through the noise of the pub. But just as quickly, the rational part of him stepped in. She was back in New York. They'd said their good-byes, promised to move on. And yet, he couldn't stop himself from scanning the room, hoping against hope for something impossible.

But as someone waved him over, the fragile spark of hope crumbled. Upon recognizing the individual, he experienced a pang of disap-pointment, realizing it was not Harper. Instead, it was another familiar face from his past. Lila. His ex-girlfriend, now a rising food blogger in Charlotte's culinary scene, sat waiting with a smile that pulled him back to another chapter of his life altogether.

"Lila! Lila Prescott!" he called with a warm smile as he approached. They hadn't crossed paths for years, but reconnecting with her felt good. Their breakup had been amicable, and he still held a lot of respect for her.

She smiled back, her eyes lighting up. "Aidan Murphy, still the man behind the curtain here, huh?"

"Guilty as charged," he said with a warm smile, wrapping her in a brief, friendly hug. "It's been a while. How've you been?"

"Good! Life's good." With a sweep of her hand, she pointed to the remnants of a special Philly Pie on her table, a testament to a hearty meal. "And I heard you've been busy experimenting in the kitchen. Had to come in and see for myself."

"Oh, the 'Philly Special,'" he said with a half-smile. "I'm so glad you liked it."

"Liked it? It was delicious, Aidan. Inspired, even," she said, tapping her fork against the empty plate. "I have to say, I've always admired your flair for pushing boundaries, especially with traditional Irish fare."

"Thanks, Lila. But, uh … don't let Da hear you say that." he said, rolling his eyes. "Seamus is still as stubborn as ever."

Lila laughed, nodding in agreement. "Yeah, that sounds about right. Same old Seamus. But you? I always thought you'd be … well, I don't know, somewhere else by now. Doing your own thing, maybe. But it's good to see you here, keeping the family legacy going."

He shrugged, his smile laced with both fondness and resignation. "Still slinging it at Murphy's. It's like family always has a way of reeling you back in, you know?

"That, I do." She rested her chin on her hand, studying him. "It's just … I remember all the ideas you used to have, the new dishes you wanted to create, that food truck dream you kept talking about. I figured you'd have made it happen by now."

Aidan laughed softly, though there was a hint of tension in it. "Life doesn't always go the way we plan, right? Sometimes, it's easier to stick to the road already paved."

"Well, from the taste of that Philly Shepherd's Pie, it sounds like you haven't lost that creative spark." Her glance swept the room, finally resting on the kitchen. "Honestly, Aidan, you are way too talented to stay trapped here forever."

He could feel her words stirring something inside him, that familiar itch for more freedom and creativity that he often pushed down. But he shrugged it off, as he always did, focusing on her instead. "Enough about me. What about you? I've heard you're making waves with your food blog."

Lila smiled, visibly excited to share. "Yeah, it's been growing faster than I ever imagined. People seem to really connect with my focus on local spots and hidden gems. And, uh …" She paused, glancing down at her left hand where a modest diamond sparkled. "I'm engaged now, actually."

Aidan leaned forward, a grin spreading across his face. "No way! Congratulations, Lila. That's amazing."

"Thank you," she said, her cheeks flushing with genuine happiness. "His name's Russ. We met a couple of years back, not too long after ... you know, we ended things. He's a nurse, working his night shift tonight, but he's the kindest guy I've ever met."

Aidan grinned. "That's great. I'm thrilled for you. You deserve it."

There was a moment of peaceful silence filled with the distant clinks of glasses and soft laughter from the dining room. Aidan thought about how life had taken them both down different paths, paths that seemed to suit them but not fulfill every dream they'd once had.

Lila's expression turned tender. "So ... how about you, Aidan? Anyone special in your life these days?"

He scratched the back of his neck, chuckling, not willing to bring up his brief fling with Harper. "Nothing like that. The restaurant keeps me pretty busy. I don't really have a lot of time for dating."

She gave him a knowing look, her voice gentle. "I remember that struggle. I know you, Aidan, and I know you're capable of a lot of love if you allow yourself to give it."

He didn't respond immediately, images of a week on the ocean flickering through his mind, memories of laughter and late-night conversations, of warm breezes and a smile that had haunted his thoughts long after he'd returned home. But he shrugged, keeping things light. "Yeah, well ... I don't think romance fits too well with colcannon potatoes and Guinness."

"You don't have to bury yourself in this place forever," Lila said, her voice warm but insistent. "Be open to happiness, Aidan. You're allowed that."

For a moment, it felt as though Harper was sitting across from him, her words woven into Lila's. *Take a chance,* Harper had told him back on the ship, her eyes sparkling with certainty. *Life's too short to play it safe.*

There was something gentle yet insistent in her words, and he felt a pang of gratitude that she cared enough to say it. They'd both moved on from each other, found separate lives and futures, yet here she was, still encouraging him.

"Well, maybe one of these days," he replied with a smile. "But I'm glad things are going well for you, Lila. Really."

She gave his arm a friendly squeeze. "You know where to find me if you ever need a little reminder to live life for yourself now and then. And seriously, that Philly Pie is brilliant, Aidan. If Seamus won't let you keep it on the menu here ... maybe there's a different kitchen out there for you."

Her words lingered in his mind as they shared a hug, her warmth and kindness leaving him with a sense of nostalgia mixed with a strange hope. Sometimes, hearing from an old friend could remind you of parts of yourself you'd forgotten.

"Take care, Aidan," she said with a smile. "Shake things up occasionally. You never know what the tide will wash up on shore."

As Lila disappeared into the night, Aidan stood there, her voice mingling with another that drifted up from his memory, a voice softer and seasoned with the sea: Maude, on the deck of the ship, her words layered with gentle mystery. *The tide always knows where it's going, even if we don't,* she'd said with that knowing smile.

Back then, he'd laughed off the words as one of Maude's poetic musings, something meant to charm the passengers and fill them with romantic notions. But now, standing in the quiet aftermath of a Friday night rush, he considered it differently.

Maybe there was something in the tide he couldn't control, something he was being drawn toward.

He sighed and shook his head, feeling a strange blend of restlessness and curiosity beginning to bubble up in him, nudged along by Maude's words and Lila's honest encouragement.

Eighteen

The house felt both familiar and too small, a comforting but confining embrace that left Aidan in a strange state of both contentment and restlessness. The living room was a portrait of their family: Declan glued to his phone, Aisling absorbed in her book, Seamus asleep in the den with the television on low, and Maureen puttering around in the kitchen, humming softly as she scrubbed the last of the dishes from their Sunday meal.

Aidan sat on the couch, remote in hand, scrolling absently through channels he had no interest in watching. Despite the quiet peace of the room, his mind buzzed with questions he couldn't silence. In a way, the calm made them louder, each thought brushing against the surface like the sea washing against rocks, relentless and unceasing.

As he flicked through channels, Declan was slouched in the armchair beside him, eyes fixed on his phone. Aisling, curled up on the other end of the couch, turned a page in her book, oblivious to her brothers.

Aidan cleared his throat, breaking the silence. "Hey, Dec," he started, trying to ease the tension building in his chest. "How's that custom table coming along? The one you're making for the Connors?"

Declan's face lit up, a rare break in his otherwise reserved demeanor. "Oh, that one's been fun, actually. Just finished the frame last week and started sanding down the top. They wanted it rustic, so I'm using this reclaimed wood I found. Gives it character," he added, leaning forward with a hint of enthusiasm. "Honestly, it's refreshing to have a project that's fully mine, you know? No one to answer to but me."

Aidan nodded, feeling a pang of envy. "That's good, Dec. Sounds like a solid project. You've always had an eye for that kind of work." He tried to keep his tone light, but a part of him couldn't ignore the contrast between Declan's freedom in his side project and his own sense of confinement within the pub's rigid expectations.

Aisling looked up, her eyes warm as she glanced between her brothers. "It's great to see you doing what you love, Declan. We all knew woodworking would be your thing."

Declan shrugged modestly. "Yeah, but ... you know. It's still a side gig. Doesn't hold a candle to the pub, not in Da's eyes anyway. And I know he expects me to step up, especially if Aidan were to ... well, go off and do something else."

Aidan shifted uncomfortably, glancing away as Declan's words hung. That was the unbreakable pattern, wasn't it? His role in the family, his obligation. Murphy's Pub was the thread that held them all together, and yet, as the years passed, it had started to feel more like a thread binding him, pulling him in a direction he wasn't sure he wanted.

Aisling fixed her attention on him, her look both perceptive and compassionate. "So ... what about you, Aidan?" she asked softly. "How have things been since you got back from the cruise? You've seemed ... quieter, somehow."

Aidan looked over, taken aback by the sharpness of her perception. He hesitated, feeling the tangle of his emotions knotting tighter. There were words he wanted to say, things he'd been bottling up, but he didn't know where to start.

"I don't know, Ais. It's ... it's just the same as it always is, I guess," he said, his voice low. "It's like every day at the pub, I'm just going through the motions. Murphy's has been the family business since Da opened the doors, but it feels like ..." He paused, searching for the right words. "It feels like it's all I am. Like I'm not allowed to be anything else."

Declan watched him with a sympathetic edge. "You're not wrong, Aidan. I mean, I feel it too. There's a lot of weight in carrying on what Dad built. But it's different for you ... You've been the face of the place for years now. I can't imagine how heavy that must get."

Aisling leaned closer, her hand resting on his arm. "Aidan, just because you're family doesn't mean you have to love every part of the family business. There's room for you to want more. You remember when I left for law school? Dad was convinced I was abandoning the family because I wanted something different. It took time, but he accepted it. He cares, even if he doesn't always know how to show it."

Aidan's lips curled into a brief smile, the weight of old tensions now feeling lighter. "Took him long enough, didn't it? I think he stayed mad at you for a full year." He cast her a sideways glance, the ghost of amusement in his eyes. "Guess he finally forgave you, huh?"

Aisling laughed. "Eventually. But only because he saw that I was happy, that I was doing what felt right for me." Her voice gentled as she studied him. "What about you, though? What would feel right for you, Aidan?"

He didn't have an answer. He couldn't bring himself to tell her about the freedom he'd felt with Harper, the spark of something he hadn't known he'd been missing. His sister's question lingered as he let himself think about the answer he'd been dodging. But even as he considered it, he felt the weight of responsibility settling on his shoulders once again, heavy and binding.

They sat in silence, and Aidan pulled out his phone, needing a distraction. He scrolled through his social media, his eyes landing on a photo that pulled him back to that week on the cruise. Brody had posted a picture of him and Paige, standing atop a misty mountain in Tennessee, the two of them grinning with a wild, unrestrained happiness that made Aidan's chest tighten. Brody looked free in a way Aidan hadn't seen before, as though he'd finally found something that grounded him and lifted him up at the same time.

As he stared at the photo, Aidan felt an inexplicable pull. His mind drifted back to the cruise, to those fleeting moments with Harper, their laughter echoing over the deck, the quiet mornings filled with easy conversation and companionship. He could still feel the warmth of her presence, even now, like a gentle hum in the background of his mind.

Without fully realizing it, he tapped over to his contacts and hovered over Harper's name. They hadn't spoken since the cruise, and he wondered if it would be strange to reach out. Would she even want to hear from him? The logical part of his mind reminded him that they'd made no promises, that the magic of those six days had belonged to the cruise and nowhere else.

But there was another part of him, a quieter part that just wanted her to know she was still on his mind.

He typed a quick message:

Aidan

Hey … how's life?

For a few moments, he simply stared at the words, his thumb hovering over the send button. He let out a slow breath and pressed send, watching as the message disappeared into the digital ether. There was no expectation of a response, no need for immediate answers. It was enough to let her know he was thinking of her, even if it was just a simple text.

As he tucked his phone back in his pocket, Aisling noticed his pensive look and tilted her head. "What's got you so deep in thought?"

Aidan shook his head, offering a half-smile. "Nothing, really. Just … thinking about things." The last thing he wanted was to bring up Harper here, to spill the weight of everything he felt in front of his family.

Aisling's smile was small but sincere. "Well, whatever it is, don't let it linger. You've got too much heart, Aidan. Don't let it get tied up in regrets or 'what ifs.'"

He nodded, her words settling over him like a gentle reminder, echoing sentiments he'd heard before from both Maude and Harper. But he was here now, in this house, in this family, with responsibilities he couldn't ignore.

Maureen's voice rang out from the kitchen, brightening the quiet, "Dessert's out, if anyone wants pie!"

Aidan got up, moving through the quiet cadence of home. The murmur of his siblings following him into the kitchen, the soft clinking of plates, the warmth of a Sunday night with his family—it was all part of the life he'd built, the life he'd returned to. And yet, as he reached for a slice of pie, he couldn't quite shake the feeling that there was something more, a possibility he hadn't yet explored.

Later, as he leaned back in his chair, watching his mother clear the dishes and listening to Declan crack a joke that set everyone laughing, he felt the bittersweet pull of the tide Maude had spoken of. It was a part of him now, that gentle but insistent urge to seek, to explore. He didn't know yet where it would lead him or if he would ever find the courage to follow it, but for now, he let himself drift in the steady current of family life.

As the evening wound down and his family's laughter filled the house, Aidan thought of his text to Harper, waiting quietly in the silence between them. He knew that, like the tide, the future had a way of coming around whether he was ready or not. For now, he'd let it be, hoping that someday he'd have the clarity—and the courage—to chase that elusive freedom he'd glimpsed so briefly on the sea.

The following weeks rolled by in a flurry of orders, plating, and long hours that blurred into one another. Between running the kitchen, keeping a watchful eye on every dish that left the pass, and managing the odd staff squabble, Aidan hardly had a moment to catch his breath, let alone reminisce about the cruise. The quiet magic of those six days had faded into the steady rhythm of life at Murphy's, the memories cropping up only in flashes—like the scent of saltwater when he opened a window or the faintest notes of laughter echoing through his mind as he lay awake at night.

He did get a response from Harper—eventually. It came in the form of a single smiling emoji, simple yet somehow resonant, as if she, too, was leaning into those memories, holding on to them without needing words. The simplicity of her response somehow felt perfect, like a brief but knowing nod, an acknowledgment that what they'd shared existed somewhere outside the boundaries of everyday life, a little pocket of time that didn't quite belong to the real world. He saved the message in his mind, letting it buoy him on the harder days.

Tonight, though, was surprisingly calm. The typical weekday lull had settled over the pub, and the dining room was quiet, save for the faint murmur of patrons lingering over their pints. Most of the regulars had already drifted home, and even the kitchen was winding down, only a few orders trickling in from the bar. Aidan exhaled, pausing to lean against the stainless steel counter, letting himself relax for the first time that evening. The din of the kitchen had dropped to a low hum, pots and pans cleaned and stowed, staff half-leaning against counters or chatting quietly as they waited for closing time.

Aidan moved out from behind the line, catching sight of the bar through the pass window. Jazz was there, chatting with the handful of regulars who lingered over their drinks. The sight of her easy smile and the way she tilted her head in laughter brought a rare moment of ease. Jazz was the type who could make anyone feel welcome, no matter how tired they were or how long they'd been on their feet. She raised her eyes to catch Aidan's, and with a quick grin, she continued wiping the bar top.

"Hey, Chef," she called with a teasing lilt in her voice. "Slow night?"

"Feels like it, finally," he replied, the hint of a smile tugging at his mouth. "Think we'll be getting out early tonight, unless something changes."

Jazz smirked, amusement dancing in her eyes as she shook her head. "Don't jinx it now."

He gave a light snort, rolling his eyes as he started to turn toward the kitchen when the door opened, letting in a gust of cool night air. At first, he barely glanced at the new arrival, but something about the figure heading toward the bar made him pause.

Aidan squinted, feeling a rush of recognition as he took in the broad frame and easy stride. The man reached the bar and leaned against it, one eyebrow raised as he took in the familiar surroundings, his mouth curving into a grin. Aidan blinked, his brain catching up with what his eyes were seeing. "Well, I'll be damned!"

Standing there, looking right at home, was Brody.

"Well, if it isn't Mr. Murphy himself," Brody drawled, his voice carrying that effortless charm Aidan had come to associate with him. He looked entirely out of place and yet oddly at ease, like a touch of adventure wrapped up in a casual blazer and jeans. "You didn't think I'd just forget about you once I was back on dry land, did you?"

Aidan felt a grin breaking through his surprise. "Brody! What the hell are you doing here?" He walked up and patted his shoulder.

"Passing through and figured I'd stop by for a proper pint," Brody replied, laughing.

Nineteen

The clinking of pint glasses and the low hum of conversations filled Murphy's Pub, casting an inviting warmth around the otherwise quiet Wednesday evening. Aidan and Brody sat across from each other in the booth, each nursing a beer as the pub lights glinted off the deep mahogany table. It had been months since they last talked, just a few texts. But now, they were catching up like old friends, having a few beers and sharing cruise stories.

"So, what really brings you to town?" Aidan asked, leaning back with a grin. "Atlanta's got a million places to eat. Don't tell me you came all this way just for a Murphy's Pub special."

Brody put a hand to his chest, feigning insult. "I'm wounded, Murphy. Here I am, trying to visit an old friend, and you're already questioning my intentions." He cracked a grin. "But yes, I came for the Murphy's bangers. Nothing like 'em back home. And ..." he paused for effect, lifting his glass toward Aidan, "well, I figured I ought to come in and check on you, make sure you hadn't turned into a complete recluse."

Aidan snorted, raising his own glass to meet Brody's with a satisfying clink. "Right. Missed this place, huh?" He shook his head. "You've never even been here before."

Brody laughed, unbothered by the truth. "Missed it all the same—the Murphy ambiance. Besides," he added, casting a look around the pub, "this place feels like you. After you called out that pub on the ship, I needed to see what a true Irish pub was all about. It's like getting a slice of Aidan without the chef's coat. Plus, I am really thirsty for a proper pint."

They laughed, the ease of camaraderie settling over them. For a moment, it was as though they'd never left the cruise like they'd been swapping stories at sea just yesterday. The memory of those carefree nights, filled with endless drinks and unrestrained laughter, lingered between them.

Brody leaned back, giving Aidan a satisfied, almost proud look. "Man, it's good to be here," he said. "And I've got some stories for you." He launched into tales of his recent escapades with Paige, from a cliff-side hike in Asheville to a spontaneous road trip that had ended with the two of them, lost and laughing, somewhere deep in the Appalachians.

"Sounds like Paige has kept you busy," Aidan said, smiling. "Still holding on with her adventurous side?"

"Yeah, more than keeping up. She moved in with me a couple of months back." Brody grinned, lifting his beer to his lips.

Aidan leaned back as surprise overtook his expression. "Wait, really? That's big news! She always struck me as someone who liked her independence."

Brody nodded, his expression breaking into a radiant grin so genuine and unrestrained that it was impossible to miss. "She does, and believe me, I was bracing myself for a long wait. But I think we both realized there was no point in dragging things out if we were that sure. She's still got her own thing going on, but now I get to be part of it every day. It's ... it's pretty great."

Aidan nodded, taking in the contentment on Brody's face. "I'm happy for you, man. You two seem like a good match. Sounds like the real thing."

Brody leaned back in his chair, his eyes dancing with mischief. "Yeah, I guess you could say that. I have to admit, I never saw myself here, but somehow, she convinced me that freedom and commitment can coexist. I actually kind of want both, with her." He paused, studying Aidan over the rim of his glass. "And what about you, my friend? You and Harper still keep in touch?"

Aidan took a slow sip of his drink before responding. "Brody, you know the answer to that one."

Brody shrugged, though he didn't look surprised. "Had to ask. But really, no texts? Not even a friendly 'Hello'?"

Aidan gave a faint smile, swirling his beer in the glass as he considered how best to respond. "I sent one of those. Got a little smiling emoji back, and that was it. I mean, we're busy people ... different lives, you know? I'm sure she's living her best life back in New York, diving back into her work."

Brody watched him for a beat, seeming to weigh his next words. Finally, he said, "Well ... Paige talks to her a lot. They're close, actually. She says they chat about once a week or so."

The pang Aidan felt caught him by surprise, a dull ache surfacing with a little more force than he'd expected. "Oh yeah?" he said, his voice casual as he took another sip. "That's nice. She's got a friend in Paige, at least."

Brody hesitated before he added, "Last I heard, Harper's back with her ex-fiancé, Dan. They reconnected a few months ago. Paige says they're ... working things out."

Aidan managed a nod, though his smile felt more like a well-practiced reflex than anything genuine. "You know, good for her. I hope it's what she needs. If she's happy, I'm happy." He forced a smile, ignoring the faint twist in his chest. He longed for the ability to be truly happy for her, to have moved on with the same ease she seemed to possess. After all, they'd only spent six days together. Surely, he could let those memories go. It was just a matter of choice, right?

Brody let the silence sit between them, watching him with a knowing look that didn't require words. But when he finally spoke, he didn't push Aidan any further on Harper.

"Actually, I come bearing some news," he said, an unexpected grin breaking across his face.

Aidan leaned forward slightly, welcoming the shift in conversation. "Yeah? What's that?"

Brody's eyes sparkled with withheld amusement as he leaned in, savoring the tension before dropping his bombshell news. "I'm getting married."

Aidan's eyes widened as he broke into a genuine smile. "No way! That's huge!" He reached across the table to clap Brody on the shoulder. "Way to bury the lead, man! You're getting married?"

Brody laughed, shrugging. "Had to warm you up a bit first. But yeah, Paige and I are tying the knot. Thought I'd make it official."

Aidan raised his glass in a toast. "To Brody Lawson, the soon-to-be married man! Congratulations, man, that's incredible. Have you set a date?"

"October. We're going all out with a fall wedding up in the Georgia mountains." Brody's smile shifted, his excitement giving way to something quieter, more reflective. "Got this whole cabin lodge reserved. Gonna be a big day. And you ..." he pointed a finger at Aidan, "I'd like you to be my best man."

"Best man, huh? I'm honored. I'll try not to let you down. Hopefully, Paige won't think I'm a bad influence or anything."

Brody snorted. "Please, she's the real bad influence around here. But really, I wouldn't want anyone else standing up there with me."

They clinked glasses again, the excitement between them palpable. Aidan felt a rare lightness, a genuine happiness for his friend that momentarily eclipsed his own tangled feelings. "So, I guess that means Harper will probably be there too, huh?"

Brody nodded, catching the slight shift in Aidan's expression. "Yeah, she's one of Paige's bridesmaids. I'd say you two are bound to cross paths," he smiled back. "Hope you're ready for a little reunion."

Aidan let out a slow breath, the reality of it sinking in. He'd see her again, in a setting that was bound to be both beautiful and emotionally charged. Imagining Brody and Paige exchanging rings amidst the beauty of the Georgia mountains, with Harper by their side, made his heart race with both joy and a touch of unease.

"I think I can handle that," he said, smiling. "It'll be good to see her, even if it's just as friends." He took another drink, letting the thought settle.

Brody shook his head with a smirk. "Friends, huh? Well, I'll believe that when I see it."

They lingered in the silence, savoring their beers and the easy familiarity of the pub. It was a stark contrast to the cruise, where everything had felt fleeting, bound up in the excitement of the unknown. Surrounded by the familiar sounds of Murphy's, and still processing Brody's revelation, Aidan experienced a renewed sense of direction, feeling as if he could navigate his own future.

As the conversation shifted back to wedding details, Brody's excitement was contagious. He shared plans for a small but lively guest list, a bonfire the night before, and a laid-back reception with good food, music, and drinks that would flow until the early hours of the morning. His friend had found something worth building a life around, and Aidan couldn't think of anything better.

"Sounds like a perfect day," he said, meaning it. "You better keep in touch, though. I'll need all the details. And you know you're both welcome here anytime."

"Same to you, Murphy," Brody replied. "Just make sure you don't disappear into the kitchen before the wedding. Paige would kill me if I let the best man go AWOL."

Aidan laughed. "Trust me, I'll be there. Wouldn't miss it for the world."

They lingered a while longer, swapping more stories and catching up, the conversation flowing with the same ease as it had on the ship. It was only when Brody looked down at his watch that Aidan realized just how late it had gotten. The pub was almost empty now, Jazz flashing Aidan a knowing grin from behind the bar as she wiped down the counters.

They gave each other a quick bro-hug before Brody headed for the door. With a grin, he took one last look back as he left. "You're not going to half-ass the bachelor party, are you? No pressure, though."

"Wouldn't dream of letting you down."

As Brody disappeared into the cool night, Aidan lingered by the door, his thoughts wandering back to places and moments he hadn't let himself dwell on for a while. Harper's laugh echoed faintly in his mind, and a bittersweet pang settled in his chest. The cruise was a flash of brightness in his otherwise monotonous life, a memory he'd assumed would fade to gray, but it lingered in pieces. His heart, however, remembered that liberating feeling of being unburdened, even if it was just for a short time. And as he thought of Brody, preparing to start a new chapter with Paige, he felt an ache not so much for what he'd lost but for what he still hadn't found.

Life had returned to its regular rhythm here, yet somehow, the beat felt off. The restaurant was his family's pride, but with each passing day, it felt more like a tether holding him in place. Love, passion, the freedom he'd felt on the cruise—all these things felt increasingly distant, elusive.

Eventually, he pushed himself off the wall, walking over to the bar where Jazz was polishing glasses and chatting with the last few regulars.

"Well, well, Chef. Who was that?" she asked, nodding her head in the direction Brody had left. "Looked like he was a good time."

Aidan grinned, sliding onto a barstool and leaning his forearms on the counter. "That's Brody, he's from that cruise I went on. He's getting married this fall. Looks like I'll have to take a weekend off for a wedding up in the Georgia mountains."

Jazz let out an exaggerated gasp, pressing a hand to her chest as if scandalized. "The Aidan Murphy, taking a weekend off? This is the second time you'll have taken some time off this year. Someone should really document this."

Aidan rolled his eyes, laughing. "Yeah, yeah. Don't let it get around. It's a rare occasion."

"So," Jazz leaned her elbows on the bar, giving him a knowing look, "he's getting hitched, huh? What about you? Any love stories waiting to be told?"

Aidan laughed, but the question caught him off guard. "I'm ... not exactly living that life right now, Jazz. You see me in here six days a week. How can I even squeeze in dating?" He gave her a small, self-conscious smile. "I've got Murphy's and my family. The whole settling down thing isn't really in the cards right now."

Jazz tilted her head, a gentle curiosity in her eyes. "Would you even want it? You know, the whole white-picket-fence deal?"

He thought about that, letting the question settle. "I don't know. Maybe." He sighed, running a hand through his hair. "Sometimes I think about it. Then again, it's hard to imagine slowing down for something that might not be any more permanent than, well ... than anything else in life."

Jazz regarded him thoughtfully, her fingers tapping against the bar. "I get that," she said softly. "I was engaged once, years back. A whole different life, it feels like now."

Aidan blinked, taken aback. Jazz never talked about her past, and he realized how little he knew about her life beyond the pub. "Really? I had no idea."

She smiled wistfully, shrugging. "Yeah. Didn't work out. He was a good guy, but ... I don't know. I guess I'm just not built for that kind of thing. I like my freedom too much."

Aidan nodded, understanding more than he let on. "Makes sense. So ... no interest in tying yourself down again?"

Jazz shook her head, her dark eyes flashing with that familiar spark. "Nah. I'm too much of a free spirit for all that. Besides," she added with a smirk, "the bar keeps me plenty busy. And let's just say I've had my fun over the years. It's easy enough to keep things light with a fling here and a fling there, avoiding the heavy weight of commitment. No heartbreak, no drama, just ... fun." Her smile faltered for the briefest moment as she added, "After the mess with Kyle, I figured I'm not built for all that emotional baggage. Here at the bar, at least, I know what I'm dealing with. Same old faces, same old routine. No surprises."

They both laughed, but Aidan noticed the subtle edge beneath her effortless charm. As Jazz turned to tend to a few customers, her words lingered, resonating with his own thoughts. He couldn't help but wonder if she'd really let go of the past or if she'd just gotten good at hiding it behind her carefree facade.

His attention fell to his phone, with his fingers hovering over the contacts list as if waiting for a cue. He scrolled to Harper's name. Her number saved there since the end of the cruise. Nearly untouched, it stared back at him like a question he wasn't ready to answer.

Taking a deep breath, Aidan typed: Hey, heard the news about Paige and Brody. Hope to see you there.

His finger hovered over the send button, a thousand thoughts swirling in his mind. He wanted to check in with her, to reach out and reconnect, even if it was just a simple acknowledgment of their mutual friends' big news.

But as he stared at the words, his hesitation grew. Brody had told him she was back with Dan, and the thought of intruding on her life, especially if she'd already found happiness, filled him with a sense of awkwardness. He paused, his thumb hovering over the button, picturing her reading the message and maybe smiling, or even feeling a twinge of nostalgia like he did.

The message lingered on the screen, taunting him with its secrets. He could almost hear the remnants of joy and hushed secrets, smell the ghosts of lost aspirations. With a heavy heart, he erased the message. Certain memories, he thought, were too precious for words, better kept alive in the silent chambers of his soul.

Jazz wiped down a glass with lazy precision, her gaze flicking to him with quiet amusement. "Something on your mind, Murph?"

"Yeah," he said softly, his voice trailing off as he glanced back toward the door Brody had walked through. "Just thinking about how much can change ... and how much stays the same."

With quiet resolve, he made his way back to the kitchen, the comforting sound of chatter and laughter from Murphy's Pub pulling him back to reality.

Twenty

Sunlight slanted through the pub's front windows, catching the worn grain of the wooden bar, filling the empty space with the last quiet moments of the day. Aidan was running through prep for the night, mentally bracing himself for another round of steady, predictable orders. It was then he heard a familiar voice call out behind him.

"Hey, Murph! Got a sec for an old friend?"

Turning, Aidan's face broke into a grin as he spotted MJ, his old high school buddy and now the proud owner of a booming craft brewery across town. He wiped his hands on his apron and extended a hand, pulling MJ into a quick shoulder hug.

"MJ, what brings you by?" Aidan asked. Though they'd crossed paths occasionally over the years, it had been a while since they'd caught up properly.

"Just thought I'd stop in, see if you were still buried under a pile of potatoes and Guinness," he quipped, giving the pub a quick scan before nodding in approval. "Place looks good. Business still steady?"

"Steady as ever," Aidan replied, his tone betraying both pride and a hint of resignation.

"Well, I might have something that could bring 'steady' to a whole new level." MJ's tone shifted slightly, his voice carrying a weight that caught Aidan's attention.

"Yeah? What's on your mind?" Aidan asked, leaning against the bar, intrigued.

MJ took a breath, his eyes lighting up with excitement as he leaned in. "Alright, here's the deal: The brewery's expanding. We're booming, so I'm thinking of opening another place with a more pub-like feel. A place that combines the craft beer vibe with something more traditional. And when I thought about where it could work ... well, Murphy's was the first place that came to mind."

Aidan's eyes widened. "Wait, are you saying ...?"

MJ grinned, nodding. "Yeah. I want to partner up. I'm talking about a full integration. Murphy's and the brewery, a combined Irish pub and craft beer spot. We keep the old-world charm, but we add a brewery twist. Think about it, Murph. It's something different, something fresh that could bring in a whole new crowd."

Aidan was momentarily stunned. His mind kicked into gear, picturing the pub bustling with a younger, livelier crowd, the tap wall lined with Murphy's regular brews alongside MJ's rich stouts, IPAs, and seasonal specials. It was a big risk, something he'd never even thought about, but maybe it's exactly what they needed.

"MJ, that's ... that's brilliant," Aidan said, feeling a spark he hadn't felt in months. "I mean, we could pair up Irish classics with the brewery's beers, do tasting nights, even create a crossover menu. It could be the breath of fresh air we've needed around here."

MJ nodded, his eyes bright with enthusiasm. "Exactly. You keep the Murphy's heart and soul but add a little edge. We'd work together on marketing, and I can bring my team in to handle any changes we need to make. I think people would go wild for it."

Aidan felt his pulse quicken, the possibilities unfolding before him. He thought of the recent weeks, the monotony he'd felt creeping in again, the familiar weight of tradition pressing down on him. Here was an opportunity to evolve Murphy's without erasing its history. It would finally allow him to add his own mark while still honoring everything his parents had built.

"This could be the thing, MJ," Aidan said, almost breathless. "It's exactly what Murphy's needs to step into something new without losing what's made it home for so many people."

"Exactly!" MJ agreed, clapping him on the shoulder. "So, you think your dad might be open to it?"

The question hung in the air like a challenge, instantly dampening Aidan's excitement. He could already imagine Seamus's reaction, his father's face setting into that familiar, immovable expression. But Aidan pushed the thought aside, steeling himself, hoping Seamus would see the value in MJ's idea. He owed it to the pub, to his family, to at least try.

"We'll find out," Aidan said, determination creeping into his voice. "I'll talk to him tonight. Lay it all out."

MJ grinned, a glimmer of pride in his eyes. "That's the Aidan I know. Let me know what he says. And hey, even if he has questions, I'm here to talk them through, alright?"

They shook hands, MJ's optimism bolstering Aidan's own as he promised to reach out soon.

Later that evening, Aidan found Seamus in the back office, hunched over the weekly accounts. His father's hair, now more salt than pepper, caught the dim light as he leaned over the numbers with the same tenacity he'd had for decades. Aidan took a steadying breath and stepped inside, closing the door gently behind him.

"Da, got a minute?" he asked, forcing a calm he didn't quite feel.

Seamus set down his glass, studying Aidan for a moment before speaking. "What's on your mind, son?"

"It's about Murphy's," Aidan began, carefully choosing his words. "I had an idea. Well, actually, it's MJ's idea, but I think it's worth considering."

Seamus leaned back in his chair, folding his arms as he nodded for Aidan to continue.

Aidan took a breath and launched into the proposal, explaining MJ's vision for a combined brewery and Irish pub, the way it could attract a new clientele while maintaining Murphy's roots. He spoke about the potential for growth, the modern edge it would add, and how it could bring life back into their family business.

But as he talked, he saw Seamus's face shift, his expression hardening with every word.

"Stop right there," Seamus interrupted, his tone sharp. "You're telling me you want to turn my pub into some ... some beer hall for hipsters?"

Aidan's heart sank, but he held his ground. "Da, it's not about that. It's about evolving, bringing in new life without destroying what's already here. MJ's brewery is huge with people around here ..."

"I don't give a damn if it's 'huge,'" Seamus snapped, standing up from his chair. "People come to Murphy's because they know what to expect. They want the traditional, no-nonsense pub experience, not some fancy crossover nonsense."

"But, Da," Aidan argued, trying to keep his voice steady, "we could do both. We keep the classics, add a few craft beers, maybe tweak the menu a bit to include some fresh flavors. It doesn't have to be one or the other."

Seamus shook his head, his face set like stone. "You think adding a few shiny new drinks and dishes is going to keep this place alive? Murphy's doesn't need gimmicks, Aidan. It's lasted because we stay true to who we are, not because we follow every trend that blows through town."

"This isn't just a trend, Da," Aidan insisted, feeling his frustration mounting. "People want a mix of tradition and innovation. We could give them that—keep our legacy alive, but make it something people are excited about again."

Seamus's jaw clenched, his eyes flashing with bitter anger. "You don't get it, do you? This place isn't a blank slate for your whims. It's my life's work, your grandfather's work. You think you know better because you've got ideas? Well, let me tell you, those ideas won't keep the doors open when people stop coming."

Aidan felt something snap inside him, a surge of resentment he'd kept locked down for too long. "You act like I don't care about this place, but I do, Da. Every day, I'm here, working my ass off to keep Murphy's going. But if you're so afraid of change that you'd rather let this place die than try something new, then maybe you're the one who doesn't understand."

The words hung in the air, heavy and unyielding. For a moment, Aidan thought he saw a flicker of hurt in his father's eyes, but it vanished as quickly as it appeared.

Seamus's voice dropped to a dangerous calm. "You want to keep it going? Then, do it the right way. Not by tearing apart everything we've built just to chase some fantasy. You're welcome to stay and run this pub as it is, but if you can't respect what Murphy's stands for, then maybe it's time you think about finding a place that suits you."

The ultimatum hit Aidan like a punch. He knew Seamus could be stubborn, but he hadn't expected his father to draw such a hard line.

"So that's it?" Aidan asked, his voice tight. "You'd rather lose me than let Murphy's change?"

Seamus didn't answer right away. He looked away, his shoulders set in the stubborn stance that Aidan recognized all too well. "This is Murphy's, Aidan. Not some playground for your ideas. I won't let you risk its legacy."

For a moment, Aidan felt the room spin around him. Suddenly, the pub, the family business he'd built his life around, felt like a prison. He thought of MJ's vision, the potential it held, and he realized that as long as he stayed here under his father's rules, he'd never be able to turn it into something that felt truly his.

Aidan stormed out of the office, Seamus's words still ringing in his ears like the clash of cymbals: *This is Murphy's, Aidan. Not some playground for your ideas.* His father's ultimatum—his refusal to even entertain the idea of change—had left Aidan reeling. He pushed through the swinging kitchen doors and paced the narrow space, his chest tight, his hands flexing at his sides as he tried to shove down the frustration threatening to boil over.

The familiar sights and smells of the kitchen—once a sanctuary—offered no comfort. The rhythm of his own steps felt hollow, the clatter of pots and the faint hum of the evening rush grated against his nerves. As his eyes swept over the prep counter, something caught his attention: a stack of papers sitting haphazardly near the edge. A few invoices he'd spotted earlier were sitting on top, their edges dog-eared and smudged with fingerprints.

He stopped. The topmost invoice was stamped in bold, unforgiving red letters: **PAST DUE.**

His lips pressed into a thin line as he picked it up, his fingers tightening around the crinkled edge. It was for a beer delivery—dated three weeks ago. The next one, stamped with the same accusatory red, was from their produce supplier. Beneath that were notices for maintenance services, utility bills, and other orders, all marked overdue. Aidan's breath caught, his stomach twisting into a tight knot as he flipped through the stack.

This wasn't just a few missed payments. It was a pattern, one Seamus had clearly tried to hide. His father's stubbornness, his refusal to adapt, was now laid bare in front of Aidan, stamped in red and screaming for attention. Murphy's wasn't 'steady,' as Seamus liked to say—it was teetering on the edge.

He sank onto a nearby stool, the papers crumpling slightly in his grip as the weight of realization settled over him. The pub wasn't just struggling—it was drowning. And if Seamus wouldn't let go of his rigid grip on tradition, they'd all go down with it.

Aidan felt a mix of anger and sadness twist in his chest. He thought of the countless hours he'd poured into this place, the years he'd spent trying to carry on his family's legacy. And yet, Seamus would rather watch the walls crumble around them than accept the possibility of change. The spark of hope MJ's idea had ignited earlier returned, faint but insistent. For the first time since the argument, Aidan allowed himself to wonder: *What if MJ's proposal wasn't just a risk?* What if it was the lifeline Murphy's desperately needed?

He stared down at the papers in his hand, the red stamps glaring back like accusations, and something in him shifted. This wasn't just about wanting to modernize Murphy's or put his own mark on the business. It was about survival—about saving everything their family had built before it was too late.

The sound of Jazz's voice broke through his thoughts as she poked her head into the kitchen. "Hey, Aidan, you good? We're wrapping up out here."

He nodded absently, setting the papers back on the counter and running a hand through his hair. "Yeah, I'm good. Just ... give me a few minutes, alright?"

Jazz hesitated briefly, as if weighing whether to say more, but she let it go. "Sure thing, boss," she said softly, slipping back through the door.

Aidan leaned forward, bracing his elbows on his knees as he exhaled slowly. The path forward wasn't clear, and the thought of confronting Seamus again made his stomach churn. But as he thought of MJ's vision, of what Murphy's could become if they took a chance, the faint flicker of determination grew stronger. Maybe Seamus couldn't see it yet, but Aidan could. Murphy's had to evolve, or it wouldn't survive.

He straightened, his jaw tightening with resolve as he reached for his phone. His thumb hovered over MJ's number before he locked the screen and set it back down. Not yet. Not tonight. But soon.

For now, he cleaned up the invoices, stacked them neatly back on Seamus's desk, and turned off the light in the office. He couldn't shake the image of the red stamps from his mind as he closed the door behind him. They felt like a countdown, a ticking clock that reminded him time was running out.

Twenty-One

Aidan pulled up to MJ's brewery, the crisp autumn air filling his lungs as he sat for a beat. The brewery, with its brick facade and industrial charm, looked familiar, but for Aidan, stepping into its doors felt like crossing into another world—a world where possibilities weren't suffocated by the weight of *how things have always been done*. A world without stacks of **PAST DUE** bills shoved into desk drawers.

He clenched his jaw at the memory of last night, the thick envelopes he'd stumbled across while leaving a note in his father's office. Distributors, suppliers, even the electric company—red **PAST DUE** stamps had been slapped across more than half the pile. They hadn't talked about it, but they didn't need to. The papers spoke for themselves: Murphy's wasn't just in a rut. It was hanging on by a thread.

Shaking off the thought, Aidan stepped inside, letting the comforting blend of hops and caramel ease the tightness in his chest. Compared to Murphy's, where the air felt thick with pressure, MJ's world seemed lighter, freer, buzzing with the energy of growth and possibility.

MJ spotted him immediately and waved him over, grinning broadly from behind the counter. "Look who finally made it out of the kitchen!" he called out. "Thought maybe you'd gotten lost in a sea of corned beef and cabbage back there."

Aidan forced a laugh, but the image of those invoices lingered like a splinter he couldn't dig out. He wasn't just stepping out of the kitchen—he was stepping out of a sinking ship, hoping to find something here that could throw them a lifeline.

MJ pulled him into a firm hug. "Could've fooled me, man. It's good to see you. Though I assumed I'd need to enlist Jazz to pull you away from the kitchen."

"Not a chance," Aidan replied, settling onto a barstool. "You know I can't resist sampling the latest brew. Got anything new?"

"You think I'd call you all the way out here for a boring lager?" MJ asked. "Nah, I've got something special lined up." He grabbed a tasting glass and filled it with a rich amber brew that smelled faintly of honey and toasted malt. "This is our seasonal offering—an autumn ale with something extra special. See what you think."

Aidan took a sip, letting the flavors settle on his tongue. Its warm, spiced flavor evoked the comfort of a fireside evening. "Damn, MJ. This is good. Could see myself drinking one of these after a long shift."

MJ crossed his arms, clearly pleased. "Yeah? That's the idea. Something that goes down smooth but still packs a bit of complexity."

A comfortable silence stretched out as Aidan took a slow sip. These moments reinforced why his friendship with MJ had endured for so long. MJ's commitment impressed Aidan, watching him build this place from the ground up, continually pushing for growth, expansion, and innovation.

"You know," MJ said, leaning against the bar, "remember that chat we had about joining forces, building MJ's and Murphy's together? I've been thinking about it more lately. I really think there's some potential there."

Aidan tried to focus, setting down his glass. "Yeah? Da wasn't too thrilled when I brought that up." The chuckle that followed was brief, but his tone carried the weight of his frustration. "But ... what are you thinking?"

MJ scratched his chin, looking thoughtful. "The more I think about it, the more I see the potential. Murphy's has the reputation, the heritage. This spot has become a local favorite. We could draw in a broader range of customers, those who appreciate the ambiance of an Irish pub but also enjoy a touch of craft beer."

Aidan nodded slowly, his mind torn between the excitement of MJ's vision and the grim reality waiting for him back at Murphy's. The bills, the outdated menu, the declining foot traffic—it was all piling up. And yet, Seamus was blind to it, stubbornly clinging to a way of doing things that no longer worked.

"That's exactly what I was thinking," Aidan said, his voice carrying a note of both hope and desperation. "And with your brews on tap, we'd be offering something nobody else around here does. Plus, it could be a chance for Murphy's to shake things up. Show people we're more than just the classics."

MJ smiled, but there was a flicker of hesitation in his eyes. "It all sounds great, but how's your old man gonna take it? Last time you brought it up, he shut it down before you even got to the details."

Aidan sighed, running a hand through his hair. "That's the problem. He's got his mind set on keeping things the same, holding on to that legacy. But ..." He hesitated, then decided to come clean. "I don't know if he realizes how bad things have gotten. Yesterday, I found a stack of overdue bills in the office. Utilities, suppliers—hell, even the beer distributor. It's not just about keeping things steady anymore, MJ. If we don't do something soon, we might not have a pub to argue about."

MJ's expression shifted to one of concern. "Shit, man. I didn't realize it was that serious. What's your dad say about it?"

"He hasn't said anything." Aidan let out a dry laugh. "That's the problem. He won't even admit there's an issue. To him, Murphy's is untouchable. It's worked for decades, so why change it now? But those bills say otherwise."

MJ leaned forward, his tone steady but firm. "Then maybe it's time you stop waiting for his permission, Murph. You've got a vision, you've got ideas—hell, you've got me. If your dad can't see the writing on the wall, maybe it's up to you to show him. Start small, like we talked about. Introduce some new brews, test the waters. But you can't sit back and let that place sink just because he's too proud to adapt."

Aidan stared into his glass, MJ's words striking a chord. He knew MJ was right. Waiting for Seamus to come around wasn't an option anymore. The pub was his father's legacy, but it was Aidan's life. And if he wanted to save it, he couldn't afford to play by Seamus's rules any longer.

"I hear you," Aidan said finally, his voice quieter but resolute. "Something has to change. I just don't know what that looks like yet."

MJ rested a hand on his shoulder. "Whatever it looks like, you're not doing it alone. Just say the word, and I'm here to help."

As if on cue, Aidan's phone buzzed, breaking him out of his thoughts. His eyes flicked to the screen, a text from Brody:

Brody

> Get a move on, man! Wedding weekend waits for no one.

"That your buddy reminding you to get on the road?"

Aidan laughed and put his phone away. "It seems he's worried I'll show up late for my best man duties."

MJ leaned back slightly, folding his arms with a chuckle. "You? Best man? Now that's a sight I'd pay to see."

"I'm getting some practice now, you know, in case you ever choose to settle down." Aidan laughed. "How is Sue anyway?"

"Sue and I split months ago," MJ clarified. "I'm with Amy now."

"Just like MJ, always on the lookout for a new girl."

With a quick brotherly hug, MJ passed a to-go growler to his friend. "Here's something for you and the wedding crew to enjoy this weekend. Tell 'em it's on the house."

Aidan smiled, grateful. "You're the best, MJ. I'll keep you updated on things with Murphy's, I promise."

MJ waved him off, grinning. "You'd better. Have a safe drive, buddy, and have a great weekend! Life's short, remember?"

With a last nod, Aidan turned and walked back out into the cool afternoon air, the excitement of seeing Brody and Paige mingling with the conversations he'd had with MJ. As the road stretched out, he felt a growing sense of anticipation, unsure if he was approaching a fresh start or merely more questions.

The highway stretched endlessly in front of him, a ribbon of asphalt winding through a blur of yellow and crimson as the trees flashed past in autumn splendor. But Aidan's mind wasn't on the scenery. It was back in Murphy's office, staring at those overdue bills, feeling the crushing weight of responsibility settle over him.

He gripped the wheel tighter, his knuckles turning white. MJ's words echoed in his mind: *Stop waiting for his permission.*

Could he really take the reins without his father's blessing? Could he risk pushing forward, knowing it would mean going head-to-head with Seamus?

His eyes flicked to the growler of autumn ale sitting on the passenger seat. It was a reminder of what Murphy's could be—what *he* could make it. If he wanted to preserve the pub's legacy, he had to evolve it, to give it a future instead of letting it crumble.

The miles passed in a blur, but Aidan's thoughts stayed sharp. He wasn't sure how it would all play out, but one thing was clear—when he got back from this wedding, avoiding the truth wouldn't be an option anymore. It was time to act.

Harper, he thought, her name like a quiet pulse beneath everything else. He wondered what she was up to, if she was still back with her ex-fiancé, or if she had found a different path altogether. She was probably knee-deep in her New York life, balancing clients and deadlines, navigating a world as far from his as one could imagine. There was an ache somewhere deep in his chest at the thought of her, a longing mixed with resignation. She belonged to that big city, to a life full of high-rise buildings and fast-paced ambition. He belonged ... well ... he belonged somewhere, but the edges of that place felt blurry and hard to define.

Maybe seeing her at the wedding would bring some clarity. Or maybe it would only remind him of how different their worlds really were.

He sighed, shaking his head as he focused back on the road. The sun was sinking, its glow turning the fields rich with color, a reminder that change was inevitable. The drive gave him space to think, and the further he went, the clearer one thing became—he was done waiting, done making excuses for a life that didn't fulfill him. The weekend was a break, a celebration, but it was also a turning point. The only question was, what exactly was he willing to do next?

His phone sat in the cup holder, MJ's number just a tap away. Aidan toyed with the idea of compromise—scaling down the vision, reshaping it into something his father might accept. He pictured the conversation: testing the waters with MJ's beers, weaving in hints of craft influence. But would that be enough? Or would it feel like pressing his dreams into a smaller frame, one that didn't quite fit what he'd once imagined?

His phone buzzed, pulling him out of his thoughts. Another text from Brody:

Brody

Dude, where are you?

Aidan smirked, rolling his eyes as he activated his phone's voice assistant. "Text Brody: 'Just enjoying the open road. Be there soon. Don't start the party without me.'"

The assistant responded, "Did you say, 'enjoying the open toad be der soon don't start the patty without me'?"

Aidan shook his head, laughing. "Nailed it," he said sarcastically, but he hit send anyway. Brody would figure it out—or just assume Aidan had finally lost it.

It was strange how Brody had become such a steady presence in his life since the cruise. They hadn't known each other long, but in some ways, Brody understood him better than people he'd known for years. Brody's easygoing, adventurous approach to life was the perfect counterpoint to Aidan's sense of responsibility and routine. There was something freeing about Brody's confidence in his choices, his refusal to settle for anything less than a life filled with excitement and joy. And as he thought about his friend, Aidan realized he was almost ... envious. Envious of Brody's ability to dive in headfirst, to embrace love and happiness without letting fears or doubts hold him back.

He eased into the seat, gripping the wheel as the scenery blurred past. There was something freeing about the road, something that made change feel within reach. But the drive wasn't endless, and the escape wasn't real. When the weekend ended, he'd be back in Charlotte, back at Murphy's, back to a life that no longer felt like his. And this time, he wasn't sure he could pretend otherwise.

Aidan grew increasingly restless as the miles went by, and whether it was Harper or the pub, the answer was clear: waiting for change wasn't an option. It was his time to take the wheel.

Twenty-Two

The grand ballroom of the mountain lodge was alive with laughter, clinking glasses, and the warm hum of conversation. Brody's and Paige's families filled the space, each group mingling, making introductions, and sharing old stories as if they'd known each other forever. Brody and Paige invited a small collection of faces from the cruise, adding a spark of familiarity to the crowd. On one side of the room, Paige was gracefully working her way through relatives, laughing and greeting with an ease Aidan could only admire. Harper was most assuredly somewhere nearby, her presence lingering in his mind like a faint, familiar melody.

As Aidan and Brody waited by the bar, sharing a pre-dinner drink, Brody raised his glass. "Well, here's to what promises to be the most chaotic, wonderful weekend of my life," he said with a grin.

"Cheers, man," Aidan said, tapping his glass against Brody's. They each took a long sip of their Old Fashioned, savoring the warmth of whiskey and bitters.

Brody exhaled, taking in the view of the buzzing ballroom before looking back at Aidan. "You know, Harper's here ... alone," he mentioned with a sideways glance.

Aidan felt the words hit like a live wire, sending an unexpected thrill through him. He nodded, attempting to play it cool, though his heart raced at the news.

"Really?" Aidan replied, forcing an easy tone. "I thought she'd be here with, you know ... someone." The words felt heavier than he wanted them to, his pulse picking up despite himself.

"Guess not. Seems she and Dan had a falling out not long ago," Brody added with a shrug. He offered Aidan a grin before downing the last of his drink. "And on that note, ready to dive into the lion's den?"

Aidan swirled the ice in his glass, the soft clink filling the silence between Brody's words. *Harper, here alone.* It stirred something restless inside him, a tension he wasn't ready to fully unpack. But perhaps it was a good thing to focus on Harper—or on Brody and Paige for that matter. The weekend felt like a much-needed distraction, a reprieve from the mounting stress back home. The past-due bills, Seamus's stubbornness, and the uncertainty of Murphy's future had been eating at him for days. For now, though, he'd leave it all behind, just for a little while.

As Aidan and Brody made their way toward the ballroom, Aidan's heart thudded with anticipation, nerves fluttering to life with each step. It had been months since he last saw Harper, months since she'd slipped into that cab at the cruise terminal, their final glance over shoulders feeling unfinished, like a door left ajar.

Now, however, with the night swirling around him, the prospect of seeing her again after all this time had an edge to it. There were so many things he'd left unsaid, things he hadn't even let himself fully process, and now, here she was, somewhere in the crowd, just a few walls away. He inhaled, steady but shallow, already feeling a quiet spark inside. As much as he tried to keep the past neatly packed away, he had a feeling Harper's presence was about to unearth all of it.

A firm slap on the back jolted Aidan from his thoughts. Brody grinned, clearly enjoying himself. "All right, man, ready to dive in?"

"As ready as I'll ever be," Aidan responded, though he could feel his pulse quicken, a hum of nerves spreading through his veins. As they entered the ballroom, a crowd of well-wishers immediately gathered around. He smiled and shook hands, nodding and laughing through a flurry of introductions, but his eyes kept drifting to the crowd, searching.

During his conversation with Paige's aunt about the wedding, he noticed a familiar figure by the entrance, a surprise that shifted his focus from the crowd.

A sea-green wrap dress flowed gracefully around Maude.

Aidan blinked, startled. "Maude?"

She turned at the sound of his voice, a warm smile spreading across her face as if she'd known he'd be there all along. "Aidan Murphy," she greeted, her voice carrying that familiar, calming lilt. "I had a feeling I'd see you here."

"Are you officiating the wedding or something?" he asked, still trying to process her presence. He could almost imagine Paige pulling a stunt like that, inviting the cruise's unofficial sage as a guest of honor.

Maude's eyes twinkled as she smiled. "Not this time, though I'd have happily accepted. No, I came as a guest. Paige invited me, and I do my best to be there for my cruise kids' special days."

"Your cruise kids?" Aidan repeated with a grin.

"That's right. Every one of you," she offered a playful wink, though her face quickly grew serene. Casting her gaze beyond his shoulder, she nodded knowingly. "It's funny how the tide brings people back together, even when they're not looking for it."

Aidan's fingers curled slightly at his sides, his intrigue tempered by wariness. Maude always had a way of reading people with unsettling clarity, and he wasn't sure he wanted to be laid bare right now. All she did was give him a gentle nudge, her eyes guiding him silently to the other side. Curiosity got the better of him, and he couldn't help but look. There, standing near a group of bridesmaids, was Harper.

In that moment, everything seemed to quiet, the lively hum of the party dimming in his mind. Harper looked every bit as radiant as he remembered, even more so in the softly lit ballroom. She wore a simple but elegant dress, her hair loosely framing her face, and though they hadn't spoken other than a select few text message exchanges since the cruise, the sight of her sent a rush of warmth through him like he'd just seen a glimmer of sunlight through clouds.

He barely registered the small squeeze Maude gave his shoulder before she disappeared back into the crowd, leaving him alone, watching Harper across the room. His heart thudded a little faster with a mix of anticipation and nerves. This wasn't some faraway memory or an abstract sense of what could have been; she was right here, just a few steps away, real and present.

Brody nudged him, grinning. "Well, there she is, man. What are you waiting for?"

Aidan swallowed, nerves twisting and mingling with a strange thrill. "Guess I'd better say hi."

He moved through the crowd, his steps deliberate, feeling like each one brought him closer to something he hadn't fully allowed himself to hope for. He closed the distance until she glanced his way, meeting his look with a bright, welcoming smile.

"Aidan," she greeted softly, her voice carrying a mixture of warmth and surprise. Her eyes held that same spark he remembered from the cruise, a spark that had lingered in his mind long after they'd said goodbye.

"Harper," he replied, his voice a little rougher than he intended. It felt surreal seeing her here after all this time, with all those months of distance and silence stretching between them. He wrestled with the desire to hold her hand, to find a sense of stability in this fleeting moment.

"You look ... amazing," he added, his words coming out softer than he'd planned.

Her cheeks flushed slightly, a faint laugh escaping her as she brushed a stray hair from her face. "Thanks. You're not looking too bad yourself."

They shared a brief laugh, the tension between them easing just a little. But beneath the surface, an unspoken current flowed, a shared awareness of something significant remaining between them, something neither could quite forget.

After a pause, Aidan gestured toward a quieter corner of the room. "Want to catch up for a bit?"

She nodded, and they moved away from the bustling crowd, finding a small alcove by the edge of the ballroom. In the quiet space, the low light softened around them, creating the hush of a private, enclosed world. Here, with the noise of the party muted, they could speak freely, just the two of them.

"It's good to see you," she began, her voice soft but sincere. "It's been a while."

Aidan nodded, swallowing as he considered his next words. "Yeah … it has. And I've been wondering …" He paused, searching her eyes. "I guess I just wondered how you've been, after … you know."

Harper seemed to understand exactly what he meant. She inhaled slowly, her attention dropping briefly before she looked up to meet his gaze once more. "Well," she began, "it's been … a strange few months. I went back to New York, got back together with Dan." She hesitated, the faintest flicker of uncertainty crossing her face as she watched for his reaction. "But that didn't last. Turns out … I was just comfortable. Not happy."

Aidan's stomach twisted. The mention of Dan sent a ripple of unease through him, though he masked it with a small nod. "Comfortable," he repeated quietly. He understood the word all too well. How often had he clung to comfort at the expense of something real?

Harper's voice turned quiet, laced with something close to relief. "Remember that text you sent a while back, 'Hey, how's life?'" She glanced away for a moment, a self-conscious laugh escaping her lips. "I don't know … it sounds silly … but it was like … that one message shook me out of my autopilot. It made me realize I was trying to go back to something that didn't really fit. Dan and I split for good that night."

Aidan froze, the weight of her words settling over him like a sudden downpour. He felt all choked up, a jumble of surprise, guilt, and maybe even a sliver of hope he didn't want to admit to. "Harper ... I didn't mean ..." He stopped, searching for the right words. "I ... um ... I didn't realize I'd had anything to do with ... with what happened."

She shook her head quickly, stepping closer, her eyes warm and reassuring. "Aidan, no. Don't think for a second that it was your fault." Her voice was steady now, her sincerity cutting through the noise of his thoughts. "Your text did not break anything that wasn't already cracked. It just ... woke me up. Made me see things clearly for the first time in a while."

Aidan's hands rubbed over his lap, his fingers briefly knotting together before he forced them still. "I guess I just ... I don't know, Harper. I don't want to think I hurt you."

She reached out, her hand resting lightly on his forearm, a quiet anchor between them. "You didn't hurt me, Aidan. You helped me." Her voice was steady, but there was something deeper in her eyes—something sure. "And for what it's worth, I'm glad you sent it. Because it reminded me of what I was missing ... not just in my relationship, but in my life."

Aidan's pulse steadied, her words landing somewhere deep, wrapping around the quiet ache he'd carried since their last goodbye. "You were always so good at saying things that make sense," he murmured, his voice low but warm. "Even when I can't figure them out myself."

Harper's lips curved into a small, wistful smile, and she dropped her hand, though her presence lingered close. "Maybe it's because I've been trying to figure it out for myself, too. And I think ... I think we were both looking for something we hadn't quite found yet."

Aidan's throat tightened, but he managed a small, tentative smile. "Yeah," he agreed, his voice barely above a whisper. "Ever since the cruise," he admitted, "I haven't been able to shake this feeling that something's missing. Like I had a glimpse of something real, something alive, and then it was just ... gone."

Harper gave him a thoughtful look. "Is it the freedom? Or just the change of scenery?"

"Maybe both," he replied. "Or maybe it's the realization that I could feel ... I don't know ... more alive. That there's a world outside of Murphy's and Charlotte."

"The cruise had a way of making things feel different, didn't it?" She hesitated, "It wasn't just the change of scenery. It was the way everything felt lighter, freer. Like, for once, the world wasn't so ... heavy. And you were a big part of that." She locked eyes as she attempted to study his expression. "For the first time in a long time, I felt like I could breathe, like I didn't have to hold everything together so tightly. It's hard to explain, but ... being with you made everything feel possible."

"Yeah," he murmured. "But sometimes I wonder if it was real or just some dream we all had together."

She shook her head, reaching out to place a hand on his arm. "It was real. For me, at least. Maybe just a different version of real than what we're used to."

The weight of her hand on his arm brought a comforting warmth. He looked over as her, and for a heartbeat, neither of them spoke, each absorbed in the quiet connection that had somehow survived months of distance and unanswered questions.

They remained there, neither rushing to move, content in the quiet space between them. Around them, the rehearsal dinner carried on, but it all felt muted, far away. Aidan's pulse steadied, a rare calm settling over him, the kind he hadn't realized he'd been missing.

But then, movement caught his eye. Across the room, Paige stood waving, her grin wide, her enthusiasm impossible to ignore.

"Looks like we're being summoned," Aidan murmured, nodding toward Paige.

Harper laughed. "Looks like it. Meet the parents?"

Aidan grinned. "Guess we're getting the full wedding experience."

Before they moved, though, he hesitated, turning back to her. "Hey, before we go ..." His fingers tapped against his thigh as he spoke. "Can we promise to spend some more time together this weekend? Really catch up?"

Harper's smile gleaned with a hint of playful spark he remembered so well from before. "I'd like that. Let's make it happen."

With a soft smile, Harper nudged him lightly before slipping her arm through his.

"Come on," she murmured, leading them toward the others. The simple act sent a quiet warmth through Aidan, steadying something inside him. Whatever came next, at least they were walking toward it together.

They reached Paige, who clasped her hands together in delight. "Finally! Come meet the family," she beamed, guiding them through the crowd. And as Aidan followed, the evening felt a little lighter, the promise of more time with Harper filling him with a quiet thrill he hadn't felt in months.

The night flowed effortlessly, a blur of introductions, easy laughter, and Brody and Paige's wildly inaccurate retellings. Over and over, they insisted that Aidan and Harper had orchestrated their romance, spinning the story with dramatic flair. Aidan met Harper's gaze more than once, both of them barely holding back their amusement—because, in reality, it had been Brody and Paige who had done everything short of locking them in a room together to make sure they hit it off. But correcting them felt unnecessary. If they wanted to rewrite history, Aidan was happy to let them.

At dinner, the room buzzed with conversation and clinking glasses. Aidan shared jokes with Brody's groomsmen, swapping lighthearted stories and banter that kept the mood lively. Harper was seated among the bridesmaids, her laughter drifting over occasionally, lifting something in him each time it reached his ears. She seemed so at ease, so herself. In a room full of strangers, she was in her element, and it reminded Aidan of their nights on the cruise, those easy, unforced moments when she could make any group feel like old friends.

As the night wore on, the conversations and laughter died down, the energy in the room shifting as Brody tapped his glass with a spoon, summoning everyone's attention. Aidan leaned back, already bracing himself for the toast that was sure to follow. Brody stood up, his voice taking on an uncharacteristic seriousness—well, as serious as Brody could manage.

"We just want to say how grateful we are to everyone who came out to celebrate with us," he began, his arm around Paige as he looked across the room. "To our family, friends, and everyone who somehow thought it was a good idea to spend a weekend out in the middle of nowhere with us."

He paused for the round of laughs and raised glasses that followed, then continued, staring directly at Harper and Aidan.

"And a special thank you to these two matchmakers over here." He pointed his glass at Aidan and Harper, his grin stretching ear to ear. "Even if they don't admit it, we know they had a master plan, orchestrating this whole setup. Couldn't have done it without you two!" He winked, the crowd chuckling and raising their glasses toward Aidan and Harper, who exchanged an amused, slightly embarrassed smile.

Aidan felt a confusing mix of emotions as Brody's voice filled the room, a mix of admiration and perhaps even envy. Brody had embraced love with open arms, never hesitating to leap toward the life he wanted. Aidan wondered if he could ever be that brave.

Brody took a moment to look at Paige. "And of course, to my beautiful Paige ... my partner, my compass ... My life is better because you're in it, and I can't wait to keep making memories with you." He paused, clearly moved, then cleared his throat, slipping back into his more comfortable humor. "And, uh ... well, as a wise woman once said, 'When the tide wants you ... it'll ... uh, find you ... or you'll find it!'"

"Cheers!"

The room erupted in laughter, glasses raised in a cheerful salute.

Aidan couldn't help but laugh, shaking his head as he raised his glass. Brody's terrible paraphrasing of Maude's sayings had somehow become its own tradition, and though it was ridiculous, it stirred something in him. Maude's words, for all their ambiguity, had a way of slipping under his skin, echoing in his mind when he least expected it. And here he was again, thinking of them now.

As the laughter died down and everyone took a drink, Aidan felt the truth of it. The tide had unexpectedly drawn him to Brody, to new friendships, and ultimately, back to Harper. He watched her laugh with the bridesmaids, her smile bright and unguarded, her joy as contagious as it had been when they'd first met.

Maybe it was time to stop letting fear dictate his choices, to stop living half a life out of obligation. If he could embrace even half the courage he saw in Brody and Paige tonight, maybe he could finally start building the life he'd only ever dreamed of. And maybe, just maybe, that life included ... her.

The tide always knows, he thought, taking a quiet sip from his glass. And this time, he was ready to see where it would lead.

Twenty-Three

Aidan squinted into the early afternoon light, a golden mist hovering over the outdoor venue. The scene felt like something out of a fairytale, tucked away in the heart of the woods. Tall trees, their leaves ablaze in autumn hues of rust, gold, and crimson, towered overhead, their colors shimmering under the gentle sunlight. Droplets from the morning's brief shower clung to the leaves, sparkling like tiny jewels. He took a deep breath of the crisp, earthy air, trying to shake off the remnants of his hangover from last night's bachelor party. It had been tame by Brody's standards but spirited enough to leave his head a little heavy.

As the best man, Aidan was next to walk down the aisle, paired with Rachel, Paige's Maid-of-Honor, who gave him a polite nod. He glanced ahead and spotted Harper walking a few rows in front of him with one of Brody's friends, Joe. She looked radiant, her soft pink dress with floral accents fitting beautifully into the autumnal color scheme. His chest fluttered as he watched her, graceful and poised, her expression serene yet warm. The white fuzzy shawl draped around her shoulders added to her charm, making her look even more captivating in the brisk air.

He regained his composure, thinking about the event and the happiness he felt for his friends. He hadn't seen Brody look this happy, maybe ever. Aidan looked back at Brody, who was right behind him, waiting for his turn, a wide grin plastered on his face. He looked almost comically stylish in his unique ensemble: a white jacket, white shirt, and black tie paired with red pants and black shoes, a choice only Brody could make work. He was beaming, a man completely in his element, his excitement practically infectious.

They'd chosen lively music for their walk-up, something with a beat that felt more like a baseball walk-up song than traditional wedding music. The rhythm buzzed in Aidan's veins, lifting the energy of the moment. As he walked with Rachel down the aisle, he took in the smiles of the guests, the colors of the forest, the gentle rustling of leaves. It was a moment of pure, unfiltered happiness, the kind that Paige and Brody both longed for, not just for this day, but for every day in the future.

Once they reached the front, Aidan split off to the right with the other groomsmen, standing shoulder to shoulder with Joe and a few of Brody's other friends. Across the aisle, the bridesmaids lined up to the left, a pastel line of soft pink dresses and fuzzy shawls, with Harper near the front. Aidan stole a glance her way, a mix of emotions stirring. There she was, the woman who'd shared that magical week with him months ago, someone who still held an unclaimed piece of his heart, despite the distance and time. Her smile was gentle as she looked out over the scene, taking in the view as if savoring it.

In an impulsive moment, Aidan reached into his pocket and quickly pulled out his phone. He was aware she wasn't carrying her phone, but he sent a message anyway.

Aidan

Hey, how's life?

Then, he hit send with a slight smile as he pocketed the phone. It was small, just a reminder that he was thinking of her, that she was still on his mind, even on this big day for his friends.

Aidan caught sight of Brody at his side, his friend practically vibrating with excitement. With a smirk, he gave Brody an encouraging slap on the behind. "Go get her, champ," he whispered, earning a wide grin and a nod of thanks.

And then Paige appeared at the back of the aisle, arm-in-arm with Brody's dad, who had proudly volunteered to walk her down the aisle in place of her late father. She looked absolutely stunning, her playful, flirty dress a perfect reflection of her spirit, the sparkling red heels peeking out beneath. Her dress flared out just below her knees, a splash of white against the colorful backdrop of trees. The plunging neckline and flower accents, as well as her choice of tiara instead of a veil, made her look less like a traditional bride and more like a free-spirited vision of joy.

The sight of her nearly took Aidan's breath away, and he could only imagine what Brody must be feeling. He looked over and saw his friend's eyes locked on Paige, a look of pure, unfiltered love on his face. Brody seemed utterly captivated, barely blinking, as if afraid he'd miss a moment of her walk down the aisle.

The gathering hushed as Paige began her journey, a palpable sense of love and happiness. Aidan watched her approach, feeling an unexpected wave of emotion. He couldn't deny the happiness he felt for his friend. Paige and Brody had found something real, something rare, and standing here, surrounded by family and friends, he felt genuinely lucky to be witnessing it.

But as he watched the couple's joy unfold, he couldn't help but think of Harper. Seeing Brody and Paige so deeply in love stirred something in him, a quiet longing he hadn't allowed himself to fully acknowledge until now. He noticed Harper one more time, catching the gentle way she was smiling as she watched Paige's approach. It was a soft, wistful expression, and he wondered if she, too, was feeling something similar.

Despite his wandering thoughts, Aidan attempted to concentrate on the vows as the ceremony began. Brody started strong, his trademark grin firmly in place. "Paige, my love for you is endless, and I promise to share it with you in every moment, big or small, whether we're gazing at the sunset, having fun in the kitchen, or ... putting our furniture to the test."

Paige stepped up, her tone equal parts mischievous and heartfelt. "Brody, I promise to stand beside you in every adventure. Whether it's surviving one of your 'shortcut' hikes that somehow ends with us ... losing track of our clothes," she quipped, her eyes sparkling, "or keeping you from turning the kitchen into a crime scene every time you cook, I'll be there to blow your mind ... and occasionally save your butt." The crowd burst into laughter as Brody ran a hand through his hair and his cheeks turned pink. "Our future is going to be wild, passionate, and a bit chaotic because ... let's face it ... calm isn't really our thing."

Aidan laughed along with everyone else, but their words cut deeper than he expected. Though masked by humor and suggestive remarks, a raw, passionate dedication to their bond shone through. It wasn't just love they were promising. It was their life, and it was anything but boring.

As the crowd cheered for the kiss that sealed their vows, Aidan's eyes wandered to Harper. Her smile was subdued, soft, and it struck something in him. Could he find a love like this? One full of laughter, heat, and unrelenting honesty? Observing Paige and Brody, he soon met Harper's eyes from across the aisle, and the thought lingered: maybe it was nearer than he realized.

As the ceremony wrapped up and Brody kissed his new bride, the crowd erupted into applause, cheers echoing through the trees. Aidan couldn't help but join in, his hands clapping with sincere happiness for his friend. Paige beamed as she and Brody walked down the aisle together, her red heels sparkling in the sunlight that filtered through the trees. The pair looked radiant and carefree like they had stepped out of a dream and brought everyone with them.

A few hours later, as the sun dipped lower in the sky, the celebration moved inside the grand hall of the lodge. The soft melody of a string quartet drifted through the open doors of the grand hall, mingling with the scent of polished wood and fresh greenery arranged along the long banquet tables. Afternoon sunlight streamed through the tall lodge windows, casting golden streaks across the rustic beams and rich mahogany floors. Laughter and conversation echoed through the space as guests filtered inside, drawn by the promise of celebration.

As Aidan stepped into the reception hall, he took in the warm, intimate setup—the flickering glow of candle centerpieces, the floral garlands winding along the tables, the vibrant hues of autumn woven into every detail. He hadn't felt this kind of quiet joy in a long time.

Across the room, Harper laughed at something one of the bridesmaids said, her easy joy lighting up her face. Aidan lingered on the sound before forcing himself to look away. This day wasn't about them—it was about Paige and Brody. Still, he couldn't shake the feeling that tonight might hold more than just a reunion with old friends.

The DJ's voice cut through the chatter, announcing the start of the toasts. Aidan exhaled, rolling his shoulders back as the attention in the room shifted toward the stage. He felt movement beside him, and a second later, Harper slipped her arm through his, guiding him forward as they weaved through clusters of chatting guests.

"You're going to do great," she murmured, her voice calm, certain. When he turned to look at her, she met his gaze without hesitation, something steady in her expression.

The tension in his chest loosened. Somehow, she always knew exactly what to say to cut through the noise in his head.

"Thanks, Harper," he said, his voice quieter now. His hand briefly covered hers where it rested against his arm, the moment small but grounding. "That means a lot."

As they reached the lead table, Harper slipped her arm away and turned to him with a teasing glint in her eye. Before he could step away, she leaned in and delivered a quick, playful slap to his butt.

"For good luck," she quipped, her grin widening as his eyebrows shot up in mock surprise.

"Bold move," he said with a soft laugh, shaking his head. "Let's hope it works."

Harper winked before taking her seat beside Paige, who was already teasing Brody about something, her laughter lighting up the room. Aidan took a slow breath, his nerves settling as he let the joy in the room wash over him. He nodded to Harper one last time before stepping up to the podium.

The room quieted, the expectant hush settling over the crowd as he picked up the mic. The sheer number of eyes on him should have rattled him, but instead, as he scanned the crowd, he felt something shift—an unexpected steadiness taking root. His focus fell on Brody, who watched him with a grin full of encouragement.

"Now, if there's one thing to know about Brody," Aidan began, "it's that subtlety has never been his strong suit." The crowd erupted in laughter, and Aidan relaxed, letting the moment carry him. "I mean, just look at those pants! Red, like his love for Paige, I guess." He stopped for a beat, allowing the room to calm, and then looked over at Brody, who beamed and nodded along with the humor.

Aidan's thoughts drifted back to the cruise, remembering the exact moment he and Brody met Paige. The night had been a whirlwind of chance encounters, the kind that wouldn't usually lead to anything lasting, and yet, here they were. "I first met Brody on a cruise that neither of us were expecting much from. I figured, at best, it would be a week of sun and drinks. But then ... Brody met Paige." He looked over at Paige, her face radiant as she laughed softly, leaning close to Brody.

"Their fire roared hot and fast from the very start," he continued, grinning at the memory of those early, intense glances the two of them had exchanged on the ship like they were the only two people in the world. "Honestly, I didn't think it'd survive the week. But here they are. And somehow, I'm not surprised anymore."

Aidan sat with the moment, letting admiration sink in, followed by the familiar ache of longing. Brody and Paige weren't just in love; they fit. They moved through life together like they were meant to. And Aidan? He wanted that. Maybe more than he cared to admit

He cleared his throat and continued, his voice warming as he spoke from the heart. "You know, you two have a free spirit about you, a natural spark that just seems to light up every room you're in together. And let me tell you, Brody ... Paige is special." He lifted his glass, looking straight at his friend. "So, promise me you'll be good to her, alright? You've got something amazing."

Brody, looking surprisingly earnest, nodded as he mouthed, "I will."

"To Brody and Paige," Aidan said, raising his glass high. "May you always keep that fire going. Cheers!"

Despite the music, the chatter, the celebration in full swing, Aidan's focus kept returning to Harper. He sipped his drink, his smile small, almost to himself. Maybe it was the moment, or maybe it was something deeper, but for the first time in a while, he found himself wondering: *What if?*

As Aidan settled back into his seat, a wave of contentment washed over him, accompanied by a gentle warmth that spread from his chest to his fingertips. The reception was lively; the room buzzing with laughter, clinking glasses, and the occasional shout as friends and family urged each other onto the dance floor. Brody and Paige were radiant, holding court at the center of it all, surrounded by love and well-wishes, basking in the joy of their new life together.

Aidan tried to keep pace with the celebration, raising his glass in various toasts and joining in on some of the revelry. But as the night wore on, he felt the pull to step away, to clear his head. Making his way outside, he found a quiet spot on a small balcony that overlooked the serene forest, the sounds of the party muffled behind him. The air was crisp, and he breathed deeply, smelling pine and damp earth.

Leaning on the railing, Aidan found himself lost in thought. His mind drifted to Harper, who had woven her way back into his life tonight as if she'd never left it. Being near her again, even just in fleeting glances across the reception, had stirred up emotions he'd nearly buried. But it was more than that. Watching Brody and Paige pledge their love had rekindled something deeper, a restlessness that had been gnawing at him since he'd come back from the cruise. Aidan desired the same passion they shared, a passion that extended beyond romance into their shared embrace of change and the unknown.

Somewhere along the line, he'd lost that fire. The kitchen, once his sanctuary and playground, had become a source of constant tension and monotony. He was proud of his family, of their legacy, yet he couldn't shake the feeling that he'd been burying his own dreams in order to uphold theirs. The urge to change, to make something that felt genuinely his, was stirring more fiercely than ever.

"Aidan Murphy, hiding away already?" a familiar voice teased.

He raised his eyes, a grin forming on his face as he spotted Harper walking toward him. With two champagne flutes in hand, she looked at him with the same mischievous gleam he remembered.

"You caught me," he admitted, taking a glass from her. "Needed some air."

"Well, I thought I saw you sneak off," she said, leaning beside him against the railing. "I was afraid you forgot your champagne."

He raised his glass to clink it gently against hers. "Good call."

They sipped in quiet companionship, the hum of the reception a distant murmur. For a moment, they simply watched the night settle around them, the silence broken only by the occasional flicker of laughter from inside.

"Tonight's been beautiful," Harper finally said, her voice soft. "Seeing Brody and Paige ... they're so happy. It's inspiring."

"Yeah," Aidan agreed, nodding slowly. "Seeing them like this ... it makes me think about what I want, you know?"

Glancing in his direction, Harper's expression remained unwavering. "And what do you want, Aidan?"

He hesitated, feeling the weight of her question, the sincerity in her voice. "I guess ... I want to feel alive. I want to wake up excited about what I'm doing every day. The kitchen used to make me feel that way, but now ... now I feel like I'm not making progress. Keeping everyone else happy and forgetting what I actually want."

Harper listened quietly, nodding as Aidan spoke about the weight of expectations and the pull of safety. "I know what you mean," she said softly. "Doing something because it's what's expected ... because it's safe or comfortable. It's hard to pull yourself out of that."

Her expression shifted, her eyes reflecting a weariness he hadn't seen in her before. "What about you?" he asked gently. "Are you ... comfortable?"

Harper let out a breath, her shoulders dropping slightly. She hesitated, as if weighing whether to answer honestly. "I'm ... comfortable," she admitted, the word carrying a heaviness that spoke volumes. "But not in a way that makes me feel alive. Work is fine. Stable. Safe. But it's like every ounce of creativity, every spark I used to have, has been stripped away. I spend my days making small tweaks to things I don't even care about anymore."

Her voice cracked slightly, but she pressed on. "I thought I wanted this. I thought stability was what I needed. But now I just ... I just feel stuck. Like I'm playing it small because it's easier than taking the risk of doing something bold, something real. And I hate it. I'm tired of safe. I'm tired of ... comfortable." She gave a rueful laugh, shaking her head. "I don't even know if that makes sense."

He said nothing, keeping his focus on her while her words bridged the gap between them. He didn't interrupt, didn't offer solutions, or quick reassurances. He simply listened, his quiet presence urging her to keep going, to let it all out.

Harper met his eyes with a vulnerability creeping into her voice. "I'm ready to be done with comfortable, Aidan. Give me more than that. I'm not sure what's next, but I know I can't stay here. Not anymore."

Aidan stepped closer, his hand brushing her arm gently before pulling her into a warm, steady embrace. He didn't speak, didn't offer solutions, he just held her, anchoring her.

Harper let herself lean into him, resting her head against his chest. After a moment, she looked up, her eyes searching his. "Aidan," she said softly, her voice just above a whisper, "kiss me."

He didn't hesitate, his lips finding hers in a kiss that was gentle, unhurried, and filled with the kind of connection they'd both been searching for. It wasn't about being comfortable; it was about what could be.

They broke apart, breathless, resting their foreheads together as they held onto each other. For a moment, neither spoke, letting the night and the quiet envelop them.

Aidan's hand traced a gentle line along her back, his voice low. "Come back to my room with me tonight?"

Harper gave him a teasing smile, her fingers lightly running down his arm. "I'd love to, but ... shouldn't we head back in for the bouquet and garter toss first?" She tapped a finger against her chin, her smile growing. "You know, for tradition's sake?"

He laughed softly, pressing another kiss to her forehead. "Alright. But after that ... I'm not letting you out of my sight."

"Deal," she whispered, her hand finding his as they turned to make their way back inside, both of them knowing that tonight there would be no more interruptions, no more missed chances. Tonight, they were exactly where they wanted to be.

As Aidan and Harper rejoined the crowd inside, the wedding party was just gearing up for the bouquet toss. Harper tried to stay toward the back of the cluster of eager bridesmaids, giving them a small smile but stepping back, clearly not too invested. She shot Aidan a sideways glance, tilting her head slightly as if to say, *Definitely not my scene.*

But as Paige let the bouquet fly, everything slowed down, like a scene out of a rom-com. The bouquet ricocheted off one bridesmaid's hand, then another, wobbling unpredictably through the air before somehow landing squarely in Harper's hands. She froze, holding the flowers like they were a live grenade, her wide eyes matched by a faint blush as the other bridesmaids erupted in cheers and clapping.

Aidan, barely able to contain himself, caught her eye and smirked. He mouthed, "Looks like fate."

Harper rolled her eyes dramatically but couldn't keep the grin off her face. "Don't start," she shot back, her voice carrying just enough for him to hear.

"Hey, I'm just saying," he teased, raising his hands in mock innocence.

She shot him a playful glare but couldn't keep a smile from breaking through. Before she could say anything, Brody announced with a grin, "Alright, it's my turn!"

Paige's laughter echoed as Brody made an elaborate show of *preparing* for the garter toss. With a dramatic wink at the crowd, he ducked under her dress, his face disappearing entirely as he attempted to remove the garter with his teeth. The crowd burst into laughter, and Paige swatted him with a laugh before he emerged, triumphantly clutching the garter in his jaw.

"Now, gentlemen, are you ready?" Brody called, brandishing the garter like a prize.

Aidan, wary after Harper's surprise bouquet catch, moved off to the side, content to avoid the same fate. But Brody's aim was as unpredictable as ever. He aimed for a graceful arc, but the garter took a sudden, unexpected turn, missing the men completely and landing right at Aidan's feet.

The crowd burst into laughter, and Aidan shook his head, grinning as he bent to pick it up. He glanced over at Harper, who was clutching her bouquet with a knowing smile, her eyes twinkling with the same spark he'd seen during the cruise.

As the evening stretched on, the celebration showed no signs of slowing. Aidan and Harper joined the newlyweds for a last dance, the sounds of laughter and music filling the air. Maude, watching from the sidelines, caught Aidan's eye and gave him a subtle wink as if this evening had gone exactly as she'd foreseen.

Aidan leaned in, his arm still wrapped around Harper's waist, their bodies swaying to the music. "What do you say we make a getaway?"

Harper looked up at him, the mischief in her eyes softening into something deeper. "I thought you'd never ask."

They made a quick round of goodbyes, sharing tight hugs and warm smiles with Brody and Paige before slipping out of the lodge hand-in-hand. The cool mountain air kissed their skin as they hurried toward Aidan's room, their pace quickening with each step. The tension that had been building for months now felt almost unbearable, thrumming between them like a string pulled taut, ready to snap.

At the door, Aidan paused, his lips curving into a mischievous smile as he slipped the garter onto the outside doorknob. "Think they'll get the message?" he asked, his emerald-green eyes gleaming with humor and heat.

Harper didn't answer with words. Instead, she gave him a playful shove through the doorway, her smile matching his but laced with something more urgent. The door clicked shut behind them, and in the next moment, her lips were on his—fierce, determined, and unapologetic. There was no hesitation, no space for words, only the raw need that had simmered between them for far too long.

They stumbled into the room, their movements frantic and uncoordinated but entirely natural. His jacket landed somewhere near the lamp; her shawl slid from her shoulders in a whisp of silk, pooling on the floor. Harper's bouquet toppled from her hand, forgotten in the corner, a quiet casualty of their rush to close the impossible distance that had separated them for months.

Their kisses deepened, growing hotter, more insistent. Harper's hands tangled in Aidan's hair, pulling him closer as her lips devoured his, and she sighed against his mouth when his hands gripped her waist. Fingers fumbled with buttons and zippers, fabric tearing slightly in their haste, each sound adding to chaos of their reunion.

Aidan pulled back for a brief moment, his chest rising and falling with uneven breaths as he looked into her eyes. Those deep, enchanting eyes had haunted him for months, filling his dreams and quiet moments with memories of what he'd lost. Now, they burned with the same longing he felt, an unspoken hunger that only she could quench.

"Six months," he murmured, his voice low and raw, his hands trembling slightly as they framed her face.

Harper silenced him with a kiss, her fingers slipping beneath his shirt, tracing the familiar lines of his chest and stomach. "No more waiting," she whispered against his lips, her tone equal parts command and plea.

Their laughter, light and full of relief, soon dissolved into breathless murmurs and soft moans as they moved together toward the bed. Layers of clothing fell away like forgotten promises each piece discarded revealing more of the skin they'd ached to touch. Bare and vulnerable, they came together like two halves of the same whole, the heat between them building into something almost tangible.

Aidan's hands found her hips, his touch reverent but possessive as he pulled her closer. She responded by arching into him, her body soft and warm against his, her legs wrapping around his waist as he lifted her effortlessly. Her breath hitched when his hands moved down, gripping the curve of her ass, holding her steady as he carried her to the bed.

They fell together in a tangle of limbs, their movements a mix of urgency and tenderness. Harper's hands roamed over his shoulders and back, her nails scraping lightly against his skin, her lips trailing heated kisses along his jawline. Aidan groaned, the sound low and guttural, as her touch sent sparks racing through him. He leaned over her, his weight pressing her into the mattress as he kissed her deeply, pouring every ounce of his longing into the connection.

As their bodies joined, she enveloped him fully, the slick heat of her body drawing him in with a sensation so overwhelming it nearly undid him. He paused, his breath catching, his forehead resting against hers as he struggled to keep himself from losing control too soon. Every fiber of his being was consumed by her—the feel of her curves beneath his hands, the way her body fluttered and tightened around him, and the quiet, breathless sounds she made as they moved together.

They found a rhythm that was both natural and desperate, each thrust a culmination of months of waiting, of longing, of imagining this very moment. Aidan's hands explored every inch of her, memorizing the softness of her skin, the curve of her waist, the swell of her breasts. Her body responded to his every touch, arching and pressing against him in perfect harmony, her moans a melody that echoed in his ears.

"Harper," he murmured, her name leaving his lips like a prayer as he buried his face against her neck, inhaling the sweet, familiar scent of her skin. He tightened his hold on her hips, his movements growing deeper, more deliberate, as he felt her body tremble beneath him.

The tension between them coiled tighter with every movement. Harper's fingers dug into his shoulders, her body arching into his as her gasps broke against his skin. Aidan felt everything—the heat, the pull, the way she clenched around him, drawing him deeper, dragging him closer to his peak.

"Don't stop," she whispered, her voice trembling with need, her eyes locking onto his with a fiery intensity that threatened to send him over the edge.

He obeyed, his pace steady but unrelenting as he gave her everything he had, his body and soul fully consumed by her. When she cried out, her body shaking with the force of her release, Aidan followed her, his own climax hitting him like a tidal wave. He groaned her name, his hands gripping her hips as he buried himself fully within her, the world narrowing to the two of them in this moment of perfect, shared ecstasy.

As the tension ebbed, their movements slowed, their breathing heavy but calming. Aidan brushed a strand of hair from Harper's face, his hand lingering on her cheek as he looked at her. Her eyes were closed, her lips parted, her expression one of pure contentment.

He lowered himself beside her, pulling her against him as the quiet aftermath wrapped around them like a warm blanket. His hand traced gentle circles on her back, his heart still racing as he tried to process everything he felt. Six months of longing, of wondering if they'd ever find their way back, and now she was here, in his arms, where she belonged.

Neither of them spoke, the silence filled only with the soft rustle of sheets and the steady rhythm of their breathing. Aidan pressed a kiss to her temple, his lips lingering as he closed his eyes. It wasn't just the culmination of six months of waiting; it was a new beginning, a promise that no matter what came next, they would face it together.

Twenty-Four

Aidan awoke slowly, the golden morning light casting soft shadows across the room, illuminating Harper beside him. She lay nestled against him, her warm breath gentle on his skin, a comforting rhythm that pulled him from the depths of sleep. His hand rested on her bare shoulder, tracing delicate patterns on her skin as he admired her peaceful expression. The night before was totally magical, like something they both really missed.

Feeling her stir, he leaned down, pressing a tender kiss to her lips. Her eyes fluttered open, and she smiled softly, returning the kiss with a gentle warmth that radiated through him. "Good morning," he murmured, his voice barely a whisper.

"Yes, indeed," she replied, her smile widening, a playful glint in her eyes.

He watched as she slowly stretched, the sheet slipping down, revealing the soft curves of her body bathed in the morning light. Aidan felt a familiar warmth in his chest, a mixture of awe and longing. The way she moved, so effortlessly graceful, as if she belonged here, left him momentarily speechless.

Harper slipped from the bed with the kind of quiet confidence that made even the simplest movements feel deliberate. Stretching lazily, she let out a soft sigh before padding over to his suitcase, rifling through his clothes with casual familiarity. Aidan watched as she pulled out his worn green shirt—the one that had absorbed years of his life, his work, his world. She slid it on, knotting it at her waist, effortlessly recreating the memory of their last morning on the cruise, as if drawing a thread between then and now.

Harper shot him a wicked smile before crouching down, her fingers curling around her thong from the floor. Aidan watched, intrigued, as she tucked it neatly into the side pocket, smoothing her hand over the fabric as if tucking away a secret only they would ever know.

She eased onto the edge of the bed beside him, tucking her legs beneath her as the quiet stretched between them—comfortable, unhurried. For a while, they simply sat there, savoring the night they'd shared, before she reached for his hand, their fingers intertwining.

"You know," she began, her voice soft but firm, "being here, with you, seeing Paige and Brody so happy ... it reminded me that I've been settling. I keep pushing my happiness aside, hoping that somehow things will change on their own."

Aidan squeezed her hand, a gentle affirmation that he understood completely. "I know what you mean," he replied, his voice filled with a quiet intensity. "I keep telling myself that things at Murphy's will improve, that somehow I'll find room to grow, to experiment, but it's like I'm just spinning my wheels, keeping the same routine to make everyone else happy."

Harper nodded, her grip on his hand tightening just slightly. "You deserve to be happy, Aidan. You deserve to wake up every day feeling excited, inspired." She paused, her thumb brushing lightly over his knuckles. "We both do."

The conviction in her words struck a chord deep within him. His fears weighed heavy, particularly the fear of letting his father down and straying from the path preordained for him. Harper's eyes met his, and suddenly, those fears didn't seem so bad.

"So, what do we do about it?" he asked, his voice barely above a murmur, yet full of a newfound resolve.

"We make a promise," she replied, her tone both serious and hopeful. "When we go back, we don't just fall back into old patterns. We chase what we want. No more settling, no more hiding behind obligations. We owe it to ourselves."

Aidan nodded, feeling the weight of her words settle over him like a mantle. "You're right. No more running in place. I'm going to have that conversation with my dad. Murphy's has been his dream, not mine. I need to create something that's truly mine."

Her face lit up with a quiet pride. "That's the Aidan I remember from the cruise—the one who dreams big, who lets nothing hold him back."

They sat in silence for a few moments, the resolve between them feeling like a bond, an unspoken pact. Harper leaned in, pressing a soft kiss to his cheek, her hand lingering on his shoulder. "You're not getting rid of me that easily, Aidan Murphy," she teased, her voice warm with affection.

Aidan felt a surge of warmth through his chest. "Good. I wouldn't want it any other way."

A sigh slipped from Harper's lips as she cast a fleeting glance toward the door, the weight of goodbye settling between them. Rising to her feet, she moved across the room with unhurried ease, gathering her scattered belongings. Aidan watched her, unable to look away, drawn to the effortless grace in her every movement. Aidan's smirk deepened, his gaze shameless as she bent to retrieve her dress, flashing him a fleeting view of bare skin—a final tease before she tossed her dress over her shoulder, the look in her eyes making it clear: she knew exactly what she was doing.

With a playful twinkle in her eyes, she made a move for the exit. As she flung open the door, she snatched the garter from the doorknob, flinging it back at him with a playful wink.

"Don't lose that, Murphy. You're going to need it next time," she teased, a smirk dancing on her lips as she slipped out into the hallway, leaving him grinning in her wake.

An unyielding smile spread across Aidan's face as he watched her leave. The garter felt like a promise in his hand, a tangible reminder that this wasn't the end. It was only the beginning.

The sound of Harper's footsteps retreating down the hallway left Aidan alone with a deep breath, allowing the weight of the morning to settle over him. He'd felt more alive in the last forty-eight hours than he had in months, maybe years, and it wasn't just the excitement of reconnecting with Harper. They had promised each other to be fearless, to stop accepting mediocrity. He carried that resolve as he packed his bag and hit the road, knowing the hardest part of his journey still lay ahead—confronting his father.

A soft buzz from his phone pulled him from his thoughts. He glanced at the screen to see Harper's reply to his message from the ceremony, the simple question he'd sent on impulse, *How's life?*

Her response was just a single, smiling emoji, the reply that needed no words. The tiny, luminous symbol held the unspoken weight of their promise, making Aidan smile with a deep, private understanding. She was ready. And he would be, too.

He tossed his bag over his shoulder, pocketing his phone as he left the hotel room, the buzz of renewed determination following him through every step. The drive back to Charlotte was a blur of autumn leaves and winding roads, Harper's words echoing in his mind as he pictured Murphy's Pub. The pub was his family's pride and joy, his father's life's work, and for years, it had been the center of Aidan's world. But now, for the first time, he felt ready to confront what that world had cost him.

By the time he pulled into Murphy's parking lot, the sun had risen higher, casting a bright, crisp light over the building's familiar brick exterior. He sat in his truck, hands resting on the steering wheel, gathering his thoughts. This conversation with his father would be anything but easy, but Aidan knew it was necessary. His mind drifted to the pile of bills he'd seen in the office last week, stamped with angry red letters that read **PAST DUE**. The memory twisted in his gut like a knife. The pub wasn't just stagnant—it was in trouble. And Seamus's refusal to adapt was dragging it further under.

He couldn't sit on this any longer. This wasn't just about Aidan's dreams anymore—it was about survival.

Glancing back at his phone, he saw Harper's smiling emoji and drew strength from it as he stepped out of the truck and headed toward Murphy's Pub. He wasn't the same Aidan anymore, the one who'd spent years in that kitchen, preparing food he'd grown indifferent to. He was ready to fight for everything he'd promised—for himself, for Harper, and for the future of Murphy's.

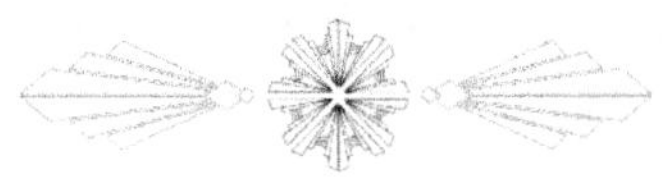

Aidan leaned against the worn wooden bar at Murphy's Pub, the familiar scent of hops and aged wood filling his lungs. The morning sun streamed through the front windows, casting long shadows across the polished floor. Returning felt strange, yet everything remained unchanged: familiar photos, the hum of the cooler, and memories of laughter. Yet today, a storm brewed within him, one that threatened to break free as he prepared for the confrontation he had been dreading.

Seamus, surrounded by awards and family photos, was in his office, a space reflecting his dedication to building Murphy's. Aidan could hear the rustle of paper and the muffled sound of his father's footsteps as he shuffled about, likely reviewing the day's inventory or preparing for the usual lunch rush. But Aidan felt the tension crackling in the air, thick and heavy, as if the walls themselves were bracing for the explosion that was about to occur.

He had returned home from the wedding the night before, the echoes of Brody and Paige's vows still fresh in his mind. The celebration had been a whirlwind of joy and laughter, a vivid contrast to the turmoil simmering within him. His time with Harper brought back the spark he believed had vanished under the weight of family customs. Yet now, as he stood in Murphy's, that moment felt distant, overshadowed by the weight of his father's expectations and the shackles of obligation.

Aidan pushed through the door to the office, the old hinges creaked in protest. Seamus looked up from his desk, a mixture of surprise and annoyance crossing his features.

"Aidan," he said, his tone clipped. "I didn't expect to see you here so early."

"Thought I'd drop in," Aidan replied, forcing a casualness into his voice. "We need to talk."

"About what? More changes to the menu? Because if it's anything like your last ideas, I'm not interested."

Aidan felt his blood boil at the dismissal. His father was inflexible, refusing to consider anything that deviated from the established ways of Murphy's. He clenched his fists, the image of the overdue bills flashing in his mind like a warning light. "It's not just about the menu, Da. It's about the future of this place."

Seamus straightened in his chair, the muscles in his jaw tightening. "What future? We've been doing just fine without any of your 'big ideas' disrupting the way we run things. Tradition matters, Aidan."

"Tradition?" Aidan's voice rose, frustration spilling over. "What good is tradition if it means stifling growth? We're losing customers to places that adapt. This pub can't survive on nostalgia alone!"

Seamus's eyes narrowed, his face reddening as the air between them thickened. "You think I built this place on nostalgia? This pub is my life's work! All I've done is for my family. You think that by bringing in some trendy brewery, you're honoring that legacy?"

"Honoring it?" Aidan snapped, his voice breaking with frustration. "Have you even looked at the bills, Da? The ones sitting in a pile?"

He jabbed a finger toward the desk, his voice trembling with barely contained anger. "We're not 'doing fine.' We're sinking. And you're too stubborn to admit it."

Seamus froze, his face a mix of indignation and unease. "What bills?"

"The ones that say **PAST DUE** in big red letters!" Aidan barked. "The ones you keep stuffing into a drawer like they'll magically go away. This place is in trouble, Dad. And if we don't do something, there won't *be* a Murphy's to argue about."

The accusation hung like a thunderclap. Seamus's face turned a deep shade of red, his eyes blazing with anger. "You think I don't know what's going on? You think I haven't been keeping track?"

"Then why aren't you doing anything about it?" Aidan demanded, his voice rising. "You're so obsessed with protecting your legacy that you're willing to let it crumble around you rather than adapt. We need MJ's brewery. We need to evolve if we're going to survive."

Seamus rose from his chair, towering over Aidan with an intensity that sent a chill down his spine. "You're not thinking straight! You're letting your dreams cloud your judgment! This pub is like an extension of our family. Any slight against it is a betrayal against the family!"

"Betrayal?" Aidan echoed incredulously, the anger boiling over. "You think I'm betraying the family by wanting to make something of my own? You're the one who's chained me to this place, living out a dream that isn't even mine!"

Their voices rose, echoing off the walls of the office like thunder, each man unyielding, caught in the cyclone of their conflicting ideologies. Aidan could feel the heat of his father's anger, the old wounds of unspoken resentments and unmet expectations surfacing, ready to explode like a violent volcano.

"Do you even realize how much you sound like a spoiled child?" Seamus shot back, eyes ablaze. "This isn't just a business, Aidan! This is our family's legacy!"

"Legacy?" Aidan laughed bitterly, the sound devoid of humor. "You're living in the past! I'm trying to build a future! You're acting like this pub is only yours, but I have a stake in it too! We all do ... your family. I want a place where I can express myself, not just be your shadow."

Seamus's expression tightened, a muscle jumping in his jaw as something unreadable flickered across his face—pain, disappointment, maybe both. For an instant, Aidan thought he saw hesitation, a fracture in his father's fury. But then the anger returned, fiercer than before, drowning out everything else.

If you can't respect what we've built, you have to question whether you really want to be part of this family." Seamus roared, his voice echoing in the small office.

Aidan stepped back, stunned by the force of the accusation. His chest tightened, a cocktail of hurt and anger bubbling. "I'm trying to honor what we've built, but you need to let go of the past! You're holding me back from pursuing my own dreams!"

"Then go! If you think you can do better without us, then leave!" Seamus shouted, the words striking Aidan like a physical blow.

The confrontation became increasingly aggressive, both men on the verge of a physical fight, their emotions a storm of frustration and hurt. The long-simmering tension finally erupted, with each accusation echoing the unspoken resentment that had built up.

With fists clenched and heart racing, Aidan was about to take a step forward when Maureen burst into the office, her arrival a calming force amidst the growing storm.

"Enough!" she commanded, stepping between them with a firm yet gentle resolve. "Both of you need to take a step back. This isn't the way to handle things."

Aidan felt his body tense, the heat of anger still pulsing in his veins, but he took a deep breath, the sound of his mother's voice anchoring him in the chaos.

"Ma, he doesn't understand," Aidan said, his voice strained but softer now. "I'm trying to make a change. He sees it as a betrayal."

"And you're pushing him away," she countered, her eyes darting between the two men. "Aidan, your father has spent his life building this pub for you and your siblings. It's more than just a business to him; it's a part of who he is. You can't just dismiss that."

"I'm not dismissing it!" Aidan protested, the frustration bubbling back to the surface. "I'm trying to build something new while honoring the past. But he won't even consider it!"

The fire in Seamus's eyes flickered as he glared at Aidan, but his wife's voice seemed to cool his anger. Maureen's kind nature acted as a unifying force between their differing perspectives, a testament to the underlying love that sustained their family, even in the face of conflict.

"Let's take a moment to breathe," she urged, her voice steady. "We can talk about this without tearing each other apart. Aidan, your ideas matter, but so do your father's feelings. Seamus, Aidan is your son, and he deserves to be heard."

Silence fell over the room, the tension still remained but less explosive. Aidan looked at his father, seeing the storm of emotions churning behind Seamus's eyes. Anger, yeah, but there was something bigger going on. He was terrified of losing his kid, scared of the changes, and maybe even sad about how things had gone between them.

"Can we try to find some common ground?" Maureen inquired, her expression growing gentler as she shifted her attention from one to the other. "Aidan, you want to bring in new ideas, and Seamus, you want to protect what you've built. What if we explored a way for both to coexist?"

Aidan took a step back, letting his mother's words wash over him. Could they really merge tradition with innovation? Seamus's face remained tight, but a glimmer of something else, possibly a trace of openness, caught his eye.

"Let's talk about MJ's proposal," Aidan began, but before he could finish, Seamus threw up his hands in frustration, his face a mask of disbelief.

"I'm done with this!" he exclaimed, his voice booming in the small office. The door slammed shut behind Seamus, the sound reverberating through the pub like a gunshot.

Aidan stood frozen in place, his heart pounding in his chest. He glanced down at the desk, his eyes falling on the familiar stack of unopened envelopes peeking out from under a folder.

He reached out, pulled one of the bills free, and stared at the red **PAST DUE** stamped across the top. His throat tightened as he scanned the numbers. They were deeper in the hole than he'd realized. This wasn't just a temporary setback—it was a slow bleed that would eventually kill the pub if nothing changed.

He tossed the bill back onto the desk, his hands trembling with frustration. How could Seamus look at this and still refuse to see the truth? How could he put his pride above everything else—above the family, above the business they'd both poured their lives into?

He turned back to his mother, his voice thick with frustration. "There's no talking to that man," he spat, the words tumbling out before he could stop them.

He turned to her, his voice raw with emotion. "Ma, you saw these, didn't you? You know how bad it is."

She hesitated, guilt flickering across her face. "Your father's been under a lot of stress, Aidan. He's been trying to handle it, but—"

"But what?" Aidan interrupted, his voice rising. "Pretending it's not happening isn't handling it! If we don't do something, Murphy's is done. Do you get that? We'll lose everything."

Maureen stepped closer. "I understand, sweetheart. But you need to give him time. He's scared, Aidan. Scared of losing what he's built. You have to approach this carefully."

Aidan shook his head, the bitterness rising in his throat. "Time? Ma?! How much more time does he need? I'm at a breaking point, Ma. It feels like I'm trapped in a story I didn't write, living in the shadow of someone else's achievements. I've tried to be the dutiful son, but it's suffocating! Maybe I just need to walk away, like Aisling when she left for law school. Maybe I'll come back in a few years and see if he's finally ready to mend fences then."

He could feel the hot sting of tears prickling at the corners of his eyes, and he fought hard to hold them back, not wanting to show weakness in front of his mother. But the pain was real, a heavy ache in his chest that seemed to swell with each passing day.

Maureen stepped forward, her hand resting on his arm. "You don't mean that," she said gently, her eyes searching his face for understanding. "You love this place. It's your home, too."

Aidan ran a hand through his hair, frustration bubbling to the surface. "It doesn't feel like home anymore, Ma. It feels like a prison. I want to create something that's mine, something that makes me feel alive. I can't keep fighting for that here if he won't even listen."

"Aidan ..." Maureen began, her voice soothing, but he could feel the tremor in his chest growing stronger.

"I'm tired of fighting!" he blurted out, the emotional weight crashing over him. It's pointless to keep banging my head against a brick wall. I just want Da to see me for who I am. But every time I try, it's like I'm betraying him! I don't know how to fix this!"

The floodgates threatened to open, and he swallowed hard, struggling to maintain his composure. A tear slipped down his cheek, a solitary testament to the hurt he had kept bottled up for so long.

Maureen she moved closer, wrapping her arms around him in a comforting embrace. "It's okay to feel this way, sweetheart. You're not alone in this. Your father loves you, even if he can't show it right now. You're both just ... stuck."

"Stuck, Ma," Aidan echoed, the word hanging heavy. "That's exactly it."

As he leaned into his mother's embrace, he felt the warmth of her support, but the storm within him raged on. He struggled with the conflict between his duty to his family and his yearning for freedom. Finally, in that moment, he realized he might have to confront not just his father, but also the fears that had been holding him back.

Aidan wiped the tear from his cheek, taking a deep breath to steady himself. "I don't know what the future holds, but I can't keep living like this. I want to create my own path—one that honors what we've built but also allows me to breathe."

Maureen stepped back, looking into his eyes with unwavering support. "Then you need to find the courage to pursue it. Even if that means taking a step back for a while, you deserve to discover what makes you happy."

As Aidan nodded, a flicker of hope ignited within him again, though he knew the road ahead would be fraught with challenges. Arguing with his father had left him shaken, but he could feel the resolve building inside, igniting a fire that had been smoldering for too long.

Aidan felt the weight of his mother's words settling in, but before he could fully process them, he could hear the tension simmering just outside the door where Seamus had stormed out.

"Let's take a step back," Maureen suggested gently, her voice laced with understanding. "I think it might be best for you to stay away from the kitchen this week. Everyone needs to cool down. Emotions are running high, and if you keep pushing, it's only going to escalate. Your father needs time to reflect."

Aidan frowned, the thought of retreating from Murphy's Pub feeling like another form of defeat. "But I can't just hide from him, Ma. At some point, I need to stand my ground."

Maureen shook her head, her eyes soft yet firm. "It's not hiding; it's allowing space for both of you to breathe. You won't get anywhere if you're both angry. Let's try to have a calm conversation about this at dinner on Sunday."

He considered her words, feeling the internal struggle rage on. "Yeah, Ma," taking space felt like the easy way out, but maybe it was also the smart choice. "I can take some space ... but right now, I'm not sure I can promise I'll make it to Sunday dinner this week," he admitted, a knot of frustration twisting in his stomach. "I can't sit across the table from him pretending everything's fine."

"Aidan, I understand," Maureen said softly, her voice filled with compassion. "But if you stay away for a few days, you might find that the conversation will be more productive. You can't change the way he thinks overnight, but you can give him a chance to consider your perspective."

With a reluctant sigh, Aidan nodded. He hated the feeling of being cornered, but perhaps stepping away would help him see things more clearly.

"Okay, I'll give it a shot. But I can't guarantee I'll feel up to it by Sunday."

"That's all I'm asking for—some space to let cooler heads prevail."

He took a deep breath, trying to center himself amidst the swirling emotions. "Thanks, Ma. I just want to figure this out."

Filled with newfound resolve, Aidan stood tall, ready to tackle the challenges in his relationship with Seamus and embrace the path he had chosen for himself.

Twenty-Five

Aidan sat on the edge of his bed, phone in hand, eyes unfocused as he traced circles on the sheets. A familiar ding pulled him from his thoughts, and he glanced down to see Harper's name light up the screen. Without a second thought, he picked up.

"Hey," he murmured, trying to push the tension from his voice.

"Hey yourself," she replied, her tone light. "What's got you so broody this morning?"

"Got a lot on my mind, I guess."

"Oh, I don't doubt it," she said with a playful lilt. "But, lucky for you, I'm a certified expert at taking minds off heavy stuff. Consider it my gift to the world." She paused, clearly waiting. Imagine you could be anywhere, doing anything right now. Where would you be?"

Aidan closed his eyes, a smile breaking his frustration. "Probably on some beach ... fishing, maybe. Just ... no responsibilities."

"Fishing? Okay, unexpected," Harper teased. "I was picturing you whipping up some culinary masterpiece over an open fire or something."

He laughed, shaking his head. "Just me, some quiet, a few beers. Simple."

"Simple sounds nice," she replied softly, letting a beat pass. "It's just you and that huge decision now, huh?"

"Yeah. And everyone waiting on it," he admitted, running a hand through his hair. "I just ... I don't know what he'll say. Or if he'll listen."

"Well, he'll have to listen eventually, Aidan. You've given him years. You've earned it," she replied. "But hey, enough of that. Let's talk about something completely ridiculous instead. Do you remember that horrible dance contest on the cruise?"

He laughed, grateful for the lighter topic. "Oh, don't remind me. I almost pulled a muscle trying to keep up with you."

"Almost?" she teased. "You simply couldn't compete. Admit it."

A knock at the door cut through their laughter. Aidan glanced at his phone, grimacing. "Looks like destiny just showed up, right on time."

"Destiny? What do you ... "

"My sister. I gotta run," he said. "But ... thanks, Harper. For this."

"Anytime," she replied, "Good luck, Murphy."

He ended the call and opened the door to see Aisling leaning against the frame, one eyebrow raised. "Who's Harper?" she asked, smirking.

Aidan rubbed the back of his neck, playing it cool. "Just a friend from the cruise."

"Just a friend?" Aisling repeated, eyes gleaming with curiosity. He shrugged, keeping his expression unreadable.

"Yep. Let's go."

In the car, the weight of her scrutiny settled between them.

"So ... just a friend from the cruise?" she asked, her tone loaded.

Aidan shrugged, staring out the window. "Yep. She's ... nice."

Aisling snorted. "Sure. Well, let's hope this mystery friend has you thinking clearly, 'cause we both know Da isn't about to welcome a big change without some kind of fight."

He nodded, sighing. "I've tried easing into it, getting him to see how bringing MJ in could help ... but you know him. Soon as I say the word 'change,' it's like he tunes out everything else."

Aisling gripped the wheel a little tighter. "Look, he's stubborn, but he's also practical. Maybe you'll be more persuasive if you explain how this affects him, Ma, and even Declan. Concentrate on the practical benefits, not just ... your own needs."

Aidan rubbed his temples. "I know. And I've thought about every angle, every way to say it. But when it comes down to it, it's about more than the pub. He wants me there because he thinks that's what family should mean."

"Then remind him that family's also about supporting each other," Aisling said gently. "Not just following a path because he expects it."

Aidan looked over, a grateful smile breaking through his nerves. "Thanks, Ash. You always know how to make things sound doable."

"Just promise you won't let him bulldoze you," she said. "You deserve this."

Sunday warmth filled the Murphy family home, as usual. The smell of Maureen's freshly baked bread and the sharp scent of coffee filled the room with a sense of comfort. Aidan and Aisling walked in, but the place felt weird like everyone was holding their breath. The family assembled early, sensing the weight of the situation that was about to develop.

Seamus, with a guarded expression, sat in the living room, arms folded across his chest and his jaw clenched. Maureen's hand rested reassuringly on his forearm, her touch an anchor against the threat of a full-blown argument. Although Declan pretended to be calm, Aidan noticed his brother's nervousness. Declan's lack of passion for the pub wasn't a secret to him, but Declan had never voiced his reservations before.

Aidan noticed MJ hanging back by the door, quietly offering support, like he knew this was something for the family to handle first. With a nod and a steady look, MJ signaled Aidan to get going.

Clearing his throat, Aidan spoke, his voice steady but low. "Thanks for being here, everyone. I know … I know it isn't easy, but this conversation is long overdue." He felt his throat tighten, but he pressed on. "I wanted to talk about what Murphy's could look like if we brought in new ideas. MJ and I are exploring a partnership with the potential to elevate things significantly."

Seamus's voice hardened, irritation seeping into every syllable. "Partnership," he repeated, the word falling from his mouth like a lead weight. "We don't need some fancy partnership to keep this place going, Aidan. We've done just fine on our own."

"Da, I know how you feel about change, but … please, hear me out," Aidan said, fighting to keep his tone calm. "Our goal isn't to alter our identity, but to provide Murphy's with the opportunity to flourish. MJ's brewery brings a different crowd, and we can introduce new things without losing what Murphy's is about."

Seamus's eyes narrowed. "And what is Murphy's about, according to you?" His voice was sharp, almost a challenge. "Is it some trendy place with fancy drinks, or is it the pub I built from nothing?"

Aidan's frustration bubbled up, but he forced himself to stay composed. "It's about family, Da. It's about connection. But if we stay the same forever, it's going to wither. I've been running the kitchen, doing the same things ... we have some good regulars, but we're not getting any new clientele."

Seamus's face reddened, his posture tightening. "So what, Aidan? You think I haven't sacrificed for this place? You think I don't know the struggles? I poured my life into this pub for all of you kids, so you'd have something steady, something strong."

"Exactly," Aidan countered, his voice firm but tinged with urgency. "You've worked yourself to the bone, Da, but you're ignoring the fact that it's not working anymore. Sales are down; fewer people are coming in, and the ones that do ... half of them ask for something we don't even have because we refuse to adapt. I see it every night. I feel it every night. And I know you see it, too."

Seamus's expression wavered momentarily, a fleeting hint of doubt or guilt before hardening back into the stubbornness Aidan expected.

"So what, Aidan? You think change is the magic fix? I've seen what happens to places that try to 'keep up.' They lose everything that mattered in the first place."

Aidan leaned forward, his voice sharp, his frustration at boiling point. "You know what really loses everything, Da? Ignoring what's right in front of you." He reached into his pocket and pulled out a crumpled overdue bill, one he'd grabbed from the office drawer before this meeting. With a sharp flick of his wrist, he slapped it down onto the coffee table. The red **PAST DUE** stamp seemed to glow in the room's heavy silence.

"This isn't 'fine,'" Aidan said, his voice trembling with emotion. "This is where we are, Da. Rent. Suppliers. Utilities. We're drowning, and all you want to do is plug your ears and pretend it'll all go away."

Seamus's eyes flicked to the bill, his jaw tightening, a flicker of unease flashing across his face. "You had no right to go through my desk," he muttered.

"I didn't have to go looking," Aidan shot back. "It was right there, shoved under some papers like it didn't exist. This isn't about a few 'fancy changes.' It's about saving Murphy's because if we don't, it'll be gone, and you'll have nothing left but your pride."

Maureen's hand tightened on Seamus's arm, her voice gentle but firm. "Seamus," she murmured, her steady look brimming with quiet understanding. "I've seen what this pub means to you, how much you've sacrificed. But I've also seen the strain—the late nights, the way you barely sleep ... and those bills piling up on your desk." Her voice carried the weight of truth, a reality they could no longer ignore. "You've carried this burden alone for so long, love. But it doesn't have to be this way anymore. You don't have to keep fighting this fight by yourself."

Seamus flinched slightly, his eyes darting toward her before narrowing at Aidan. "So that's what this is about, is it?" he asked, voice hardening. "You've all decided I can't handle things anymore?"

"No," Aidan replied quickly, the frustration rising. He leaned forward, his voice soft but steady. "This isn't about saying you can't handle it, Da. It's about us wanting to help. I don't want to walk away from the family, from the pub, but I can't keep sinking with a ship that's going down if we don't make some changes. You've worked yourself to the bone, but the business is struggling. We're all trying to figure out how we can make it work—not just survive … but thrive. But if we don't change something, this place won't make it."

Seamus's expression darkened, his fists tightening on the armrests. "So, you're saying I've failed, that I've ruined everything?" His voice was strained with hurt, and he didn't bother to mask the anger in it. "This is my life's work. And now you want to just throw it all away?"

A heavy silence filled the room, the tension thick and suffocating. Aidan felt the weight of his words linger, and he realized it wasn't just about the pub anymore—it was about everything they had built, the expectations, the weight of his father's legacy. Declan cleared his throat, and Aidan saw the discomfort in his brother's posture, his eyes shifting downward.

"It's not just Aidan, Da," Declan said quietly, his voice barely above a whisper. He cast his eyes down to his hands, as if the mere thought of speaking his truth was too laden with shame. "I've been in the kitchen too, working my share. But it's not my dream either. I've been thinking about other things. Things that matter to me."

Seamus turned to Declan, his face hardening with a mix of disbelief and hurt. "So that's it, then? All these years, and neither of you have it in you to carry on what I've built?"

Declan's words hit like a bitter realization. He looked down, frustration and shame etched into his features. "It's not that simple, Da. I'm grateful for everything we have here, but I want to do something that feels like it's … mine."

Seamus's face reddened, his fists tightening as he sat forward. "So now I'm supposed to just let go? Just throw away everything I've worked for because you both want something different? What's next, huh? Are you both going to leave and leave me here alone with all of this?"

Aidan felt the sharp sting of his father's words, and it set off a chain reaction within him. His irritation, already simmering beneath the surface, finally boiled over.

He threw his hands up in exasperation, the words tumbling out in a rush. "I don't know why I even bothered to come over here today," he muttered, his voice sharp with bitter finality as he turned toward the door, feeling the anger and helplessness mix together. "We keep talking in circles, and nothing's changing. I don't want to be part of a legacy that doesn't let me breathe. This place has become a prison, Da. You're holding onto something that's dying, and you're dragging us all down with it!"

"Enough!" Seamus's voice cut through the room, booming with raw anger. It halted Aidan mid-step, the force of it making him flinch. "You think you can just walk away, don't you? Leave all of this like it meant nothing? You don't know what it took to get here. None of you do."

Aidan slowly turned back, his anger raw and his voice trembling with hurt. "Then tell us, Da. Tell us why keeping us here—trapped in this—matters more than letting us live our own lives." His words were strained, thick with the frustration that had been building for so long, too much for him to hold in anymore.

He watched his father closely, searching his face for any sign of a shift, any sign that he might finally understand. But Seamus was staring at the floor, his jaw clenched tight, his forehead furrowed as he struggled to process Aidan's words—and the proposal MJ had made.

For a long moment, Seamus said nothing. The room fell into an uneasy silence, thick with tension. Aidan felt a mix of hindrance and sympathy rising in him. He could see that Seamus wasn't just weighing the offer; he was wrestling with something deeper, something that seemed to take him far from this room.

Seamus finally looked up, his eyes settling on an old photo hanging on the wall. It showed his family outside Murphy's, taken during one of his grandfather's last visits to the restaurant. Aidan observed that his father's attention remained fixed, growing tender as the familiar face came into view. Seamus had shared the tale of the man in the picture over and over, a gruff, dedicated immigrant who arrived in America with almost nothing, driven by a desire to build a better future for his family.

Seamus's expression shifted, the tightness in his features loosening, replaced by something almost vulnerable. Aidan realized his father wasn't just seeing a photo on the wall; he was reliving a piece of his own history.

"When my father came here," Seamus began, his voice low, almost as if he were speaking more to himself than to anyone else, "he worked his fingers raw. In construction, mostly. Came home every night covered in dust, his back shot to hell. But he told me ... he told me he did it, so I'd never have to." Seamus swallowed hard, his focus unyielding as he stared at the photo.

Aidan felt a lump form in his throat. He was aware of the importance his father placed on the legacy, but as he listened, he detected a subtle undercurrent of fear beneath the outward pride. A fear that, by letting go of Murphy's, Seamus would let go of everything his own father had worked for.

Seamus shook his head, letting out a shaky breath. "I made a vow to him, way back when, that I'd build something substantial, something that would endure." Aidan watched as his father's fingers loosened, then tightened again as if he were holding on to some invisible thread.

For a moment, Seamus looked lost, torn between the weight of his promise and the future he could feel slipping out of his control. In his father's eyes, Aidan recognized a chilling fear: the fear of being unneeded, of losing the significance in the family he'd spent his life building.

Shifting his focus to Aidan, Seamus reached for another photo from the mantle. The picture captured a moment from years past: Seamus in the kitchen with Aidan, when he was maybe seven or eight years old, both covered in food and grinning with a joy that could light up the darkest night.

Seamus took a heavy breath, his shoulders sinking as he resigned himself to the weight of his own mind. "I just wanted to make sure you'd be all right," he said softly, almost apologetically. "That you'd have something ... something solid to stand on."

Aidan's heart swelled with a mixture of sadness and gratitude. He wanted to reach out, to tell his father that the strength and stability he'd given them was real, that it would always be there, even if Murphy's looked a little different in the years to come.

His attention fell to the photo in his hands, and he examined it as if the man pictured was a stranger. "But somewhere along the way, I ... I started seeing it as the only way. As if Murphy's was all I had to give. My fear kept me from letting go. I was scared that if I let go, I'd lose you. That you'd leave and never look back."

Aidan felt the anger in his chest dissolve, replaced by an ache he hadn't expected. "Da ... we're not trying to leave you behind. We want to carry on what you started, but in our own way. You taught us to work hard, to be proud. That's part of us. But so is this need to be ourselves."

Seamus looked up, his face weary. For the first time, Aidan saw not a stubborn man but a father grappling with fears he had buried beneath years of hard work.

"I don't want you to be tied to Murphy's if it makes you feel trapped," Seamus admitted, his voice barely above a whisper. "I thought ... I thought this would be our family's pride, our legacy. But maybe I was wrong."

Maureen reached over, taking Seamus's hand, her eyes glistening with tears. "You haven't failed us, Seamus. The legacy is this family, not just the pub."

MJ spoke up then, his voice calm but warm. "Seamus, your dream gave this family a foundation. Murphy's doesn't mark the end, it sets the stage. Let us build on what you started, in a way that lets them be who they need to be."

Seamus closed his eyes, nodding slowly as he processed their words. He seemed smaller, the burden of years melting away. "I see that now. I wanted to give you a foundation, but maybe I forgot to let you build your own house."

Aidan felt the tension drain away as he stepped closer to his father. "We can still make Murphy's something we're all proud of. But we need to make it our own. And with MJ's help, we can keep it going strong."

Seamus looked at him, his eyes tired but resigned. "Aidan ... if that's what you truly want, then ... then let's make it work. For all of us."

The room exhaled with him, the weight of years lifting in that single moment of surrender. The silence that filled the room felt like peace, a sense of resolution slipping in at last. They each recognized the time had come for a new chapter, one that valued their shared past but also allowed for unique personal growth.

As the tension settled, MJ cleared his throat, glancing at his phone. "I should step out and make a quick call. I'll be right back," he said, nodding to Seamus with a quiet smile before slipping out of the room, leaving the family with a newfound sense of stillness.

For a few long moments, silence wrapped around them, each of them absorbing the conversation, the relief in the room almost tangible. Aidan leaned back, exhaling deeply, the load he'd carried for so long easing from his shoulders. Declan shifted in his seat, rubbing the back of his neck, and Maureen reached over, giving Seamus's hand a soft squeeze.

"That was ... a long time coming," Aidan said, his voice quiet but relieved.

Seamus nodded slowly, his own expression tempered. "Guess I had it coming," he murmured, the corner of his mouth lifting in a half-smile as he looked at his sons, the weariness on his face now touched by something warmer. "But if we're going to make this work, we'll do it together. All of us."

Aisling broke the silence with a gentle, almost tentative laugh, drawing everyone's attention. "I have to admit," she said, her tone self-conscious, "I feel like I'm partly to blame here. I remember all the years I stayed away after law school, how long it took me and Da to work things out ... I should've come back sooner, tried harder. Maybe if I had, we wouldn't be here, fighting over the same things."

"Ais, don't do that to yourself. We both made our choices," Seamus replied gently. "You were just following your path. It took me too long to see that."

Aidan reached over, giving Aisling's shoulder a light squeeze. "None of this is on you. We all have to find our way, even if it means butting heads. And look at us now," he said, offering her a reassuring smile. "We're here, together, sorting it out."

Declan nodded, looking around at them, his own face tinged with guilt. "I just want to say I'm grateful—for all of you. This whole thing, the pub, it means a lot. But not more than this family," he added, motioning to the family gathered around him. "We need to stick together, no matter where we end up."

Maureen's eyes grew misty as she looked at each of them. "No matter what happens, I want you to know that what matters most is this family." She looked at Seamus, her eyes full of pride and love, and squeezed his hand. "It's been a journey, but maybe that's the whole idea—growing and learning together."

Seamus gave her hand a gentle pat and looked at his children. "I may not have always shown it, but you three ... you're my pride. And I know now that it doesn't matter how you do things, so long as you're happy. That's all any father can ask for."

Aisling leaned in, putting an arm around her mother's shoulders, and Declan and Aidan shared a smile. For the first time in ages, the family felt united. The tension had lifted, replaced by a quiet, steady sense of peace.

MJ returned from his call, his expression thoughtful, as though he carried a weight he hadn't fully placed down. Stepping back into the room, he glanced around, noting the softened atmosphere, the quiet peace that had settled over the Murphy family.

"Alright," he began, his voice calm but direct. "If you're all open to hearing me out, I'd like to put a different offer on the table."

Seamus shifted in his seat, his eyes narrowing with both curiosity and residual wariness. "I thought we were clear on the partnership," he said, his tone even but cautious.

MJ held up a hand. "I know, and the partnership idea is still an option. But after talking it over with my business partner, we thought maybe something ... more straightforward could work."

The Murphys exchanged confused glances, Aidan leaning forward as if trying to read MJ's face. "More straightforward?" Aidan asked, the tension flickering back into his tone. "What do you mean?"

MJ took a breath, looking straight at Seamus. "Seamus, we'd like to buy Murphy's. Outright. From you."

Seamus's eyes widened in disbelief, and Maureen placed a hand over her mouth in shock. Before anyone could speak, MJ continued, his tone measured but sincere. "I know what you're thinking. But hear me out. I've seen the overdue notices. I know the suppliers are knocking, the rent's behind, and margins are shrinking. This isn't about pointing fingers—it's just the reality of the business right now."

He paused. "This is why we want to step in. Let us shoulder the financial strain. Let us take the pressure off you, so you can finally breathe. You've done your part, Seamus. No one's asking you to let go of the pub's spirit. We're asking you to let us make sure it *survives.*"

Staring at MJ with a tightening jaw, Seamus's attention momentarily shifted to the table, where the overdue bill remained. For the first time, his shoulders slumped just slightly as though the weight of it all was pressing down harder than he could bear.

"Buy it?" Seamus repeated slowly, the words catching in his throat.

"Yes," MJ said, nodding. "We want to take over Murphy's entirely. Full ownership. And that means you'd get a clean break if you want one. This money is completely yours to use. You're free to decide where you go, how you spend it, everything. Retire, travel, help your kids ... whatever you feel is right."

Seamus opened his mouth to respond but stopped short, his face creased with confusion and something else, perhaps a hint of intrigue. "And ... and what would you do with Murphy's, then?" he asked, his tone measured as if weighing each word carefully.

MJ's expression mellowed as he carried on. "We'd keep it as Murphy's, make no mistake about that. We want to acknowledge and pay tribute to everything you've created: the reputation, the community, and the warm atmosphere that everyone knows. But we'd also want the freedom to evolve, to introduce new ideas. We want to grow it in a way that respects the past but also makes room for the future. And that means letting us make changes. Tastefully, of course."

Seamus drummed his fingers against the table, his expression unreadable. Aidan shot MJ a doubtful look. "What about Da? Where does he fit into all this?"

MJ smiled, looking directly at Seamus. "Seamus, I'm asking you to stay on as a managing consultant. We need someone who works part-time, someone who isn't caught up in the daily routine, but can keep us accountable, uphold our standards, and represent the spirit of

Seamus Murphy. You'd be our guide, our touchstone. But you'd need to let us handle the evolution of the place."

Seamus's face was a mixture of shock and deep thought, his eyes locked onto MJ as if he were seeing him for the first time. "So ... you want me to stay involved? Just not in control."

"Exactly," MJ confirmed. "This way, Murphy's continues, the community doesn't lose what it loves, and you get the chance to step back without giving up the spirit of what you built. And," he added, glancing meaningfully at Aidan and Declan, "your kids get a chance to build their own lives, too. It's the best of both worlds."

A silence fell over the room, each family member absorbing the implications of MJ's proposal. Aisling's eyes were bright with unspoken hope, and Maureen's hand found Seamus's, squeezing it tightly as if to say, *This could be it.*

Seamus looked around at his family, his expression a mixture of pride, resistance, and raw emotion. Finally, he turned back to MJ, his voice gruff but softened. "You want me to believe you'll protect Murphy's, our way. Not just as a name, but as a place that matters to people."

MJ advanced a step, his steady look underscoring the quiet intensity in his measured tone. "Sir, I've known the Murphy family for close to twenty years, since I went to school with Aidan. I've watched what you built here. And I like to think of you all as my extended family, too."

He paused, glancing around the room at each member of the Murphy family. "You know me, Seamus. You know I don't just jump into things. I admire the work, the pride, and the soul you've poured into this place. You can trust me when I say that if you let us take this over, we're gonna honor your legacy. Absolutely everything."

MJ's voice grew even stronger, his conviction clear. "We're not just looking to make changes for the sake of change. We're gonna keep Murphy's alive in a way that respects everything you've poured into it. You have my word that you'll be there to guide us. This place will always be yours, Seamus. We'll just make sure it can keep going strong for years to come."

MJ extended a hand, his eyes unwavering. "Trust me to carry this forward. The Seamus Murphy way."

Seamus sat still for a long moment, his face unreadable as he processed MJ's words. Then, with a deep exhale, he stood up, signaling to Maureen with a gentle nod. She rose to follow, placing a reassuring hand on his shoulder as they walked out of the room, leaving the others in tense silence.

The click of the door closing behind them seemed to echo. The quiet settled thickly over the room, each of them wrapped in their own thoughts as they waited.

Declan shifted on the couch, casting a wary glance toward the closed door. "You think he's actually considering it?" he asked, his tone uncertain. "Or is he just in there, cooling down before he comes out swinging again?"

Aidan rubbed his temples, exhaustion mingling with frustration. "I don't know," he admitted. "It'd be like him to stew on it a bit, then march back in here, telling us how this whole idea's a waste of time."

Aisling leaned forward, her hands clasped tightly in her lap. "Maybe Ma will talk him down if he starts up again. She's always been the one who can reach him, even when he's convinced himself he's right about everything."

Declan snorted softly, crossing his arms. "The real question is whether he's open to having his mind changed. I mean, all we've done today is show him we're not happy, and he's always taken that as some kind of personal slight."

Aidan sighed, shaking his head. "I tried telling him … it's not about leaving him or abandoning the pub. It's about … finally making it something all of us can live with. But that's hard for him to hear."

MJ, who'd been listening quietly, spoke up, his voice low. "I get it. Change is hard, especially when you've built something like he has. But sometimes … the love you have for something has to mean letting it grow beyond you."

They all fell silent, their eyes occasionally drifting to the doorway, waiting.

Seamus emerged from the den sooner than any of them expected. The heavy silence shattered as he stepped back into the room, his arms crossed, fingers tapping idly against his bicep. His gaze traveled across his children and MJ, but he kept quiet, pausing by the doorway as though he were undecided about rejoining the discussion or withdrawing into introspection.

Seamus cleared his throat before turning his focus to Declan. "Tell me something, Declan," he began, his tone gruff but steady. "If it weren't for the restaurant, if you weren't in that kitchen every day … what would you be doing?"

Declan blinked, thrown by the unexpected question. He shifted, glancing down at his hands before looking back at his father. "Well … woodworking, probably. I've loved it for years. Always thought about starting my own business. Maybe furniture-making. I ... I don't know if it'd ever amount to much, but I'd want to give it a try."

Seamus nodded, his face remaining impassive. "And you, Aidan?"

Under his father's penetrating look, Aidan felt a sudden twinge of anxiety. He paused before clearing his throat. "I'd keep cooking," he said slowly. "You got that part right, Da. But ... maybe I'd try something new, push some boundaries. Open a food truck, maybe. Experiment, do something that feels like ... me."

Holding Aidan's stare for one last moment, Seamus released a deep sigh and ambled over to his armchair. He lowered himself down, settling in, still silent as he seemed to consider their answers. The family waited, breaths held, tension mounting as Seamus's silence stretched on. Finally, he lifted his head, meeting each of their eyes with a look of reluctant resolution.

"Well, then," he said, his voice low but steady, "I'll agree to the sale."

A shocked silence filled the room, followed quickly by an outpouring of relieved breaths and tentative smiles. But Seamus stopped him, raising his hand to show he still had more to say.

"There's one more stipulation," he added, his attention fixing firmly on Aisling. "You, Aisling, will negotiate all the terms."

Aisling's eyes widened, her mouth falling open. "But, Da, I'm a family attorney. Selling and buying a business isn't in my scope."

Seamus's expression softened, and he leaned forward, his eyes filled with a rare tenderness. "Nonsense! You're a family attorney, yes. And this is family business," he said, his voice filled with pride. "I place my full support in your dealings, my love. I trust you to handle this better than anyone else could."

"Da, I've never ..." she started, only to pause when she caught the look in his eyes. For once, they weren't filled with frustration or expectation. They were trusting. And that trust, she realized, was all she needed. She nodded, determination settling in her chest. "I'll do it. I'll make sure this is done right."

The room filled with a burst of excitement as Seamus's words sank in. For a moment, it was as though years of tension and worry melted away, replaced by a shared sense of relief and newfound possibility. Maureen reached over, her hand resting on Seamus's, her eyes shining with pride and love. Declan let out a low whistle, clapping Aidan on the back, and Aidan felt a grin spread across his face, relief and gratitude swelling inside him.

MJ gave them all a nod, his own smile quiet but full of satisfaction. He stepped back toward the door, catching Aisling's eye. "I'll be looking forward to hearing from you soon," he said with a grin. "Sounds like we'll have a lot of details to settle."

Aisling grinned back, shaking his hand firmly. "You certainly will. You'd better be prepared because I intend to make this deal beneficial for everyone."

MJ laughed, raising his hands in mock surrender. "Wouldn't expect anything less." With a last nod to Seamus, he exited, leaving the family to bask in the victory.

As the door clicked shut, Declan nudged Aisling playfully. "Alright, sis," he teased, winking. "If you're taking the lead on negotiations, make sure you get a great deal for all of us, not just Da!"

Aisling rolled her eyes, but her grin didn't waver. "Oh, believe me, I plan to make sure everyone's taken care of. And I think I know exactly how to make it work."

Seamus cleared his throat, drawing their attention back to him. "Speaking of making sure everyone's taken care of ... I want to be the first official investor in your next ventures," he said, looking between Aidan and Declan. "I mean it. Whatever you need to get started, I'm here to back you, with both my heart and my checkbook."

A lump formed in Aidan's throat, a blend of gratitude and love welling up as he locked eyes with his father. Declan's face broke into a broad grin, and he crossed his arms, nodding at Seamus.

"Well," Declan said, his tone light but filled with emotion, "looks like we've got ourselves quite the business partner."

They all shared a laugh, the air between them light and full of promise for the future.

Twenty-Six

The pub buzzed with life, the sounds of celebration filling the space as if the pub itself was determined to go out on a high note. Aidan stepped inside, earlier than most, his gaze sweeping over the photos lining the walls. Generations of faces stared back at him, their presence both comforting and heavy. This was the last night Murphy's would be in his family's hands, and though the warmth of nostalgia lingered, it was edged with something bittersweet—a quiet goodbye woven into the familiar hum of laughter and clinking glasses.

The kitchen, now under new management, ran smoothly without him, thanks to the past couple of months spent training MJ's chosen replacement. Unlike usual, Aidan didn't have to deal with the hectic pace of preparing orders and calling out times tonight. Unconstrained, he explored, savoring each element, reflecting on the pub's impact and the possibilities that awaited him.

He walked the length of the bar, fingers trailing lightly over the polished wood that had witnessed countless toasts, raucous laughter, and a few whispered secrets over the years. The old barstools creaked under the weight of regulars who had been coming here since before he could remember. He smiled, nodding to the familiar faces, each one carrying a memory of Murphy's.

"Hey, Aidan!" Bernie called out. He was a rosy-cheeked regular, an old friend of his father's, who sat with a pint in hand. "Your dad tells me you're leavin' soon, yeah? Finally chasing that big dream of yours?"

Aidan snickered, nodding. "Yeah, Bernie, something like that. Trying to see what's out there for me."

Bernie raised his glass in salute. "You've got that Murphy fire in you, kid. Just remember where you came from, eh?"

"Always," Aidan said with a grin, patting the bar. "Rest assured, you'll still run into me. Maybe for a pint or two."

Moving through the crowd, Aidan found himself surrounded by friends and patrons congratulating him on the new venture, sharing stories of the pub that felt woven into the very fabric of his life. Every handshake and clap on the shoulder felt like a testament to the community Murphy's had built, a legacy MJ would carry forward even as Aidan ventured out on his own.

As he reached the bar, Jazz gave him a wide, teasing grin. "It's gonna feel weird not having you here, Murphy. I mean, who else am I gonna roast when they mess up a drink order?"

Aidan laughed, leaning against the bar. "Oh, come on, Jazz, we both know you've already got a line of people you're waiting to torment." He nodded toward the two new bartenders she'd been training for the transition. "Pretty sure they're fair game."

Jazz tossed a knowing glint over her shoulder at the newbies, who were busy stocking glasses. "Maybe. But they're not Murphy. Can't say it won't feel different around here without you stirring things up."

MJ, who had been listening in from the other side of the bar, raised a glass toward Aidan. "Don't go getting sentimental on us now, Jazz. Besides, she's staying with us for the long haul," he said with a grin. "Turns out I finally managed to hire her away from Murphy's, after all."

Jazz laughed, giving MJ a mock salute. "Yeah, well, you finally sweetened the deal, boss. And I've got to keep these rookies in line, right?"

MJ chuckled, turning to Aidan. "This whole thing's getting bigger than any of us thought. We're converting my old brewery into a second pub location. It'll be 'Murphy's Legacy Brew Pub,' just like here. Carry the family name and spirit forward."

Aidan took in the news, nodding slowly, feeling both humbled and excited. "Murphy's Legacy," he echoed, letting the name sink in. "I like it, MJ. Sounds ... fitting."

MJ clinked his glass with Aidan's, a shared understanding passing between them. "Thanks, man. And don't think we're letting you disappear completely. Wherever you're headed next, we'll find a way to rope you back in for a special Murphy's night."

"Deal," Aidan said, grinning. "As long as someone else handles the dishes."

They all shared a laugh, and as the conversation shifted, Aidan glanced around the pub once more. There was something uniquely freeing about this night. His future wasn't tied to these walls anymore, yet he could still feel Murphy's spirit everywhere, in every laugh and every toast.

Just then, Seamus walked by, catching Aidan's eye. He clapped him on the shoulder, giving a small nod that needed no words. For all their differences and clashes over the years, tonight was a shared triumph. Murphy's was still their legacy, and that wasn't going to change, no matter where life took them next.

As Aidan watched his father disappear back into the crowd, a sense of pride settled over him, warming his chest. This wasn't an ending; it was a new beginning for each of them. With the food truck, he'd have the freedom to go wherever he wanted, cooking on his own terms while MJ carried on the Murphy's namesake.

Jazz tapped him on the shoulder, jolting him from his thoughts. "Better make the rounds, Murphy," she said with a grin. "These people are here to see you, after all. Give 'em a wonderful memory to go home with."

Aidan nodded, grinning back. "Don't worry, Jazz. I've got an entire night left, and I'm planning to make every minute count."

As the night carried on, laughter and stories mingled with the familiar scents of hops and wood smoke. Aidan made his way through the crowd, sharing quick hugs, handshakes, and a few heartfelt words with the faces that had been a part of his life for so long. Glasses clinked, old friends exchanged grins, and the hum of voices filled every corner of the pub.

Then, from near the bar, a sharp tap of glass cut through the noise. Aidan turned to see his father, Seamus, standing tall, holding a pint high above his head. The room fell into a respectful hush as Seamus cleared his throat, his eyes sweeping over the crowd, filled with pride and nostalgia. A quiet anticipation settled, and everyone leaned in, sensing the weight of this departing toast.

Seamus took a deep breath, his voice steady but swelling with emotion. "Thank you all for being here tonight," he began, his voice carrying across the room. "This place, Murphy's ... well, it wouldn't have been half of what it is without every one of you."

A few cheers erupted, and Seamus cleared his throat, his eyes misting slightly. He hesitated, his mouth working to form words he'd probably rehearsed a dozen times. "I still remember the day we opened the doors. Truth be told, I wasn't sure this pub would even last a month." A murmur of laughter rippled through the crowd. "Didn't have much more than a handful of recipes, a few tables, and a prayer. And if I'm honest, most of that first month's business was probably just my own mates drinkin' me nearly out of stock!

"It wasn't easy. There were long nights and plenty of worry about keepin' this place open. I was just a childish fool with a lot of grit and not a lot of sense. But we scraped by, day by day. And slowly, Murphy's became more than a pub. It became a place to come together. I've seen friendships born here, hearts broken, and lives celebrated."

A hush fell again, and Seamus swallowed, closing his eyes as he collected his thoughts. "To our dedicated regulars who stood by us through thick and thin, we wouldn't be here celebrating without you. I couldn't have done it alone. Murphy's has always been a family, and you are all a part of that."

Aidan felt his throat tighten. This was a side of his father he seldom saw: open, vulnerable, and grateful for the support he received. For a moment, Aidan glimpsed the man who had poured his whole heart into Murphy's, even when it meant long hours and late nights away from home.

Seamus continued, his voice catching slightly as he spoke of the staff. "To all those who have worked here throughout the years, both in the front of house, the kitchen, and the bar, you have all played a part in making this place what it is. Your hard work, your laughter, your loyalty. Without you, Murphy's would've been just another empty pub."

From behind the bar, Jazz gave Seamus a playful salute and Seamus raised his glass back in her direction. "And now, as we move forward, we've got MJ to thank. This pub's not going away. It'll keep growing, keep changing, but it'll always stay Murphy's at heart." He looked over at MJ, his voice thickening. "It's not been easy, lettin' go. Truth is, I held on tighter than I should've, but I can't think of a better person to carry on what we started here."

MJ raised his glass, the two men sharing a nod of respect. The crowd's applause echoed as Seamus paused, visibly composing himself before turning toward his family with gentler eyes. His voice lowered, touched with an uncommon tenderness. "And to my family ... Maureen, Declan, Aisling, and Aidan. You've given more than I could ever ask. You've supported me through every rough patch, every late night, and every stubborn idea I had."

He tried blinking back some tears as he turned toward Declan. "Declan," he said, his voice gaining strength, "I've always appreciated your hard work and dedication to the pub, even though you might not have always been completely passionate about it."

With a grin, Seamus reached into his pocket and tossed Declan a set of keys. "These are the keys to your new woodworking shop. Just outside town. A whole place to build and create whatever you want. It's yours."

The crowd broke into applause, and Declan's face transformed with shock, then delight. "You're serious?" he asked, barely able to contain his excitement. Seamus simply nodded, and Declan, overcome, pulled his father into a hug to the cheers and whistles of the crowd.

Seamus then turned to Aisling, his expression weighed down with a look of deep, unspoken regret. He took a breath, steadying himself, before speaking. "Aisling, you've always been strong and independent," he began, his voice unsteady, "brave enough to chase your dreams, even when I didn't understand. When you left for law school … I didn't understand. I thought you were turning your back on what I'd built, and I was too proud and too stubborn to listen."

He paused, his hand reaching up to rub at his eyes, blinking back a tear.

"I fought against it, and against you. I held on tighter because I thought … I thought if I just kept everything in one piece, I'd be doing right by you. But in trying to hold on, I know I pushed you away. And for that …" his voice broke slightly, "for that, I am so very sorry."

Aisling's eyes filled with tears, her hands shaking as she pressed them to her mouth, absorbing the words she had waited years to hear. Seamus continued, swallowing hard, "You deserve to live your life without guilt. And now, with that little one on the way, you're about to begin a whole new journey."

He pulled out an envelope, holding it out with both hands, as though it were a sacred offering. "Here's a head start for the college fund," he said, a small, prideful smile breaking through. "A gift of one hundred thousand dollars, to give that child the freedom to pursue any dream, unhindered by judgment or limitations."

The crowd erupted in applause, their cheers ringing through the pub, and Aisling's composure crumbled as she covered her face, a few quiet sobs escaping. She threw her arms around her father, clinging to him tightly. "Thank you, Da," she whispered, her voice thick with gratitude and relief. Seamus wrapped his arms around her, holding her close, his voice a gentle murmur meant just for her.

He took a shaky breath. "You've done us proud, Aisling," he whispered. "You always have."

Then, turning last to Aidan, Seamus hesitated, a slight tremor in his voice. "And Aidan," he began, "I know you've got big dreams, and you've got a gift." He gestured toward the door. "I wanted to give you a proper send-off, something that'll let you make your own way."

Aidan trailed Seamus's attention toward the entrance, Aidan's breath hitched as he noticed a gleaming new food truck outside, equipped with all the essentials. It was almost too astonishing to process.

Seamus steadied himself, voice rough with emotion. "It's all set up," he murmured, pausing as if the weight of the moment hit him all over again. "Just needs your name on the front and a new coat of paint." His chest rose and fell in a shaky breath, but he managed to push through. "It's yours now, lad. Go on ... make it something incredible."

Aidan could only stare, his heart pounding, gratitude swelling so fiercely he could hardly speak. He turned to his father, pulling him into a tight hug as the crowd cheered again, their applause echoing around them.

At last, Seamus turned to Maureen, his features easing into something unguarded, something rare. He stepped closer to her, reaching out to take her hand, and as he did, the years of hard work, the long nights, and unspoken sacrifices seemed to flicker across his face. His eyes, misted with emotion, held hers with a depth that was both tender and vulnerable.

"Maureen," he began, his voice barely more than a whisper, yet thick with feeling. "I don't think I've said it enough, or maybe even at all, over the years, but ... thank you." He looked down, as if gathering his words, then back up at her, a bit of his usual gruffness giving way. You stayed by my side, even during the long nights and difficult periods, even when my stubbornness made me blind to the strain it was putting on our relationship. Without you, Murphy's would never have lasted. I would never have lasted."

A tear slid down Maureen's cheek, and Seamus reached up, gently brushing it away. "I've been so busy holding on to this pub ... maybe I forgot to hold on to you the way I should've. And I'm sorry for that." He paused, a bittersweet smile fighting off tears. "I know I haven't always been easy to love. And yet, here you are."

The room was so quiet you could hear a pin drop, everyone witnessing a rare moment of unguarded honesty from the man they all knew as the steadfast, sometimes immovable Seamus Murphy.

Clearing his throat, Seamus paused before a glimmer of boyish excitement returned to his eyes. "So, Maureen ... I think it's about time we took a little trip, don't you?" He squeezed her hand, his voice breaking slightly with the enormity of his promise. "In a few weeks, we're going back to Ireland. Just the two of us. I want us to relive every moment of that honeymoon. All of it."

Maureen let out a soft, disbelieving laugh, her tears now mingling with a radiant smile. She shook her head, cupping his face in her hands as if she were looking at the young man she'd fallen in love with all those years ago. "Seamus, are you serious?" she whispered, her voice thick with joy and surprise.

Seamus nodded, his hands trembling slightly as he held hers. "Serious as I've ever been, love." He drew her close, his forehead resting gently against hers. "It's time I give you the part of me that I've held back too long. I think ... I think we both need that spark back."

With tears streaming down her face, Maureen kissed him, a kiss full of years and history, of things unspoken but deeply felt. The room burst into applause once more. Everyone was caught in the spell of this raw, heartfelt moment.

The cheers and claps washed over Aidan, a wave of appreciation for the legacy he inherited. He saw the love woven into the pub's fabric, the sacrifices that cemented its foundation, and the strength that had sustained his family through thick and thin. This night, this farewell, was more than just an ending; it was a promise, an unbreakable bond woven into each of them, one that would follow Aidan wherever the road led next.

As the applause gradually quieted, Seamus and Maureen held each other a moment longer, sharing quiet words that only they could hear. Around them, friends and family exchanged smiles and knowing glances, their eyes reflecting the warmth that had filled Murphy's for decades. A bittersweet ache filled Aidan as he watched his parents, recognizing the finality of this stage and the hopeful start of a new one.

At last, Seamus gently released Maureen, clearing his throat as he straightened and looked around the pub. He raised his glass one last time, a silent invitation for everyone to join him. The crowd stilled, all eyes on the Murphys, sensing that this closing toast was a farewell not only to the pub as they knew it, but to an era.

"Now," Seamus said, his voice carrying a mixture of pride and nostalgia, "let's raise a glass to the journey ahead."

Near the bar, Aidan leaned back against the wood-paneled wall, letting the evening's quiet lull wash over him as he surveyed the pub. It was late now, and most of the crowd had filtered out, leaving behind only the closest family and friends. The last remnants of laughter and conversation echoed softly in the nearly empty room, blending with the lingering scent of ale and Irish stew.

He took a deep breath, his eyes tracing every corner of the pub that had been his whole world for so long. There were the faded pictures of his parents in the early days, Seamus beaming with pride and Maureen by his side, bright-eyed and full of hope. He glanced to the scuffed wood floorboards where he'd learned to take his first steps, and the barstools worn smooth from the generations of patrons who had come, stayed, and come again. Murphy's wasn't just a place; it was a living memory, each corner brimming with decades of stories, of joy and struggle.

Aidan felt the burdens of his past, but for the first time, they didn't feel like a heavy weight. Instead, they provided a sense of stability, a quiet assurance that he was prepared for the future. Tonight had been a turning point, not just for his family but for himself. He'd finally seen a glimpse of his future, one filled with the freedom and creativity he'd longed for, yet still connected to everything Murphy's had taught him.

He spotted MJ across the room, talking quietly with Jazz, who was still wiping down glasses with her usual no-nonsense determination. MJ caught Aidan's eye, offering a small nod as if sensing the gravity of the moment. With a deep breath, Aidan fished the pub keys from his pocket, the coolness of the metal against his skin a comforting reminder of his father. These were the very same keys his father had used to unlock the doors each morning, and to lock them again at night, a symbol of the love and dedication that had been poured into this place.

Aidan approached MJ, his usual easygoing smile met with quiet respect. Neither of them spoke at first, letting the weight of the moment settle between them. He turned the keys over in his palm, tracing their worn edges—the grooves, the scratches, each one a quiet record of years spent building something that mattered.

"Here you go, mate," he said, his voice low but firm as he extended the keys out to his friend. "Murphy's is yours now. Take care of her."

MJ took the keys with reverence, nodding. "I promise you, Aidan," he replied, his tone sincere, "we'll honor everything you, your father, and your family have built here."

Aidan smiled, feeling a profound sense of peace settle over him. "I know you will. And hey," he said, a mischievous grin emerging, "you'll be hard-pressed to find a stew recipe that's better than mine."

MJ laughed, pocketing the keys. "Wouldn't dream of it, Murphy. Some things don't need changing."

A shared clasp of hands brought forth a surge of pride in Aidan, not just for Murphy's, but for the restaurant's impact on his life. From his first kitchen lessons to his recent clashes with his father over its future, Murphy's had given him a sense of belonging and purpose. Somehow, all of it had led him here, to this ultimate act of letting go, and he could feel something like peace settling over them both.

Aidan looked at MJ, the new bearer of Murphy's legacy, and felt a sense of finality that was both bittersweet and freeing. This was no longer his burden to bear. It was a chapter closing, not in defeat, but in triumph, with the promise of rejuvenated stories to come.

Beside him, Seamus stood in stillness, his gaze tracing the familiar walls, the worn bar, the photos that had witnessed generations. But there was no regret in his stance—only something quieter, something closer to reverence. Aidan realized, then, that his father had finally let go. The pub no longer held them in place, no longer dictated the shape of their futures. Instead, it stood as a marker of what had been—and a symbol of the lives they were both free to build beyond it.

Seamus turned to Aidan, a small smile breaking through his usual stoic expression. "You've got big things ahead, son. We both do." His words were simple, but they carried the depth of years' worth of struggle, stubborn pride, and, finally, reconciliation. There was a happiness in his father's eyes that Aidan hadn't seen in a long time, a genuine excitement about the life still to be lived.

Aidan felt his own smile spreading as he looked at Seamus, feeling their bond settle into something new, something easier and stronger than it had been before. "Yeah, Da. We do."

With Seamus's hand on Aidan's shoulder, they walked out of Murphy's, ready for a future of freedom.

Twenty-Seven

The Myrtle Beach Food and Art Fest brimmed with energy. Bright flags fluttered above vendor tents that stretched along the sandy path, guiding crowds through a sensory feast of sizzling foods, vibrant artisan displays, and laughter that rippled beneath the steady pulse of live music. Excited voices rose above the chatter as festival-goers admired everything from handcrafted jewelry and vivid paintings to the mouthwatering aromas wafting from the food trucks.

Inside the Emerald Tide food truck, Aidan moved with purpose and ease, his whole being vibrating with the energy of the crowd outside and the upbeat, soulful music playing over his speakers. A symphony of tantalizing scents filled the small kitchen: garlic seared with whiskey glaze, fresh herbs mingling with sizzling butter, and the earthy fragrance of Guinness-braised ribs. Aidan's hands, moving quickly yet carefully, crafted each dish with a passion long bottled up back in Charlotte.

His truck, a striking emerald green with ocean-blue highlights, brought to mind the dramatic landscape of Ireland's coastline. Celtic knots framed the window where festival-goers lined up, eagerly waiting to try Aidan's signature creations. From the start, Emerald Tide had drawn a steady crowd, each person curious about the fusion of Irish tradition with American street food.

"Next up, Guinness-braised short rib sliders!"" Aidan called, plating the tender, slow-cooked ribs with a dollop of horseradish aioli and a handful of peppery arugula on fresh brioche buns. With a wide grin and a knack for conversation, Sam expertly managed the window, serving sliders and interacting with each customer. Sam, a line cook who'd worked with Aidan at Murphy's, was doing well in his new position.

"These are so good!" Sam laughed as he handed the sliders to a couple at the window. "Aidan, we're making people very happy over here."

Aidan grinned, feeling a thrill shoot through him. This wasn't just ordinary cooking, it was an act of liberation, creation, and pure joy. Murphy's Pub was all about following a strict schedule, but his food truck kitchen embraced creativity and improvisation. He could test new dishes on a whim, switch up the menu, and see the reactions right in front of him.

He worked through the next few orders with an almost effortless rhythm, blending smoky, salty, and savory flavors that combined seamlessly on his compact griddle. Just as he was putting the finishing touches on a batch of whiskey-glazed wings, Sam leaned out of the window, calling his name.

"Hey, Aidan!" Sam turned back, smirking. "There's someone here asking for you ... says she's an old 'sea buddy' or something."

Aidan paused, his heart giving a quick leap. He wiped his hands on his apron and turned toward the window.

Harper.

Aidan froze mid-step as he looked up to see her standing at the window, smiling in that familiar way that always seemed to light up everything around her. The sound of sizzling pans and shouted orders faded into the background, his usual rhythm faltering. Her hair danced in the breeze, and her eyes sparkled as she took in the sight of him behind the grill.

"Harper!" he said, grinning widely, his heart jumping as he walked up to the window. Months of brief texts and unanswered calls culminated in this incredible moment—she was finally standing before him.

"Didn't think you'd recognize me, Murphy," she teased. "Saw your post and figured I'd see what all the fuss was about."

Aidan felt a rush of excitement mixed with that old, easy warmth between them. "You found me," he said, running a hand through his hair. "And here I am, drowning in sliders and whiskey wings."

"I'd say you're thriving," she replied, glancing past him at the sizzling griddle.

Aidan laughed, glancing over his shoulder as more orders piled up. "Look, I'm swamped right now, but can you stick around? Come back later, and we can really talk and catch up."

She nodded with a radiant smile. "I'll be here, Aidan."

"Great." He gave her a quick, candid smile and paused momentarily before diving back into the chaos of the kitchen. He called back out to her, "Harper ..." he started. "It really is good to see you again."

The hours melted into a rhythmic blur, the afternoon and evening passing in a satisfying, steady stream of orders. With the food festival's lively chatter and energetic music drifting in through the open window, Aidan and Sam worked together effortlessly, their movements synchronized and familiar. The griddle sizzled with Guinness-braised sliders, the fryer churned out batches of golden potato wedges, and the aroma of whiskey-glazed wings filled the air, blending with the scents of neighboring food stalls.

Sam shouted out order numbers to the line outside, his voice half-lost in the festival crowd's excited chatter. Between flipping sliders and drizzling sauces, Aidan stole the occasional glance out the window, catching fleeting glimpses of people enjoying their meals, some snapping photos as they took their first bites.

As the last wave of orders tapered off, Aidan felt the buzz of satisfaction settle over him, the type of fulfillment he'd always hoped cooking could bring. By the time the last order left the window, he and Sam were laughing, drenched in the heat of the kitchen and the messy pride of a job well done. With a quick grin, Aidan gave Sam a fist bump, signaling the close of service.

"All right, let's tackle this chaos," Aidan said, glancing around at the scattered bits of lettuce, sauce splatters, and crumb-covered countertops. The two moved into cleanup mode, the energy finally calming as they worked in practiced unison, each swipe of a rag and clink of a washed dish a minor victory in the satisfying close to a long, rewarding day.

Aidan tied off the trash bag with a quick twist and hefted it out the back of the truck. The cool evening air hit him, refreshing after hours in the heat of the kitchen. He stepped onto the festival grounds, making his way toward the dumpster, but his attention was captured by a familiar face seated at a nearby picnic table. Harper was there, idly scrolling through her phone, looking both relaxed and completely at home under the dim festival lights.

He paused, a wave of déjà vu washing over him. It was the same feeling he always got when he saw her across a crowd.

As he returned from the dumpster, Sam poked his head out the truck's side door, wiping his hands on a dishtowel. "Go on, boss," he said with a knowing grin. "I'll take care of the rest. You've got someone waiting."

Aidan shook his head as he tossed the towel over his shoulder. "Thanks, Sam. I owe you one."

"Just put me on your menu board someday," Sam quipped, already back at the sink.

Aidan made his way over to Harper, the buzz of the festival fading to the background as he approached. She looked up and flashed him a warm, amiable smile, tucking a loose strand of hair behind her ear.

"Thought you might've forgotten about me," she teased, leaning back and crossing her arms.

Aidan shrugged with a playful grin. "You know how it is, no rest for the road-weary chef."

Harper's eyes twinkled as she looked him over, taking in the splatters and smudges on his apron. With a smirk, she reached out and playfully brushed a streak of flour from his chest. "Well, you look like a mess. A yummy mess, but a mess nonetheless," she teased. "Are you wearing half your menu?"

Aidan laughed as he inspected his sauce-streaked apron. "Should've seen us last weekend," he replied. "Had a hand pie explode in the fryer. That was the kind of mess you don't forget."

Harper laughed, shaking her head. "Why does it sound like every kitchen you work in turns into a war zone?"

"Hey, chaos makes for great food," he replied, flashing her a wink. "Besides, Sam and I are doing just fine. But you ..." he trailed off, looking at her more closely, "you look great. Happy. I'd even say ... vibrant?"

She smiled, tilting her head a little, and he could tell she was savoring his words. "Thanks, Aidan. I think it's this beach air. Kind of hard not to feel good living here."

"Back to Myrtle, huh?" he said, nodding as he remembered her saying something about it after the wedding. "I knew you'd moved back after blowing up the NY agency, but it didn't really cross my mind that I'd actually run into you here."

"Well, I saw on your Instagram that Emerald Tide would be here, so I figured I had to come by and see if the food's as good as you claimed it would be," she said, grinning. "Honestly, I'm not sure I'd have believed it was you behind that account if it weren't for the occasional picture of Sam looking exasperated in the background."

Aidan laughed, nodding. "Yeah, he's had a lot of 'why did I sign up for this' moments. "It's been a good time. We started traveling a little over a month ago and it's been non-stop."

"You've really got this whole food truck thing going, huh?" Harper asked, a trace of pride in her voice. "It's amazing, Aidan."

Aidan felt a warmth spread through him as he spoke. "Yeah," he admitted, a note of satisfaction in his voice. "It's been ... a lot. Hard work, messy, sometimes just plain crazy. But I think I've finally found that thing I've been looking for. It feels good, you know? To actually see it happen."

Harper nodded, her look growing tender, and Aidan realized that she shared his sense of fulfillment, that special satisfaction in creating something personal.

"So," he continued, his curiosity getting the best of him, "how's Blue Horizon going? I remember you saying you were picking up a few clients. Has it turned out like you imagined?"

She laughed softly, glancing down as if gathering her thoughts. "Honestly? It's a whirlwind," she admitted, a little self-conscious. "Some days, it feels like I'm just figuring it out as I go along. But it's good. I'm partnering with some incredible local businesses, like surf shops, cafés, and a charming artisan jewelry store. Helping them find their voice, telling their stories ... it's like I'm finally doing something meaningful."

Aidan grinned. "I had no doubt you'd make it work."

She laughed lightly and shrugged. "It's a little strange, to be honest, doing things my way instead of answering to some executive or client who wants a million revisions on every campaign. But, I like it. It's low key. I can work with people I actually care about ... I think it's what I was missing."

He nodded thoughtfully, letting her words sink in. "I'll admit, you look ... different," he said. "Not just the vibrant thing. It's like you've finally figured it all out. Kind of like you're back in your element?"

"I think so," she agreed. "I got so caught up in everything back in New York, chasing things that didn't bring me undisputable happiness. It's good to feel alive again. Here, I'm on my own schedule, my own rules. Plus, I get to go to food festivals in the middle of the week and sample great food," she added, giving him a playful smile.

"Speaking of which," Aidan said, leaning forward, "what'd you think of those nachos? Not too much cheese?"

"Impossible," she replied, smirking. "They were perfect. You've got a great thing going, Aidan. I can see this really taking off."

Aidan grinned. "I'm doing what I can. Right now, my marketing plan is just Sam yelling at me to post something on Instagram every few days."

She laughed, rolling her eyes. "Well, I can't say I'm surprised. But ... what if I told you I could help take Emerald Tide to a whole new level?"

He raised an eyebrow, intrigued. "I'm listening."

"Well," she began, leaning closer, "I'm serious about my new agency. And I'd love to work with you if you're interested. I can help you spread the word more effectively than just relying on sporadic Instagram posts. We could develop a brand, reach people all over. With your food and a solid marketing plan, we could make Emerald Tide the next big thing."

Aidan stared at her, the offer hanging in the air. He was aware of her success in New York, but now there was a new depth to her, an authenticity that made her offer feel sincere and personal. She wanted to be a part of this, just as much as he did.

"That sounds ..." he began, trying to gather his thoughts, "Harper, that sounds amazing. I can't even imagine how much easier it'd be with you helping me out. Are you sure you want to take on this crazy circus of a food truck, though?"

"Absolutely," she replied, her eyes sparkling. "I came all the way out here tonight, didn't I? Plus," she added, "I believe in you, Aidan. And I believe in what you're doing."

Aidan felt a lump in his throat, an overwhelming sense of gratitude. "You're making it hard to say no," he said with a grin, trying to lighten the moment.

"Good," she said, laughing softly. "Then don't."

Aidan felt his pulse quicken as he looked at Harper, letting her offer sink in. "Alright," he said, a warm grin spreading across his face. "I accept. Let's do this. Emerald Tide and Blue Horizon Creative."

Her face lit up, and for a moment, Aidan could have sworn time froze. "Perfect," she replied, her voice just above a whisper. "I can't wait to get started."

Aidan let the quiet linger a second longer before clearing his throat, shifting slightly on his feet. His fingers brushed the back of his neck as he shot her a half-smile. "So, Harper ... any chance you might like to get some dinner sometime?"

Her eyes sparkled as they came up to meet his. "Like ... a date?"

Aidan shifted as he could feel his cheeks warm. "Yeah. Like an actual date. You in?"

She looked at him for a beat, then nodded, her smile growing even brighter. "That sounds ..." she paused for a moment as if she was contemplating the decision, "Yes. I would love that."

"Fabulous," he said with a relieving sigh before suggesting, "the festival wraps up tomorrow, then I'm free Monday."

"Monday it is," she responded. Then, without thinking, Aidan opened his arms, and she leaned into them, hugging him tightly. The world faded as he held her, feeling a rush of warmth and gratitude for this reunion he hadn't known he was waiting for. She lingered in his embrace, and when she finally pulled back, there was a spark in her eyes that felt like a promise.

"Well then, Murph," she said with a grin, "I guess I need you to get back to your truck before Sam sends a search party."

"It was fantastic to see you, Harper. I'm glad you came out."

"Me too," she replied and shared a smile so electric it sent chills down Aidan's spine. "I'll see you Monday."

Aidan reached up and gently brushed a rogue hair from Harper's forehead to behind her ear. "I can't wait."

Harper turned and began walking away but momentarily later turned back as if she had forgotten something. "Hey, Aidan ..."

"Yeah?" he called back.

"Maybe wear a clean shirt," she said with a joking grin before turning back and walking toward the festival exit.

After watching her for a few moments longer, Aidan turned to walk back to his food truck. Along the way, he pulled his phone from his pocket for the first time since before lunch to check his missed alerts. Among them was a message from Harper that she must've sent earlier.

Harper

Hey, how's life?

The memory of their shared messages, almost like an inside joke, flashed before him. They'd exchanged similar thoughts several times in the year since they met on the Elysian Serenade.

This time, he felt his response would be simple but communicate just how far he had come since that cruise. He responded with a simple smiling emoji, both mirroring her preceding responses and symbolizing both his newfound happiness in the food truck and the hopeful promise of possibility with Harper.

Try as he might, there was no chance to hide his smile when he returned to the truck.

"All good, boss?" Sam asked.

"Yeah, everything is great, Sam." Aidan replied. "Everything ... is great."

About The Author

I'm J.D. Harbor, a romance novelist drawn to love stories set on the high seas. A former military photojournalist, I found my writing voice capturing real-life moments in the field. Now, I craft tales of connection, adventure, and self-discovery aboard cruise ships.

My RomantiSea Serenades series begins with Emerald Tide and Sapphire Seas, companion novels following two souls brought together by fate on a cruise. While their romance spans both books, each story delves into one character's personal journey. Inspired by my own experience of meeting my wife on a voyage, these novels embrace the magic of love unfolding when least expected.

Originally from Utah, I now live in Central Florida with my wife and two kids, always dreaming up our next adventure on the open water. I believe the best love stories begin with self-discovery—because only when we truly know ourselves can we fully open our hearts to love.

Also by J.D. Harbor

Embark on the journey of a lifetime with RomantiSea Serenades, a planned 15-book romance series set aboard the glistening Elysian Serenade cruise ship. This sweeping saga explores love, adventure, and personal growth against the stunning backdrop of the open sea.

Aboard RomantiSea Serenades, each Mingle at Sea cruise brings two solo travelers together, their love story spanning two companion novels. Each book offers a fresh perspective, following one protagonist's path through love, self-discovery, and transformation.

The series drops anchor with Emerald Tide and Sapphire Seas, companion novels that introduce readers to this vibrant world. As new couples set sail, they prove the best journeys aren't just about destinations—they're about the people who change us along the way. If you believe in love's power to surprise, this series is your escape.

One of the debut voyages in the RomantiSea Serenades series, Sapphire Seas is the companion to Emerald Tide, offering a dual perspective on an unforgettable love story. This heartfelt novel follows Harper, a successful New York City advertising executive on the verge of burnout. Reeling from creative exhaustion and a painful breakup, she accepts her best friend's invitation to come aboard a singles cruise, hoping for a much-needed escape.

Onboard, she meets Aidan, a grounded chef facing his own crossroads. As their connection deepens, Harper realizes that the life she once worked so hard to build no longer aligns with the woman she's becoming. Set against the romance and adventure of the open sea, Sapphire Seas—alongside Emerald Tide—is a deep dive into self-discovery, healing, and love found when you least expect it.

So, grab your boarding pass, find your sea legs, and get ready for a romance-filled adventure that proves sometimes, love is just a tide change away.